About the Author

Martin Morton lives mostly in the Adriatic on a boat.

Visit Martin Morton at www.martinmorton.co.uk

The Water's Depth

Martin Morton

The Water's Depth

Chimera

CHIMERA PAPERBACK

© Copyright 2019
Martin Morton

The right of Martin Morton to be identified as author of
this work has been asserted by him in accordance with the
Copyright, Designs and Patents Act 1988.

All Rights Reserved

No reproduction, copy or transmission of this publication
may be made without written permission.
No paragraph of this publication may be reproduced,
copied or transmitted save with the written permission or in
accordance with the provisions
of the Copyright Act 1956 (as amended).

Any person who commits any unauthorised act in relation to
this publication may be liable to criminal
prosecution and civil claims for damages.

A CIP catalogue record for this title is
available from the British Library.

ISBN: 978 1 903136 66 9

Chimera is an imprint of
Pegasus Elliot MacKenzie Publishers Ltd.
www.pegasuspublishers.com

First Published in 2019

Chimera
**Sheraton House Castle Park
Cambridge England**

Printed & Bound in Great Britain

1

No delay out of Dulles. She would see the kids before school and then get a full, clear weekend with them. Work had piled up but a good day on her own should see her catch up with the important things before they got home, although she knew the first hour now would belong to Pat. She'd slept quite well on the flight, as she usually did, so she expected to get through the day without flagging. The re-entry process, she knew, was important, however much work priorities were pushing in. A week in headquarters was always intense so tea and gossip with Pat was her decompression chamber and it gave her, she always felt, a better perspective on work and life.

The kids had been wonderful, Pat said, but Pat always said that so Claudia had to push to uncover the tensions she was sure must have arisen. After all, they didn't often see their dad, and Mum was away half the time during the week, but everyone seemed quite content so probably it was just her simple paranoia — the guilt that she was, in the main, enjoying life in ways she never had done before and had never really expected to.

Now the boy was twelve, the kids were at the same school together and went off chattering, not giving a backward glance. She watched them down the road and round the corner. They seemed fine, she hadn't tried to force conversation at breakfast, which she had made them take at the table. Pat, no doubt, let them sit in front of the television or their iPads.

Pat was pouring tea when she got back to the kitchen. "Did you sleep on the plane?"

"Yes, quite well, you know I'm lucky like that. But the week's so full-on anyway I'm knackered when I get to the airport."

"What do you want for breakfast? I don't suppose you've eaten." Pat was taking eggs out of the fridge. The table was laid.

"You're right. Sleep always seems more important and I like catching up with you like this."

"Well, I need to catch up with you" but Pat was smiling. "You've got a sleepover tomorrow night. Abbi's got some of her friends coming round, and Jonah's arranged to go and stay with a mate." She laughed. "He's a year or two away from finding girls interesting."

"So much for me planning to bond with my children!"

"I wouldn't let it worry you, Claudie, I think it shows they're happy. I know you keep looking for the warning signs, but I honestly haven't seen any."

"Well, I've you to thank for that, you're always here for them."

"And I love it, you know I do, they mean the world to me, but don't do yourself down, they're very proud of you — and they always ask what you'll say about anything. I just guessed you wouldn't mind the sleepover. I was right, wasn't I?"

"Oh completely, it's fun to hear them chattering and laughing. Well, up to a point, it was nearly four before it went quiet last time. No wonder he's going to his mate's."

Then Pat told her about Dave. He was drinking less, smartening himself up — and he was seeing someone. Pat looked closely for a reaction.

"Finally! Well, I'm glad about that." And she was.

"I don't know that it's serious. I wouldn't raise the divorce thing again yet."

"Oh no. No, I wouldn't do that. This suits me quite well while you're around, as long as he keeps the money coming." Pat was cooking and had her back turned. The money came via Pat and Claudia doubted that its source was always Dave but, in her new job, she had much more coming in, so life had become easier. She could even think about moving if she wanted to, but Pat was irreplaceable so that was out of the question.

"So, you're in no rush to do anything permanent with this man of yours?" Pat kept her back turned as she busied herself at the hob.

Claudia laughed ruefully, "No, I've no idea how that would work. I love him to bits but even I'm a bit cynical about making anything permanent. I'm lucky my two guys are doing so well. They have enough to put up with already, I'd hate to rock their boat with a new man in their life. Anyway," she laughed again, "he hasn't asked me!"

Pat laughed with her and dished up the scrambled eggs.

2

He rang at lunchtime.

"Oh, I thought you'd ring later."

"You may believe it, or you may not, but I happen to know you've just got back from DC and you'll want the evening with the kids. You don't want that interrupted by a dirty phone call."

"I'm impressed, I admit. So, is this my dirty phone call? It's a bit early for you, you're boring until you've had a drink."

"That would earn you six."

"Yup. That's what I'd be aiming for."

He laughed, "But you protested last time."

"Well, you went a bit heavy, I'm not Martha, you know, still, that was six weeks ago now — and it was twelve strokes, not six — but I've started to miss it."

"It takes you six weeks to miss me?"

"No, dumbo, I miss you every stupid minute, but it takes a while to begin to want some of your more extreme perversions again."

"Perversions? Me?"

"I know, I know. It's not perverted, it's just what we do. It's us. It just surprises me sometimes when I think about it but then I start wanting it again."

"It, or me?"

"You are being provocatively stupid today, aren't you? Or maybe it's stupidly provocative. You know it's the same thing for me. I can't get as detached as you about these things." There was a pause. "Don't worry, this isn't the start of a challenging conversation. Tell me what you've been up to."

And he talked about his travels and his people. Now that she'd met some of them on her three trips out there, she could put faces to many of the names. When she talked about her week in DC, he, of course, knew everybody she spoke about. "How well do you know Rod Henderson?"

"Rod, the man on the board? The one who got you set up in your job?"

"Yes."

"Hardly at all. I've only spent any time with him when he came to Singapore for the conference. My God, that's nearly two years ago now. Why do you ask?"

"Well, on the odd occasion our paths have crossed he always takes time to ask how the programme's going and tell me how important it is."

"Well, it is."

"I know, I know, but directors never normally descend to talk to mortals."

"That's true. I never interact with them. The visit here was a one-off."

"Well, I got invited to a little soirée at his place this week. It just seemed very unusual to be asked. Wonderful place though, very plush, lots of dark marble and a huge balcony overlooking the Potomac. It must be worth millions. Davis got quite sniffy when he heard I was going — he's never been. I think he thinks because Henderson's focus is on HR, the HR VP ought to be included in that sort of gathering. I hope it doesn't make him take a closer interest in what I'm doing; I quite like my independence."

"Who was there, then?"

"Well, not Davis obviously, but I recognised a few from the office, mostly senior people. Fortunately, he'd asked Sarah Jacobs, so I had someone to go with. I thought he was just adding us as eye candy — that would have been outrageous, of course, but I wasn't going to turn it down."

"You're telling me Sarah gets invited as eye candy?"

"Jack, that's unkind — and not fair either. Anyway, you know she's important to me. I need someone in Finance to make sure the units allocate funds to the programme, it can get forgotten but she's a terrier when the plans come in; even your finance guy tried to forget me last year. Anyway, we weren't just there as decoration. Henderson led me off soon after we got there and introduced me to some big honchos from other corporations and asked me to talk about our programme.

I don't know that they were really that interested, well, one of them maybe."

"Was Henderson's wife there?"

"Yes, very elegant woman, seemed a bit cold though. Why?"

"Well, doesn't he have a reputation?"

"It's funny you say that. Sarah said something on the way there, but I didn't pick up anything myself. He was the perfect host. He even managed to smile a little."

"What did Sarah say?"

"Just gossip about some relationships at work, unusual at our place, I mean, I think we're quite modern really, but one or two careers have still been advanced in the time-honoured manner, apparently. Perhaps he's worth sticking close to."

"And you're the one who can't stay detached?"

"I said I couldn't detach, not that I couldn't exploit. Your lot only sometimes get what they want but they usually get what they deserve, especially nowadays."

"My, my, who's a big girl now?"

She sighed, "I don't know, Jack, I'm not really, but I've had to learn a lot these past two years to make it work with you."

"That sounds regretful."

"No, no, definitely not — and I knew I'd have to fight that feeling of wishing things were different when I signed on with you. Look, I don't want this conversation to go down that route. Tell me how much you'd love to fuck me!"

"Go to your room!"

"My room?"

"Yes, I'm going to fuck you. Well, my stand-in will. I want to think of the big black guy pushing deep into your cunt."

"I'm supposed to be working!"

"No, you're supposed to be doing as you're told. My little man here is getting excited thinking about you. I'm leaning back on my bed, I've just showered and my bathrobe's open and he's starting to look up at me."

"Are you helping him?"

"I am now a little, I'm holding him. Are you going upstairs? You're going to be naked from the waist with your arse in the air. Get moving! Tell me what you're doing!"

"OK, OK, I'm going up the stairs now. I'm going into my room. Oh, sweet, Pat's put flowers by the bedside."

"That isn't getting your knickers off."

She woke with a start, feeling disorientated. Two o'clock. Oh, not bad, over an hour before the kids got home. Plenty time to shower and unpack. OK, less work done than she'd wanted but it sounded like she'd have some free time over the weekend.

She sat up and laughed quietly at herself. She felt relaxed. Making herself come was no longer a rarity and it did calm her down and make some problems melt into the distance. It was a feature of her relationship with Jack — the long-distance dirty phone calls that kept things going in the long separation times. She looked at the large black dildo, lying against her thigh, her juices now dry and crusty on it. She picked it up and kissed its tip. "Good boy!" and she laughed again. It was bigger than Jack and had more stamina, but she still longed for the real thing. "That's three weeks away, big boy, you and I might need to have some more fun before then."

She was changed and tidied up when they wandered in together, Abbi looking cool (too cool? she wondered), Jonah dishevelled. She hugged them in turn, a little harder than they wanted to be hugged.

"Did Gran say about the sleepover?"

"Yes."

"And it's OK?"

"Of course it is. I like your friends being here," and there was another hug, much bigger this time.

"And I'm at Damian's."

She laughed. "I know, and I don't blame you one little bit. Now, am I cooking tonight or are we going for a Chinese?"

"Chinese," they chorused, and she was glad. She would have them undistracted for an hour.

"OK, get your homework done. We're going out at six."

3

She loved eating out with them, and had done ever since they were small. Even when things were bad with Dave — and when hadn't they been bad with Dave? — the kids' chatter kept her entertained and kept Dave more calm and quiet. Sometimes there was a little provocative banter but mostly the two got on surprisingly well.

She had been distracted by giving their order when she overheard them talk about eating out with Dave and his girlfriend. She was sure they didn't see her react. *How dare he! Without asking me! And Pat had said nothing about this! Pat, why hadn't you told me?* She stuttered over the order, went over it twice, partly to make sure and partly to calm down. As her brain was still saying *'arsehole'*, her face had begun trying to smile again and they were too distracted arguing about the Italian where they'd eaten to notice her, she hoped.

"So, what's she like?" she asked as casually as she could when the waiter had gone — not very casually, she knew.

Abbi's eyes flitted between hers and the Jonah's — *oops, hadn't fooled her* — but he, less sensitive of course, dived in. "She's a bit boring. She talked a lot at first and tried to be friendly. I suppose she wasn't that bad really." He slowed and stopped munching prawn crackers, sensing something was wrong.

"It's OK, really it is. I'm glad. I don't like to think of your dad just drinking beer in front of the telly. Gran says it's made him smarten himself up, I'd been trying to do that for years." She paused. "Gran's told me that, you see." That was meant to reassure them, and the girl smiled. *But she hadn't told me about him letting her fucking well meet you two!*

"But you've got a friend too, Mum, haven't you? Dad said."

Arsehole, arsehole, arsehole! "Well, I've got quite a lot of friends."

"No, a special boyfriend I mean. You have, haven't you?"

"Well, there is one man I like a lot, but he lives on the other side of the world now." This was unwelcome and embarrassing — but maybe it wasn't so bad, maybe it was an easy way in to talking about Jack. But she'd never let them meet him without telling Dave first. Well, wouldn't have before now.

"So, you like him a lot," said Abbi, she paused, glanced at Jonah. "Does that mean you…" and she and the boy, catching each other's looks, burst out laughing.

"Abbi!" she said, much louder than she meant to, the next table looked round, and she knew she was blushing, which made the kids laugh even more.

"You do, you do, you do!" and Abbi was almost bouncing in her chair. "Can we meet him? We want to meet him."

"Yes, we want to meet him" came the echo from Jonah. She always thought of him as Jonah, always called him Jonah, but he made everyone else call him Joe — although he'd started to spell it Jo. She'd noticed but hadn't teased him about it. She was sure Abbi would have — and told him that was the girl's spelling.

"Of course you can meet him but he's not in this country very often."

"Where does he live?"

"He travels a lot, but he has a home in Singapore. He works for the same business as me, so I sometimes see him in America."

"Oh," said Abbi, crestfallen.

"Can we come to America with you then?" said Jonah, alert to an opportunity.

Somehow the conversation moved boisterously on, as it usually did, to school and friends and music and whatever was most gross on TV, without her having to admit that Jack would be in London in three weeks. Or admit that she certainly would not be introducing them.

4

The kids were in their rooms, Jonah probably sleeping, Abbi probably not. It wasn't late but she'd gone to bed with that now familiar sensation of feeling tired but not sleepy. The first night back was always fitful — she'd just take what sleep she could and let the UK clock reimpose itself on her body tomorrow.

The big boy was in the bedside drawer and she felt no inclination to reach for him. He'd done his job for the day but given the luxury of being back and having dealt with all the immediate stresses and pressures, she could relax and rewind six weeks and think about her last trip to Singapore.

It was seriously business — she'd needed to pull the regional programme together again and that was an intense three days — but she'd left the hotel for the rest of the stay, spending the time in Jack's apartment and a couple of days on a boat.

The boat had been a surprise and a thrill for her, something she'd always wanted to try, Jack knew. *My God, the man listened sometimes.* He had borrowed a friend's motor cruiser and he seemed quite competent in managing it. Although she did encounter the po-faced Jack when she teased him during the pre-sail briefing he'd insisted on giving. He made her learn how to use the VHF to make a Mayday call. She had to study the maps ('Charts!' — 'Phooey!') of where he intended to take her. She'd also had an hour's training on throwing lines ("They're lines, not ropes," and it had been wrong to laugh then, too) and tying up. He had even bought her a pair of sailing gloves which she'd brought home as souvenirs.

She was glad they had taken the trip on their own. He'd offered to hire a crewman, but she wanted privacy — and liked the idea of learning how to help him drive and dock the boat. She hadn't expected the process to be quite so serious, but it would be worth it. Also, she wanted to sunbathe but couldn't show the marks off to anyone.

Marks disappeared quickly normally — she'd learnt that with Jack and the games they played. But she'd also learned with Dave that facial lumps and bruises last longer, so she'd acquired a good deal of expertise with make-up and arnica gel, but she would have needed to wear shorts to conceal the evidence of the previous night in the apartment and it was much too warm for that.

In her reverie she could feel the hot sun on her skin and the prickling of the humidity as the sweat beads trickled down her face and made every part of her slippery. They'd found an anchorage where she could lie on the foredeck and feel the heat pressing her into immobility on the sunpads with the towel growing damp beneath her.

Their boat was alone at first but, when the new arrivals came into the bay and anchored near them, she moved carefully and lay only on her back. Her arse stung if she brushed it carelessly against anything when moving. Even lying motionless it still tingled. The evening before hadn't exactly been a surprise. They'd talked about trying a bench and even watched a couple of porn movies where one featured prominently, but their playtime, as Jack called it, normally needed no more than the available furniture and pillows in addition to the various toys they took with them to every encounter. Their collection continued to grow — and she was responsible for almost half of it, including the strap-on that he'd let her try only once. She'd been curious. She'd also been careful not to buy anything too big — she knew from the plugs she played with when he lay across her to fuck her that he was a wimp, he said he enjoyed it, and sometimes he put the small plug in readiness on the table, but he would shake his head if she reached for anything bigger. She had teased him, of course, about what he subjected her to but, as he rightly responded, she liked all of that.

But the bench was startling, the padded red fabric, washable of course, the solid mahogany frame and the shiny brass fittings, it stood like a small horse between the foot of the bed and the wall of mirrors on the wardrobe. She would lie along it, she guessed, there were pads for knees on the sides and padded straps for legs and arms.

She had grown used to the cold contemplation of toys and instruments. She knew when the moment came, and pleasure began to rise, that there were dozens of ways to prolong and enhance the intensity. Many would have puzzled her before the Jack time but now they could integrate everything into a deepening intimacy. But now was the time for playful speculation. She lay on top of it. "The knee pads are too high, can you adjust them?"

"Of course," he said, and positioned himself behind her, between her knees. "The legs need to be lengthened a bit too." He rubbed his bulge against her crotch.

"If we're going to enjoy this fully later, we don't want to get distracted now. Stand back from me, brute!"

He stepped back. "But you don't mind though?"

She unsaddled herself, stood in front of him and hugged him. "Of course I don't mind. I've wanted to try it, you know I have, but I am wondering what your cleaning lady will think."

"Oh, it comes apart and stores discreetly in a box in the wardrobe. If she opens the box, she'll get a shock but I'm sure her curiosity has taken her through the bedside drawers before now and she still comes to clean in spite of those nasty surprises. She even sends her daughter as a stand-in sometimes, so I can't have put her off that much."

"Are you going to adjust it now? I don't want to come in here after dinner and have you messing around with spanners or whatever it takes."

She left him to work on it and unpacked her case into the wardrobe section he left clear for her — nice, it was only her third visit in the two years, yet she thought of the space as her own. In some dark moments of the longer separations she thought that anyone else could feel it was their special space too but, in the main, she thought that Jack was staying honest about his other friendships and that none was very deep.

"Try it now!"

She knelt on it, lay on it. "Feels good for me. Stand behind me" and he did, and the bulge, less prominent now, seemed to be exactly the right height. "Perfect, now you can buy me dinner."

They strolled the three blocks to the restaurant. She loved the warm evening walks, the air fresh again after the thunderstorm had cleared. She would have loved his arm around her shoulder but he was still cautious about being seen together. Dining was OK, she was a visiting executive, but public displays of intimacy would have attracted more dangerous gossip if anyone were to see them — the office wasn't far away — and, although she wanted more, she had enjoyed intimacy every night in her hotel room when he had joined her. One night she'd come back and found him asleep in the bed, she'd had a wonderful time waking him up, with him still pretending to be sleeping after her mouth had coaxed his cock into vigorous life.

She glanced up at him occasionally as they walked. The grey flecks were spreading though his hair, still mostly dark and always tidy — she would have liked it longer. The street and shop lights didn't flatter his tan, making his face look greenish instead of its daylight soft bronze.

They stopped at a corner. He turned and caught her looking — she loved the grey eyes. "What's up?" He looked quizzical.

"Just thinking, you scrub up quite well," she patted his belly, "even this isn't suffering too much."

"How dare you!" he spluttered with mock indignation, "I still use the same hole on my belts."

The lights changed and they moved on and were soon in the restaurant. It was an Australian Asian fusion that he had taken her to once before. She had liked it very much — exotic variants of recognisable fish and meat. On the three evenings that week with the team she'd been taken on different gastronomic adventures and they'd taken a childish delight in her reactions to some of the dishes. She had enjoyed almost all of them, but she knew that the birds' claws would live long in her memory. She had rotated the lazy susan on quickly and they had laughed. They had been watching for that —

waiting for it — and then they'd fallen on them voraciously.

The maître d' smiled. "Ah mister Jack, so nice to see you again, sir," and he led them smoothly to the window table where they had sat before. It looked out from the first floor onto the bustling square, fringed by the waterway and many high buildings.

The irritating mosquito thought of who had also sat in this chair opposite Jack would catch her sometimes but tonight it was easily banished. She'd had three nights of sleeping in his arms and making love at night and every morning, the evenings slow and sensual and the mornings urgent and rough — and she had enjoyed that almost as much. But now a few days where they could take their time — she looked at him studying the menu — he would order for her — and she began to think of those hands on her body later.

She wanted just two starters, he would do the same and add only a small flask of sake. Good, she thought, their main meal would be later, it would be each other,

She would have scallops first, he abalone. He asked her to try it too, but she'd seen the price on the menu and her resistance to excessive indulgence kicked in. "I know it's heresy, but I didn't like it that much the one time I tried it." Anyway, she knew the scallops would be wonderful, very lightly seared on a bed of perfectly-textured risotto, drizzled with a creamy sauce with its sharp but faint tang of wasabi.

"You had that last time."

"I'd compliment you on your romantic memory if you hadn't made it sound like a criticism. I've had three nights out eating all sorts this week, a lot of it unrecognisable, and what was recognisable was often horrible — birds' claws, for God's sake, so no-one's going to call me unadventurous. Tonight, I'm eating what I like, that's why I'm ordering sashimi second and you're ordering tempura prawns, please. We can share and not eat too much. Is that OK?"

He had laughed. "Of course it's OK, bossy boots. That's what I'll order then."

It was leisurely, they even lingered over the tea at the end, she loved looking out on the tables spilling out from the bars, full of people drinking and laughing. It always seemed a happy place to her but just then he reached for her hand, she looked at him and returned his smile and realised that it seemed a happy place because she was always so happy here. She also had the suppressed excitement about the evening ahead and she knew she wouldn't be tired. She'd almost worked through the jet lag but adrenaline would keep her alert anyway for hours yet.

They began walking back, the gorgeous warmth still enveloping them, his arm reached round her shoulder. She nestled in as they walked but looked up to see him smiling at her. "Should you?"

"This secrecy thing gets a bit tiring, doesn't it? And it doesn't feel like us, or how we should be." He squeezed her shoulder gently and kept his arm in place.

"So, what is us? I'm not pushing for a serious answer, I'm very happy with what we've got and I can't see that changing while we do what we're doing. I'd love more, of course I would, but I sometimes think this way of life suits you" and she prodded him with her elbow, "but if you want to change it, you'd better let me know."

"I would but I don't see how; the jobs seem to stop that. Since I came out here, we've only spent time with each other eight times."

"Nine!"

He laughed. "OK, nine, I'm not sure which one I missed — was it good?" she prodded him again. "But it's not nearly enough."

She felt warm hearing him say that. "I think we should maybe be glad we can have what we've got. I don't know that either of us is ready for major changes — let's just go on exploring us as we are."

"Ah, yes, exploring, my dear," and his body seemed to relax a little beside her, "that was our agenda for this evening." A chuckle came from deep in his throat.

They embraced and kissed as soon as the door closed. She'd wanted to kiss him many times during the evening but, even without the fear of discovery, there was a decorum about the place that stopped her.

The kiss was lingering and sensual. The three nights together had enabled them to find a more natural tempo than the urgent coupling on her arrival, when they'd come before their clothes had been fully discarded.

This time the clothes were dropped slowly, item by item, until they were naked in each other's arms and she felt his gratifying stiffness against her belly. She slid down to her knees and held him, admired him — she liked his cock — slowly closed her mouth over its head and gently moved back and forth.

"That's very nice, my dearest, but tonight you're going to do as you're told."

She leaned back a little, still holding him, wanking him gently, and she looked up. "So, I should stop sucking your cock, master?" They both laughed.

"No, suck my cock some more, slut, but don't make him come. You're getting very, very good at it; it makes me wonder about all the practice you're getting."

She looked up again and smiled, she hoped wickedly. "Oh, my mouth is only for you, my master." And this was almost, but not quite, true.

"No, it isn't, slut, I know you've been sucking other men's cocks. That's why you have to be punished tonight. You need to get on the bench." She kept her rhythm unbroken. "But you can stay there a while longer."

She liked the challenge of taking him deeper but that would be for the time when she wanted him to come. That wasn't yet, so she focused on the head, letting it move rhythmically in and out of her mouth, running her tongue around it. She leaned back again and admired it, she would enjoy the toys on the bench but she would still want the real thing inside her, and soon, so she took him deeper in her mouth this time, enough to make him say, "Stop, you're going too far, now it's time to strap you down."

It was the first time since Peter's party that she'd been strapped onto a device. She draped herself on it, feeling momentarily awkward until Jack's hands moved all over her skin while his lips ran kisses down her back. She turned her head towards the mirror and enjoyed the sight of him admiring her and touching her.

When he moved behind her, she could see his cock still standing stiff, his hands stroked her buttocks. "OK, slut, you can have a little now" and he pushed deeply into her. She closed her eyes and smiled to herself at how easy it was to take him.

He kept a slow rhythm going, pushing deeply but not roughly, his hands running up and down her back. She watched him in the mirror, pushed back to take him deeper. His face turned to hers in the mirror, he smiled, but then withdrew enough to give himself space to slap her hard with his hand. "Stay where you are, slut! I'll make you stay where you are," and he slipped out and knelt behind her and began buckling the straps just below her knees, pausing at times to push his face onto her pussy and lick her clit. She moved gently with the arousal but found space in another part of her mind to think about those straps with the brass buckles — Velcro would have been simpler, cheaper, easier but it would have just felt wrong. There was a strangely Victorian authenticity about the dark wood and the brass fittings — but that thought passed as his mouth pushed more urgently onto her and his tongue moved inside her. She had felt exposed before, her legs spread as she'd mounted the device, but now, with her legs secured, she felt completely open to him and whatever he wanted to do to her. But he left her pussy now and moved to strap her wrists to the forward legs. "But I can't play with you if you tie my hands!"

He stepped away and picked up the paddle from the small table on which he had placed a number of toys, a tube of lube, and that cane — her cane, she remembered insisting.

He stood beside her hip, paddle in hand, their eyes met again in the mirror, he had a wicked smile on his face, the paddle came down heavily, first on her left, then on her right. She gasped loudly.

"Slut will do as she's told." Then he paddled her twice more and returned to strapping her wrists. Now she couldn't move, merely turn her head on the headrest. He moved to the mirror side and pointed his stiff cock to her mouth; she opened for him. For a while they moved as they had done before although it felt strange not to hold him in her hands, but slowly she began to enjoy the moment, his stiffness, the taste of their juices, and he seemed to have found a plateau of pleasure they could stay on — but then she felt his hand on her head. "I know you can take it deeper, slut, like you do with the others," and he pushed his cock to the back of her throat, making her choke and splutter. He eased back, the first push had been scary, she never took him that deep but, as he withdrew slightly, she knew he was looking after her and she began sucking again as just the head stayed in her mouth. His hand stayed where it was, however, but the next time he pushed deeper she was ready. It was thrilling to feel him so excited, so needy, but the feeling of him right back in her throat was unnerving and she wondered how he would control his own obvious excitement. Just as she felt he was getting too close he pulled back completely. "You have a wonderfully fuckable mouth," he said, "no wonder the guys love it so much." And as he moved around behind her again, she thought briefly of the only two real guys of recent memory instead of the many fantasy lovers of his imagination.

But now he was kneeling again and licking her. She could relax and find her own plateau. He was good, he tuned in to her, he would ease back if he felt her excitement rising too high. His hands moved slowly over her back, her arse, her thighs. She loved the wantonness of being open to him. She closed her eyes and focused on his mouth, licking and sucking her clit, moving between her cheeks which he spread with his hands, she felt his tongue tickling her, pushing gently into her then, as he moved away slightly, leaving one hand on the small of her back, she knew to expect the heavy hand slaps on her buttocks. The first few were loud but not especially painful. It was when he stood up beside her, she felt his stiff cock on her hip, that she waited for the full arm swing, his hand falling heavily on each side in turn. They stung, but when he paused between each two to press himself against her, she could feel how excited he was becoming. She wasn't counting, she wasn't even feeling the sharp pain any more; it was melting into a burning glow. He stopped suddenly, with her wanting even more but, when she felt his hands on her hips as he stood behind her, she knew she was about to enjoy that stiff cock again. He returned to the earlier rhythm, playing the slow game, not the rapid, rough fuck they'd had before breakfast in the hotel that morning but something more sensual — even loving she might have said, except for the heat on her arse.

He moved away again to the small table. She could have turned to see but she trusted him. Yes, she knew her body excited him, she knew his desires were what she would have called kinky two years ago but now she knew that everything he did was meant to stimulate her, to excite her, to touch new senses and desires in her. She knew that later on the cane would come, she knew it would be very painful, she knew she would think herself insane as the strokes landed but she knew that the culminating high was like nothing else she had ever felt.

But now the familiar buzz was from a vibrator. She couldn't tell which but when it entered her, she knew it was large, larger than the cock that had just been fucking her. She relaxed and let him push it deeply, moving it slowly in and out. Then she felt his fingers feeling her clit and her excitement mounted. This would take her to the edge if he wasn't careful. She couldn't stop if he carried on but then, just as she thought it was too late, he took his fingers away and eased the dildo out. "Don't leave me," she gasped, but very quickly felt his cock inside her again, rocking gently.

"We know the slut likes us to take turns," he said, gruffly.

And it was true. It was a weird feeling, but it was what they often did in their lovemaking. He would have her arse in the air and keep changing places with the big boy in particular and she loved it. If she was ready with the big boy inside her she would let his fingers, playing on her clit, make her come and then welcome his cock into her. If he was ready first then her fingers, usually playing with his balls, would slide to her clit and she would help herself to climax immediately after feeling him let go.

But now he had eased the big boy out, his fingers had left her clit, he just pushed his cock gently, letting her breathing ease. His other hand stroked her back and her arse. "You have such a beautiful body, my love." Somehow that startled her but not enough to distract her from the gorgeous cock moving in and out of her cunt, leaving her feeling like she was floating in a warm bath.

The stroking hand stopped; something new would happen and a moment later a large dollop of cold lube landed between her cheeks. It was massaged around and into her anus. She loved feeling his fingers enter her. How strange that had seemed at first yet now, how much a part of what they did. She felt more lube drop and more fingers pushed inside her, gently but insistently, he left only his pinkie to play with her. She knew he would have to be careful, she so often came just like this.

But she knew also that he would have to manage himself. She felt sure he wouldn't want to come yet. She could, and she felt nearer the climax again as his fingers pushed deeper — but then he eased them out as she began to get noisier in her enjoyment again.

She felt him position himself directly behind her again; she so wanted what she now expected and then his cock was pushing at her anus. She was relaxed by now, but he was still, as always, careful and slow, and that added to the overwhelming feeling that overcame her as he pushed slowly, deeply in. His hands gripped her waist as he pushed. This was a voluptuous feeling and, with nothing to play with her clit, she could sustain it indefinitely.

But she knew he couldn't. He was pushing harder, breathing more heavily, groaning more loudly and he pulled away suddenly. "Oh." She breathed in mock disappointment. His hand slapped her arse sharply. "Don't worry, slut will get more."

Then came a moment when he just stood behind her, running his hands up and down her back, seemingly to relax her but really, she knew, to relax himself. As he moved back and forth, she felt his stiff cock prod against her. He had been too close to coming, and that would have complicated his evening.

When their breathing had slowed and they had relaxed a little more, she felt him move again. She felt more lube drop but the big dildo, when it came, slid deeply into her vagina, soon followed by the head of his cock pressing into her arse. This was wonderful, she loved being so completely stretched, but she knew it couldn't last, they always came so quickly like this, especially when she could play with her clit, but it was always he who got overexcited first. It thrilled him to have her like this so, when he pulled out fairly soon, she wasn't surprised, only disappointed. And now the big dildo left her too.

"We know the slut loves two cocks at once — that's why she must be punished."

She smiled inwardly. She knew what was coming. She wanted it and dreaded it intensely and she wouldn't have needed his little punishment scenario to intensify her excitement, but it seemed to thrill him and prepare him. She only waited with that tense feeling in her stomach.

"The slut will take twelve!"

"Yes, master." Again, it wasn't what she needed but he enjoyed his little element of play and she knew how it roused him. "I have let too many men fuck me. Too many all at once."

"We must correct you."

"Yes, master, you must." She felt light-hearted and slightly amused but that changed very suddenly as she felt him rubbing the cane across her buttocks. He tapped lightly a few times. They had not played this often but those few memories were startling.

She heard the swish, she heard the thwack, both sensations quite detached until, that split second later, that searing pain completely gripped her. She gasped, barely managed to stifle the scream. That first, agonising stroke had clicked that switch inside her. She was somewhere else, deep inside her own feelings and sensations. He left her a long time after the first one, he always did. Her breathing slowed but the pain knifed even more sharply until, just as it seemed about to subside, she felt the cane sliding over her buttocks again, warning of the next stroke to come.

The noises, the slight delay before the pain hit were the same but, this time, she was somewhere else. She was inside a cocoon of feelings and sensations, dreading each stroke — but wanting more. She never counted. She just loved being in this strange and horrible place. She seemed to hover above herself and see the strokes fall on her but, as each one fell, again that searing stab of pain went through her until, finally, with her lost in her strange place, the pause was longer. She felt his hands stroking her back and her thighs and she seemed to float down from somewhere into herself again. She welcomed the dildo into herself again, she welcomed the fingers onto her clit although no sensations approached the intense fire in her arse. But she gave herself to the toy, to his fingers, enjoyed his kisses on her back, his skin against her side and she let it come from a long way off, nothing more certain than its arrival, moments later, announced by her loud howl.

She slumped onto the bench, relaxed into the straps. "Baby, I'm the boss again now, put him inside me, come inside me."

"I want to come behind you — won't it sting?"

"Of course it will sting, dumbo, but I'm desperate for your cock to come in me."

This time he was almost quick but careful not to push too deep, she'd gasped when his skin had pushed against her. His hands held her hips, she loved enveloping him and she felt him quicken, she gasped when he pushed deeper but he couldn't stop, she didn't want him to, she wanted this beautiful man's cum inside her. Once he started, he eased out slightly and kept a rhythm going, on and on, she loved it, astonished by how much cum he seemed to have, until finally she began to feel him soften. Then, when he pulled out, he moved quickly to unstrap her, helped her off the bench, embraced her passionately and pulled her onto the bed where they lay silent in each other's arms.

Claudia shook herself. That had been almost like a dream although the memory was very vivid and very real and she almost chuckled as she realised that she'd been touching herself while enjoying the reverie. Now, perhaps, she could sleep.

5

The house was quiet, almost eerily so, even for a Sunday morning, but she'd gone to sleep with the noise still loud from the girls downstairs. She hadn't heard them come up. Two were asleep on the sofas, there must be two more bodies besides Abbi in the rooms upstairs.

The kitchen, of course, had been a mess but hardly a disaster, barely enough even to complain about later — why spoil the girls' night? That had been her first job when she came down. Then coffee and just a piece of toast. She could eat a full breakfast with them later - but that would be much later if previous experiences were an indicator. They could all sleep deeply, even in uncomfortable positions.

She opened the email page, taken aback, as usual, at how many could accumulate in so short a time. She tried to discipline herself: flag the important ones to deal with in a block later; instantly delete the obviously unnecessary (by far the majority); and get onto the occasional urgent.

Was Alphonse urgent? No, but there were very few people who only made her smile. Alphonse, smooth, saturnine, but for her, oddly safe — the few memories were thrilling and spectacular but also warm and truly comforting. Alphonse, tall, slim, absurdly handsome and always stylish in his chosen monochrome. Always? She'd met him only three times in total: black, on that first night at the party; light brown, in the spring last year after his call; and dark blue, in the winter, when he'd caught her, as if by magic, at a difficult time. So 'always' was an exaggeration, but a forgivable one. And here he was again, wanting to meet, or at least to talk 'if your schedule doesn't permit a meeting' (if I don't have an urgent need to be fucked, she thought, smiling).

The first meeting, at the party, had been intense but was embedded in a sequence of even more astonishing memories from that night, the most vivid she had ever experienced in her life. But she had categorised him as a single, isolated and charming memory that had faded (only into the back of her mind; it would have stayed there always, she knew that) when suddenly his first email had appeared: brief, charming, modestly remembering himself to her ('I don't know if you remember' — was she flattered to have him imply that she often slept with strange men at parties?) and suggesting that they meet for lunch 'to talk about some possible business interests'. It had seemed altogether puzzling, but it was to be lunch; it would be safe and he was, she told herself, charming company. But her big girl kicked in: would he go out of his way? So: she would love to meet but was too busy to make it into town, where she assumed he was based, could he meet her halfway? She gave three dates when she could make it — she had more, of course, but this was the big girl again, playing what she assumed was a big girl's game.

His reply had come quickly. He'd picked the 26th and had already booked Coworth Park. She was taken aback; she'd not been there but she knew of it. She googled to confirm her assumptions, wow! What sort of business would she be discussing?

She was pleased he'd chosen the 26th. It was her birthday and she hadn't been looking forward to it much. The kids would remember, Pat would see to that, and they would all go out for a Chinese in the evening, but Jack was somewhere deep in China itself and she had managed her expectations down to an Interflora delivery, and maybe not even that. There had been difficult moments in some of the last calls.

Alphonse had been waiting when she got there, even though she was punctual. He unfolded himself from a chair in reception, a vision in light brown, perfect for a sunny spring day: the beautiful suit, the open necked shirt with a very light pattern, and elegant well-shone shoes. He smiled, took her hands, air-kissed her cheeks, held her hands still and looked at her. "My, you look even lovelier than my feeble memory wanted to let me believe, I'm so pleased you could make it."

"Well, I'm delighted I could make it of course, and, also of course, I was intrigued. But all will become clear, no doubt."

He let her hands drop. "All will become clear, of course," and he turned to the hovering woman from reception who led them through to the restaurant.

It was a gorgeous day and they looked out of their tall window onto carefully tended gardens, the rectangles of box hedging with occasional chairs and wooden sofas creating intimate little spaces for guests to meet in the sunshine.

"I honestly hadn't expected to see you again," she blurted, just as the maître d' arrived.

Alphonse held a hand politely to halt her. "We would like two glasses of champagne, please, the rosé."

"Champagne?"

"Birthday," he said, smiling.

She frowned at him. "You had better start explaining; this is getting too curious. Did you really research my birthday?"

"Of course, when Peter's interested in someone, we do our research. But, well, I hadn't expected to see you again either. I mean, I had fallen a little bit in love with you — but you knew that."

"But Peter said you do that quite often." She smiled.

He smiled back. "That's both unfair and unkind. Anyway, we both knew you had someone else, someone you cared about deeply."

"That's true," she nodded, "and I still do but I don't see him any more often than I expected to, unfortunately."

"But you are still committed, you see, I had no chance," he smiled.

"Alphonse, you're being too charming, stop it." His smile broadened. "I thought we were here to talk business."

"We are, although I have nothing specific, this is just Peter's way of exploring opportunities and he wanted to keep an eye on you anyway so, when we discussed it, it just gave me the chance I wanted."

"Peter? Where does that fit in? I thought he was adorable of course, but he and his businesses were all very mysterious to me — and as for me somehow fitting into that picture…"

"Then I should tell you more about Peter."

"Yes," she nodded, "I really wish you would." But they were interrupted by the waiter wanting an order. She decided quickly, keen to get back to the conversation. Alphonse deliberated a little, then simply repeated her order.

"It makes the wine choice easier."

"Wine?"

"Of course, we're civilised people and I'm half French, as you may remember." (Of course she remembered.)

"I have to work later," she paused, thought, "no, I don't suppose I do really. I work so many hours anyway. But I do have to take the kids out this evening."

"I understand. I'll make sure your consumption is modest."

"Aren't you driving?"

"No, I'll be collected. Now, to Peter" but then the Sommelier appeared at his elbow. "Excuse me," he said to her; "a Sancerre?" he asked, "What do you have?"

"The Vincent Pinard is very good, sir."

"That will be fine, thank you." He smiled and turned back to her.

She wanted to ask why he hadn't checked the price but managed to stop herself; she was a big girl today.

"Peter is a wealthy man, as you've seen, and most of it he's made himself. He had some family money thirty years ago and he made a couple of spectacular tech investments. He doesn't talk about them much, just says he was lucky. He'll tell you more about his failures if you ever ask him — they're the things you learn from, he always says. But he was making a lot of money when he made contact with a couple of young guys who were getting a hedge fund going. He got involved with them because he thought they had some clever ideas and they really were very good. They were on the right side of the financial crisis and came out of that much richer, unlike most people, especially bankers. Then he moved into property, which is where I came in. He plucked me out of a London agent, where I'd been doing well, if I may admit that modestly, but Peter wanted to set up a property arm of his own and asked me to do that. That sort of freedom is hard to turn down."

"But what does he know about property?"

"About as much as he knows about high tech or hedge funds. What you'll probably remember from that night at the party, I'm sure someone will have said, is that what Peter knows about is people."

"Yes, someone did, Yvonne, I think, but I thought that anyway, just listening to him."

"Well, he's got it into his head that there's something in what you do that should be given more space. He wants to know if you would think about setting up on your own." She frowned as a dozen questions crowded in at once. Best just listen, she thought, or ask minimum questions; that's what Jack would do. She tilted her head and raised an eyebrow. "It will now become obvious to you that I know little about your job and what's special about it. I've been sent on a quest and asked to report back."

"Report on what?"

"On what I find." He was interrupted by a waiter bringing the compliments of the chef and that gave him the chance to raise his glass to say, "Happy Birthday to a very beautiful lady." She raised her glass and hoped she'd remained cool enough not to blush.

"Thank you," she said, "but how would I fit into what he does?"

"I don't know yet, so I'm going to ask you to tell me more about what you do. But before you start, it might help you to think about his first area of business. He's kept stakes in the first two companies that made him wealthy — smaller stakes now; they've become less interesting to him — but he has big stakes in a group of businesses and consultancies, quite a large group, more than twenty. He likes to find people with interesting skills and ideas that can branch out by themselves with his help and also interact with the other businesses and people under his umbrella. It's a pretty loose consortium but it hangs together mostly because of the people he chooses and their attitudes and approaches. So, can I ask what you do? Beyond you working for a global corporation, I know little about it."

"Well, I have my own little niche, I think, but I'd never thought about taking it outside. I just work to get everybody in each business in the corporation engaged in what it's trying to do. I've only been doing it globally for a year." She paused; oh dear, where had the big girl gone? She was sounding naïve. Anyway, best just to plunge in, he could draw his own conclusions. If it led to something new, so be it, but she was, for the first time probably ever, content, excited even, about what she was doing at work and, with Dave gone and Pat helping, she finally had some freedom to do a job properly.

She talked, only realising how much she'd talked when she found herself declining dessert. Alphonse had remained very attentive throughout, asking questions about working across cultures and through local organisational structures and hierarchies that showed a man far more familiar with a global corporate world than she had assumed.

"No dessert, but will you have coffee?"

She shook her head. "I'm happy finishing the water, thank you, but the wine was wonderful, by the way."

He smiled. "Yes, I liked it too. One of the advantages of being half-French is that people assume your knowledge of wine is wide and profound, but I just wing it mostly. But that was one that I happened to know — pure coincidence — well, that and checking the wine list before I came." He even managed a small laugh at himself and she was relaxed enough to laugh with him.

"I'll have an espresso," he said to the waiter, then, turning to her again, "Do you have time? Have I kept you too long?"

"Good Lord, Alphonse, it's me who's been keeping you. How long have I been rabbiting on? But no, no, you've not kept me. I was planning to go back to the office, but I think I'll go straight home from here."

"I'm delighted. I really want to talk some more."

And they talked, and when he'd finished coffee and resisted the ridiculous petits fours, they made their way into the gardens and found a quiet corner.

"It's a flattering idea, of course it is, starting up on my own, but I don't think it's a step I'd have the courage to make. I have too little security in my life as it is." She had talked a little about her domestic arrangements.

"It didn't sound like there were too many barriers. You seem to travel very freely now."

"Very freely is putting it too strongly. I don't travel without giving a lot of thought to the kids — and to my mother-in-law. But I admit it's much easier than it used to be, but there's also the security aspect of working in a big corporation."

"Oh, you'd be surprised at how much security Peter could give you. He goes a long way for people he believes in" and here his hand moved on to hers, he squeezed it gently and held it longer than simple reassurance needed. She moved her hand away but kept looking into his eyes. She knew now that sleeping with him had not just been a mad aberration. She smiled.

"I really will have to go soon but it's been truly wonderful catching up again — and I'll admit to being very surprised and very flattered. I'm sorry if I sound like a girl but I don't think I conceal my feelings very well anyway."

"No, you don't," he smiled, "but that's just one of the things I fell in love with."

"Yes," she smiled again, "that and my perfect arse."

He smiled too. "I admit it, and I'm thrilled to see it's still perfect. Thank you for wearing a skirt that showed it off so well." Now she probably did blush, remembering how carefully she'd selected the slim fitting skirt in a light material — it would be a warm day, she'd checked — and she'd chosen the thong with care.

"I will talk with Peter. If I know him, he will respect your feelings and your circumstances, but he will make sure I stay in touch." He stood up and held out his hands to hold her hands — she took them and stood. "And I, of course, will very much stay in touch anyway. I hadn't forgotten falling in love with you and now I'm doing it again" and it seemed perfectly natural to fall into his arms and kiss him.

She'd wondered, driving home, whether she should have stayed. Could have? Oh, she was certain he would have asked but the big girl had abandoned her and she'd fled rather quickly from the kiss to her car.

That wasn't a mistake she would make the next time they met in the winter. Then the big girl had stayed with her. It had left her with just the right amount of longing and the right amount of regret.

And now he needed to talk again.

Coworth would become 'their' place if they met there for a third time but this might be serious business so she should schedule a call to explore his intentions — without, she smiled to herself, ruling out Coworth as an option. He had her number, she emailed him to call next week to arrange something. That started a train of thought about where she truly was with Jack but, fortunately, a bleary-eyed fourteen-year-old in PJs blundered into the kitchen.

"Good morning, Amanda. Did you have a fun evening?"

"Oh, it was brilliant, Mrs Brodie, thank you so much for letting us stay. Gosh, we did quite a good job of clearing up, didn't we?"

She could only smile.

Once she had three of them in the kitchen she started on breakfast. "Was Abbi moving? Who was in her room?"

"She was moving, Mrs Brodie, but not looking like she was about to get up."

Claudia paused — oh, why worry, let's stay relaxed.

Within fifteen minutes they were all up, however, moving in a random ballet of preparation, service and consumption. Claudia abandoned all hope of order and merely let them bring her the things she said she wanted. Nothing was being dropped; there seemed to be no collisions. There was only such a rising cacophony that she barely heard her phone. Private number. She declined.

It rang again a moment later: private number again. It might be Damian's mother about Jonah. She moved out of the kitchen. "Hello."

"Claudia, it's Alphonse. It's lovely to hear your voice, is this a bad time?"

"Alphonse, er, no, no it's fine. But Sunday morning's a surprise. I've only just replied to your email is it urgent?"

"Well, Peter will always tell you that nothing is urgent. And then he will ask you the next day, so the correct answer is that I don't know. But my question is quite simple. Will you be in the US in September?"

"Yes, yes I will be, but I can't tell you the exact dates without checking the diary. What's the idea?"

"Peter would like you to join him for a weekend on Yvonne D."

"Yvonne? That's his wife."

"It's also his boat. He changes his boat every time he gets divorced. No new wife wants to share the spaces with memories of her predecessor. It's a funny mind set. Houses they can strip and completely redecorate but somehow boats are more personal."

"Isn't that frighteningly expensive?"

"Not really. We sell them on with a full charter book so we always get a good price and we've always bought, shall we say, advantageously. Someone, somewhere has always pulled out of a deal late on. My job is to persuade the new wife that this particular boat, that the shipyard is now finishing and is desperate to sell, has been designed with only her in mind. It's the original selling trick, listen to what a person says they want and then persuade them that what you have exactly matches that. It's much the best way. Boat lead times are three years, most couples divorce before their project's finished. Anyway, the point is, do you have a weekend free while you're there?"

"I don't usually stay for the weekend. I get the six o'clock out of Dulles on a Thursday."

"But you could fly to Miami on a Thursday evening, yes?"

She hesitated. "I could, but what's this about?"

"You know what it's about. He wants to talk to you about starting your own business. He wonders if the time is right. You and I have talked about it a couple of times."

"That wasn't all we did the last time, my dear Alphonse, but I do remember the serious conversation, of course I do, and I guess I'm now wondering what I do next. The corporation tends not to let people stay still. Maybe I have two more years of doing what I'm doing but then, who knows?"

"So, you'll come. May I tell him that?"

"Let me think. I'll email you tomorrow morning with the date. It could only be one specific weekend at the end of a DC week and that's fixed."

"I understand, you'll let me know tomorrow. The date won't be a problem. Peter has the boat in the area for the whole month. Now, what else is going on in your life? How's Jack?"

"Jack is fine, thank you. Well, he was six weeks ago when I last saw him but I'm sorry, Alphonse, I have a kitchen full of young ladies and I think I've just heard a plate drop."

He laughed. "I understand. I'll hear from you tomorrow."

"You'll hear from me tomorrow, and Alphonse…"

"Yes."

"Thank you for calling."

"It really is my pleasure. I am still in love with you, you know."

She laughed. "Yes, yes, but seriously, thank you. Bye."

She didn't rush to the kitchen. They could clear up the broken plate. Could Pat cover a weekend, she wondered. It wouldn't have been the first — and she would be away with the kids very soon for two weeks on their holidays. She had also kept the work diary light for most of their time off school in summer anyway. It could work.

6

The gentlemen rose from the armchairs as the concierge brought her to their table. Henderson, iron-haired, tight-jawed, looking, as always, ready to spring. His companion a little taller, greyer hair, probably the same age. He looked a little familiar, but she had checked the Giddings Group's website. The chairman's picture, stiffly formal but recognisably the same man, *but Rod's party, she'd met him there, what was his name?* and there was some recognition in his smile.

Rod took her hand and shook it firmly a man's greeting.

"Arthur, I don't know if you remember…"

"Of course I remember. It's Claudia, isn't it? Who could forget?" It was a deep drawl, slightly Southern, and a warm smile went with it. He took her hand now shook it more gently. "We met at Rod's place, didn't we, a couple of months back. I was fascinated by what you were doing."

"You're very kind," she said, and allowed herself to be guided to her chair. She didn't want to risk saying anything. As this year of surprises unfolded, their intensity only increased. Thank God for google, at least she entered this charming, strangely old-world environment a little prepared. And she'd checked the menus, simple and unintimidating.

DC was at its luscious best. She was staying at the Hilton this time, just two blocks from HQ, a short walk in the mornings. Jack always stayed at the Ritz with most of the others.

She'd booked the cab very early, having got used to the American habit of uber-punctuality. If she was way too early at the George Town Club she could hop out and enjoy a stroll in Georgetown, hence the slightly sensible shoes but they didn't detract from the killer dress, she didn't think: blue, sleek, high-necked, classy and glam (sexy would obviously be wrong).

And she'd been amazed by the price. The sales had already started at Needless Markup, Sarah's joke name for Neimann Marcus but now she couldn't call it anything else, and the discounts brought many unthinkable things into her price range. But a Valentino, that had been a real find, and she was, she knew, blessed with the figure for it.

The ride into the city along the GW Parkway, through the arching trees, still in full, green summer dress, dappled by shafts of sunlight, was enchanting. The occasional glimpse of river meant they were getting nearer, still very early but it would be the bridges where the traffic fouled up. Still, she'd had evenings when it had built even this far back but the cars were still moving. Slowing, yes, but no holdups yet.

Finally, the vista opened up, the Washington monument and the dome of the Capitol beyond, dazzling in the full evening sunlight. It was a city of vistas. She and Jack had met for one late afternoon walk, *they were old colleagues catching up, she had work in his region, nothing to gossip about there.* She'd loved it; they'd walked all the way from the Lincoln memorial up to the Capitol steps. They had detoured through the Vietnam memorial which she'd found sombre but deeply affecting. But that mood was lifted as they watched the groups enjoying the National Mall: guys throwing footballs; dogs chasing Frisbees; and laughing children playing incomprehensible games. They turned at the Capitol and walked into Georgetown. They found a Japanese restaurant Jack knew ("If I have to eat another one of those enormous American steaks, I'll explode!") and then went back to her room at the Hilton. He hung back for a couple of minutes before joining her. They'd fallen asleep in each other's arms as soon as they got into bed, but she smiled to herself when she remembered how early they'd woken and how fresh and vibrant their lovemaking had been.

They were edging down to the Francis Scott Key Bridge, moving very slowly now *(it wasn't that impressive, did it deserve such a name? Nah, Key Bridge was enough)* and her ETA was edging towards her appointed time. There would be no need or time for a Georgetown stroll.

The invitation had come the previous week from a name she barely recognised Lavinia, Henderson's PA, the source of the cocktail evening invitation: would she have dinner next Tuesday at The George Town Club with Mr Henderson? He would like to introduce her to Mr Gunter of the Giddings Group.

"Maybe you're wondering why I've asked to meet you like this. Am I right?" Arthur Gunter's eyes were very blue, very smiley.

"Well." She looked to Henderson, whose face, as usual, betrayed nothing. She turned back to Gunter, "Yes. I didn't even know who specifically had asked for a meeting."

"Well, it was me. You see, I think you can help me. I was very interested in what you were saying back at Rod here's and I thought yep, we need some of that." It was a very homespun delivery but those clear, smiling eyes hinted at a bright mind. "But we can talk about that later. I'd like to know more about you first and you might even want to know a little more about us old buffers." She laughed, but he was already laughing. Henderson's face moved but she would have hesitated to call it a smile. "Now, where do you live? Or should I ask you, where do you stay?"

She laughed gently with him. Henderson looked puzzled. "You see, you haven't completely lost the accent, have you?"

"No, but when I go home, they tell me I've gone all terribly posh."

"There's an accent?" asked Henderson.

"She's Scottish, man, can you no hear that?" It was butchered but it was an attempt. "My grandmother was from Arbroath, you see, damn near incomprehensible to us kids in Atlanta and, my God, she was a strict woman. Were your folks strict?"

"No, not at all," she smiled, "but they'd no reason to be, of course."

"Young woman. I've had daughters and they've always told me I had no reason to be strict," he laughed, shaking his head. "All three of them beautiful and not one takes a blind bit of notice of me. Well, I get a bit of attention when one of them wants a car or something. Poor Rod only has sons. He's missing half of life."

"Your stories don't exactly make me envious," and, for the first time, he seemed to relax a little. "You have kids, Claudia?"

"Girl and boy, fourteen and twelve."

"Aw, wonderful," said Gunter, "but how do they get on with you being away? Oops, I'm sorry, that may not be a question I can ask nowadays."

"Oh, that's fine," she said, "I have a wonderful mother-in-law who's retired and lives near us. It works out very well."

"You'll have to forgive me, well you don't have to, of course, you can sue me and my HR people keep telling me someone will do that someday soon but Rodney, Rodney, we're sat here all this time and this young lady doesn't even have a drink." He broke off and began to wave to a waiter.

"You see," said Henderson conspiratorially, "all this guff about Southern hospitality is purest moonshine. That should have been his first thought. What would you like? Champagne okay?"

The waiter arrived. "Hello Ernesto, how are you?"

"I'm fine, Mr Gunter, and how are you?"

"I'm wonderful, thank you Ernesto, but our guest here is missing something to welcome her. I do believe I heard her say champagne and you'd better bring a glass for Mr Henderson. I'll just stick with sparkling water for the time being. But you could bring me the wine list. Oh, and the menus, I do believe we have a table booked."

"Yes, Mr Gunter, I believe it's in Mr Henderson's name." Henderson nodded.

By the time the mains were being cleared away she knew far more about Gunter's grandmother than she truly cared to know but he was a very engaging conversationalist. She'd also been peppered with questions about home and travel, particularly about Asia and her view of its cultures — dangerous ground with senior people, who sometimes barely hid antagonistic prejudices — but she loved the places she'd been to, loved the positive attitudes. Gunter's encouraging 'you don't say's' could have concealed anything, but she'd decided there was no point in second guessing. They could have her frank and honest, but by no means trenchant, views. Henderson said very little.

The waiter with the dessert menus was politely waved away. "Now see here, Claudia, here's my problem." His tone was more earnest, but he still spoke warmly. "Our corporations are pretty close, as you probably know and not just because we're two old Yaleys who've been friends for years. There's a number of areas where Giddings and Collins Corp work closely. Giddings is more than just a logistics provider to Collins, we try to work together on IT development and things like that but it's fair to say that you're more progressive than little old Giddings, particularly in things like engaging your people. Now Rod here, he's on our board as well, did we say that?" She shook her head. "Well, he is, and he talks a lot to me about what you're doing and about the impact you're having."

She was prickling a little, this was very exciting, this was real recognition.

"Now I'd been real impressed by what he'd told me, and I was real impressed when I first met you so I wanted to get to know you better and I think you could help us a lot" and, smiling, he reached out and covered her hand with his, squeezing gently. She held still but smiled slightly. "Oops, I'm really sorry, that's another court case HR will have to defend me on."

He pulled his hand back and laughed. She laughed with him. "So, can I ask, what are you looking for, apart from another court case?" He laughed suddenly as she smiled. Even Henderson smiled with her.

"I like you a lot," he said, reaching out to pat her shoulder but withdrawing his hand at the last instant only to laugh again, even louder this time. Then he settled quite quickly into a more serious tone. "I'd like you to come and talk to us, tell us what you're doing, what resources and commitments you need and what we might have to commit to could you do that?"

Wow! She turned to Henderson. "Could I do that?"

"I do know you're very busy now, but I'd encourage them to give you more support at Collins. Just to put your mind at rest, we'd charge a fee to Giddings for your time — you'd have to do quite a lot of prep about their business. It's not a small commitment, Arthur understands that."

"Oh, I fully support it," he interjected. "No point in coming if you don't understand our business."

"But quite a large part of that fee would be your bonus. Does that sound good?"

She tried to look like she was considering it, hiding her 'that's amazing' thoughts. "Well, I admit I'm intrigued — and very flattered, of course — I've often wondered how it would be to plant the ideas in fresh soil. The programme had already started when I came into it at Collins. I'd love to see if it could work somewhere else. This could be an ideal opportunity."

"Attagirl," said Gunter, not stopping himself this time from patting her shoulder. He leaned back. "Look, I have to fly now but I'd like to see you down with us in the next six weeks, could you do that?" She looked to Henderson. "Oh, don't worry about him, he's on board, I mean, can you fit us into your schedule? You're a busy woman with big travel commitments and a family, let's not forget," he laughed, "although sometimes my girls make me wish I could forget mine. Anyway, see what you can do, please."

"Of course I will. I'm pretty sure I can work something out."

"Thank you, now I can leave with a lighter heart," and he stood up, she moved to stand too. "No, no, please stay where you are. I'll leave you to make your protests to Rod about this dam-fool thing he's got you into." The men nodded to each other. "And don't worry, I've taken care of the bill. He's a skinflint and this place is lovely but it's not extravagant," and with an airy wave he left the room.

"Where does he have to get to?"

"Atlanta." His eyes narrowed and he smiled slightly as he watched her process the information. "He uses a private jet, of course."

"Oh, of course," she said, trying to remain calm although he might as well have said 'magic carpet'.

Then she calmed down. Gunter would surely have had bigger things to deal with in DC. She was merely an add-on. But a significant one, she reassured herself, the two of them had committed an evening to her.

"Well, are you pleased with the proposition?"

"I don't know if I'm allowed to say I'm thrilled, but I am," and there was, finally, a full smile on Henderson's face. He took her hand, squeezed it, and released it. "But I need to be honest up front, we're coming into my busy time of year. The corporation's finals are in December and the regions all want some hand-holding before then."

"What support would help?"

"Well, there's a lot of basic admin, making sure all event plans come together, and I've got good people in each region, but they're all helping part-time and their line managers sometimes pull them away from the programme just when things are busy."

"Well, Lavinia has some capacity and she often says she'd would like to see deeper into the companies. That would help with admin, and if we say one manager in each region is on full-time secondment until after the finals?"

"Mr Henderson, that would make a huge difference, to the guys as well. They're torn, they love helping but can't go against line bosses."

"Well, I can see a triple benefit: you get our programme properly supported; we show line managers what life's bigger priorities are; and you can give Arthur some help — that place has to change, and the change has to start with his people." He squeezed her hand again, "And it's Rod, please." She didn't react but it did register this time. Benefit of the doubt, yes, but the alert mode had been triggered. If he was in Atlanta when she travelled there, she would definitely be careful.

In the cab on the way back she was buzzing. This was real affirmation, for her and for the programme — taking it somewhere else, wow, she'd meant what she'd said to Arthur, she was keen to see it tried in a different place. And Henderson? How supersensitive was she being? He'd seen her to the cab, he'd given her his manly goodnight handshake, but she'd felt his hand on the bare skin of her back as she climbed into the cab. Jury out, she thought. She would make time to talk to Sarah tomorrow about the gossip.

7

"They want me to go to Atlanta to help Giddings."

"What happened to: it's wonderful to hear your warm sexy voice this glorious morning, my dearest darling?"

"It's wonderful to hear your warm, sexy voice etcetera, etcetera but they still want me to go to Atlanta. I think that's amazing. It is, isn't it? Sometimes I can't work this corporation out. Correction, most times."

"This is your dinner with Henderson and the other guy, yes?"

"Yes, the other guy is Gunter he's chairman of Giddings, I met him at that Henderson party and he wants to put our programme into his business. I get more support with our own programme and free up some time for this. It is brilliant, isn't it? I need some help, Jack, bring me down to earth a bit."

"I'm not bringing you down to earth, I think it's amazing too and Gunter's a bit more than chairman. He owns a huge chunk of Giddings, it's the family business. If he wants something to happen, it will. I'm blown away for you. Exciting times, and it's the boat trip tomorrow, isn't it?"

An edge had crept into his voice. This was Peter of the dungeon she was visiting. She knew Jack's feelings were ambiguous. He enjoyed how free she'd become to enjoy all they did, but she knew he grew very uneasy when he thought of her having been there.

"Jack, this is just business. I have to follow it up. I would love to get started on my own outside the corporation and put these secret trysts behind us. You even got a bit twitchy in London last month and we knew we'd see nobody there."

"I know, I know, I'm probably over-cautious but if you could start up on your own that would be wonderful."

"It would be, Jack. Look, I'm not trying to commit you to anything, but I would like us to have more freedom to choose. Still, you have plenty of that anyway. What have you been up to? Where are you going this evening?"

"It's a bit intense here, everyone's putting next year's plans together and that's full of the usual problems: people sandbagging; people trying to lower their profit projections and convince me they're investing. So, I've got the heads of the bigger units and their finance guys here for a couple of days this week. I'm out to dinner with them later."

"Am I keeping you?"

"No, I've rung early to make sure we've got time to talk. Sorry to wake you but you function quite well at

6 a.m. I'm delighted to remember. But anyway, when will you be doing Atlanta?"

"He's asked me to go within six weeks. What's on your mind?"

"I'm in the US in four weeks; could we tie that in? Go somewhere for a few days? Have a dirty weekend on the coast?"

"Oh, Jack, yes. I didn't know how we'd organise anything before Christmas. If you email me your dates, I'll try to work something out. No, I will work something out. Can you do either weekend of your stay?"

"I don't see why not. I'll make it work, whatever works best for you and Pat."

It was sweet how he talked about this person he'd never met as if she were an old friend, but she was essential to managing even what little time they had. Claudia sometimes wondered how helpful Dave would have been if he'd had to look after the kids on her travel weekends. Not very, she knew, he would screw things up, probably at the last minute, and probably deliberately. She knew he was still festering, in spite of his new friend.

"Well, even the kids want a say now. If they think I'm seeing you, they'll want to come with me. I'll have to make sure it doesn't coincide with their half-term week. That would give them a chance to argue."

"We could think about that."

"My dear sweet man, there are so many reasons why that would be wrong."

"Would it?"

"Jack! Just one for starters. When we get together, we spend every spare minute fucking for the first two days. It just wouldn't work. I need your body and now I know I can have it in four weeks' time. I know you have ways of filling the gaps in your life, but I have only you and a collection of vibrators. And talking of gaps, I haven't put you on the spot lately who have you seen? That little Asian lady with the smart mouth?"

"Jaaaack," she said, as teasingly as she could when he didn't respond, "you can't say I haven't done well. The best blowjobs since Joanna you said that night when you'd drunk too much. I obviously found that personally hard to take."

"That's an old tease now," he said, a little tetchily. "I must have said a dozen times since then that nobody is like you. I couldn't and wouldn't even begin to compare."

"It's only eight times but I'm a big person, I'm prepared to call it quits provided you book somewhere nice for next month. So, have you seen her? I'm much better knowing than speculating."

"It's been a couple of weeks. She thinks her husband's getting suspicious."

"I think it's funny that she has that American attitude. Blowjobs aren't adultery. It's so strange. So, who have you fucked?"

Another long pause before he said, "Martha asked to see me."

"Martha?" and she knew she hadn't controlled the slight shock in her voice. She tried to compose herself. "I thought that finished ages ago."

"It did. I hadn't seen her outside of business functions for a year or so but, as you know, she has a special set of needs and she was getting frustrated, so she asked to see me for a one-off, she said."

"And how did that work?" She was trying hard to rationalise this. Martha had never been a danger before and Jack seemed to have closed off the relationship in a civilised way. So, what would be the harm if it really was a one-off? "Where did you see her?"

The slowness of his responses was putting her on edge. "She came here. As she said, I had her favourite cane. That was a funny conversation to have with a powerful woman in her big office on the twenty-eighth floor. But, yes, she wanted to come here."

A very unwelcome thought was dawning, she would have to manage the next part of the conversation carefully. "So, I suppose you introduced her to the new bench."

Again, he was slow. "Yes. She was fascinated, of course."

"I bet she was." It was going to be hard to keep up this jocular façade, but she had to get through it and process her feelings later. "Did you have to adjust it much?"

"A little, she's a bit shorter than you."

"And what did she do while you were busy with the spanners?"

"She kept talking. She does that when she's nervous. And she was walking around the thing, running her hands over it. Then she started undressing."

"And was she ready for a sexy evening? Thong and push-up bra? Exotic colours?"

"Yes, she was, Claudie." He sounded a little exasperated, she needed to be careful. The trick was always to get all the information and deal with it later — but we were talking about 'her' bench. Why was her brain signalling that this was even more personal than a cane? *Stop it, Claudia!* "But it was only a small adjustment. That was done quite quickly."

"And did she climb on straight away?"

"Are you getting off on this?"

"I might be. No, it's more that I do better with these things if I know all about them." This, at least, was true. "But I do want to hear that it was very painful for her."

There was a noise, almost like a laugh, from Jack. "It certainly was that. I have to talk really dirty to her. As you know, there has to be a little humiliation involved, that goes on with a lot of paddling, and then I leave a long pause. The talk and the paddling get her quite excited and she's breathing heavily by then, so I walk round her a few times just tapping the cane on my hand."

"Her cane."

"Yes, her cane, of course. Yours is sacrosanct." It was good that he was getting almost jovial and she knew she was being a little ridiculous thinking the bench should be even more sacrosanct than a cane, but she was managing to encourage him to talk.

"And did she manage to take a good dozen?"

"Oh, a dozen's never enough for Martha. She likes to count, and she always gets to twenty-five and sometimes wants more."

"Wow, I know I get in a zone with you. It's very strange, I could probably handle more, but it's dealing with the consequences the next day that's usually a problem. Anyway, how hard were you with her? As hard as with me?"

"At first, yes, but then she wanted harder."

"Harder?"

"Yes, she's a really tough woman, and her wrists were strapped so she couldn't play with herself to bring herself off."

"Ah, I'm getting the picture. Our gallant knight now has to play with the desperate lady."

"That's pretty much it. Once I started touching her she came very quickly — and very loudly, I have to say, I was beginning to worry about the neighbours."

"And then you helped yourself?"

"A bit like that, yes."

"A bit like that? What does that mean?" *Try not to sound querulous, Claudia.*

"Well, she'd seen the lube in the wardrobe. She said, 'Stick him in my ass, Jack, I'm a dirty girl, I want to try anal'. I was nervous, her arse must have seriously stung already and if she'd really never tried it, well, you need to help people relax but I wanted to finish fairly quickly."

"You mean he wanted to finish fairly quickly. I know what he's like."

"Well, we both did, so I grabbed the lube and put a big dollop between her cheeks. I have to say, I wasn't as gentle as I am with you."

"And did it work?"

"It wasn't easy. She was very tight and started making pained noises but when I pulled him away, she kept shouting, 'no, stick him in, fuck my ass, I'm a filthy, naughty girl,' so I pushed again, trying a bit slower. She was still almost screaming but saying, 'no, go on, stick him in, make me take it, do it' in between them. Finally, I squeezed half of him in and it was so tight he just came very quickly." *He did — Jack didn't — it was him, not you, you're innocent — the ultimate man excuse — the disembodied, morality-free appendage did it!*

"As he does," she said, trying to affect a levity that she absolutely did not feel. "So, does your new bench mean that she'll want to come again? And is she now a fan of anal?" She'd managed to avoid saying 'our bench'.

"I'm afraid it might. I had an email the next morning thanking me for a wonderful time and for everything, underlined, I'd done. Do we need to talk more about this? I'm sure you've got the complete picture now."

"No, we don't, really we don't. I'm a big girl about it, really, I am. I'd like to hope it was a one-off, but it doesn't sound like it will be. Still, you've been managing Martha's special needs for a couple of years and you know I don't expect you to remain a hermit. That's our deal and I'm very grateful you've been honest about it. But like I said, I hope it was really painful, especially the anal," and she tried to manage a laugh. She thought it worked. "Anyway, I've enjoyed the story, but you've got to get out and meet your guys and I've got to shower. Now tell me you love me and I'm fabulous and don't forget to send me your US dates."

"I love you very much and you're more than fabulous and I've already written 'remember US dates' on the bedside pad."

"I'll tell you I love you when I get that email. Have a lovely evening, Jack."

She hung up, she really couldn't talk to him any more.

8

It felt strange to be leaving at lunchtime. She wouldn't be in Miami until seven but there were no direct flights that she could use. She felt some old-fashioned pangs at leaving at that time of day on private business, but she'd worked with such intensity for a day and a half that she was sure she'd paid her dues so, finally, in the cab on the way to the airport, she began to relax.

Lavinia had been an unexpected boon:

'Mr Henderson has suggested I might support you on the Collins engagement programme and I would be very keen to do so. In addition, may I offer you some assistance with your upcoming Giddings activities? I can access a great deal of material which may help you in understanding their business.'

That was a massive boost. The email had come before ten in the morning so he must have briefed her first thing. She had already googled the public information, annual reports, corporate presentations and the typical investor data which was going to be plenty to absorb but she was at a loss about what to ask for beyond that or how to access it. She had misgivings about what she could expect from the mysterious Lavinia, the faceless issuer of two surprising invitations but this was not a time to overthink what might get reported to Henderson — she was a long way from thinking of him as Rod. So, she had plunged in:

'Dear Lavinia, I was delighted to hear from you, and I will be seriously grateful for all the help I can get in both areas...'

She committed to provide an overview of everything going on in the engagement programme by the end of the day (she did do) and then simply outlined the areas of the Giddings business she wanted to know more about:

'I don't know quite how to put this, but I'm looking for dirty laundry; how can I tell where their vulnerabilities are? The public information has a positive gloss at all times. Is there information on the sensitive issues?'

That was a brief that would test anyone, but she was amazed at what came back by the end of the day: a number of reports ('internal circulation only') on delivery reliability (poor), service performance (patchy) and HR issues which gave a lot of support to Henderson's view that they needed help. The reports would keep her busy for all of the evening after the early dinner she'd persuaded Sarah to take with her.

The dinner had been quite informative. There was gossip about two or three relationships in Henderson's past and his suspected partners had usually done well in their careers — but this could just be jealous gossip spawned by resentment about talented women getting on — they agreed this was an area where, for all their posturing, men could show considerable spite. Sarah was nevertheless, she said, in the 'no smoke without fire' camp and advised watchfulness. And Lavinia was thought to be closer than she should be to her boss. Sarah saw her once a year at the annual Christmas event, always elegant, always alone. Someone to be handled carefully, Claudia thought.

That didn't stop her writing enthusiastically the following morning:

'Dear Lavinia, thank you so much for all your support on Giddings. I am only part way through the material you have sent but it is already clearly illustrating the areas I shall need to focus on. On our Collins programme, Mr Henderson had suggested that we might arrange for three of the regional team leaders to be seconded full time for the months leading up to the finals in December. I wondered if he had mentioned how we might implement this step. It will be immensely helpful in making our programme run well but I am

sensitive to the tensions that might arise between our team leaders and their line managers.'

The response had been slightly chilling:

'Mr Henderson has already communicated with Collins corporate HR that this step was to be implemented and that the relevant line managers were to be informed that failure to give continuing ongoing support would have serious consequences for them. I have already noted the names of team leaders and line managers and have diarised six month and one-year reviews of their career progress following the event.'

She didn't know whether to be more scared of Lavinia or Henderson. Both needed handling with care, she decided.

Those thoughts began to recede as the cab moved smoothly past the now familiar buildings in Reston on the Dulles access road. She was trying to look forward to Miami but yesterday morning's phone call with Jack kept trying to force its way into her head. Her usual mechanism was failing her. She would normally allow three days to elapse before rationalising the events into her familiar mantra: we agreed no constraints and we committed to honesty — and, strictly, he had observed both of those conditions. *Yes, Jack, particularly the first.* She was nevertheless troubled, in spite of laughing at herself for making something almost sacred out of a mere kinky bench which would, if she tried to be detached about it, be considered by anyone normal as somewhat sordid. Well, many of the things they did would, out of context, be seen that way. But she loved him and the lengthy absences were not diminishing that and when, in quiet times, she let herself think of how passionately and imaginatively they made love — and fucked, dammit, I love him fucking me — she still found the memories thrilling. And the latest Martha episode might damage that if she allowed herself to keep thinking about it now.

So, she tried to focus on Yvonne D. There had been detailed photos on the 'available for charter' websites. There had been two Yvonnes: one stationed in the Med, and one, Yvonne D, that seemed to move between the Med and the Caribbean. That must be Peter's, she thought — and it was the bigger of the two! She felt a little-girl excitement when she allowed herself to think about it. She wondered if she could sustain a sophisticated pose when she got there. The photos were fascinating — a window on an entirely different world — but by steeping herself in them she hoped she would be able to avoid the danger of looking awe-struck when she went on board. She'd even been impressed by the boat Jack had borrowed in Singapore and Yvonne D was vastly grander than that; a mansion compared to the cottage Jack had sailed.

The journey itself was already beginning with her in brighter spirits. She would not have to face the dread of coach class. Alphonse had emailed the day before:

'Arrive refreshed. Please upgrade. Seats are available. Your expenses will be covered. You will be met at the airport. Love Alphonse.'

It was a sweet, welcome gesture and when she followed up, he was right, there were seats but Alphonse clearly had no understanding of managing domestic cash flow in her circumstances. She didn't think the outlay would take her into the red — she was very keen to avoid that. She'd not been there since taking on the new job, but she needed to check her balance. She found that GBP 2000 had been deposited that morning with the reference 'Flights'. She almost laughed when the line came up on the screen: so, bigger seats; service; lounges — she might even enjoy the journey instead of finding it a struggle.

The additional benefit of being able to work easily helped the journey pass more quickly. She was reviewing all the material Lavinia had sent her on Giddings and making a list of what else she might need: how did they communicate with employees; how did they reward them; how did they recognise special contributions; did everyone know what the business was aiming for? The programme in Collins had given a focus to direct everyone's efforts towards important business goals. But Collins had a history of being progressive in these ways; the programme enhanced efforts in the desired directions. How would she start in a business where nothing existed? She managed an existing programme at Collins. Regional leaders, like Jack, mostly gave her lots of support. She didn't have to work miracles. But maybe Gunter himself would give a real impetus. She would know more in four weeks. Jack had sent his dates. She'd taken note but not attempted to think of the weekend they would spend together. She would have to get over Martha before she could allow herself to do that.

She'd emailed Lavinia straight away and let her know when her best three days would be. She wanted to spend two days meeting people in the business before presenting her first thoughts to Gunter and whoever he wanted to involve. Lavinia had already responded: the dates were fine for Gunter. Would she let him know, through Lavinia, who she would like to meet for her research and who she would like to present her ideas to at the end, in addition to himself? He'd suggested the names of four VPs who he thought should be there, but he would take her input on that. And would she have dinner at his home the evening before the presentation? The whole process was leaving her in a state of suspended excitement. And now Miami lay ahead; the pilot announced the descent.

The bonus of no immigration checks brought a little anxiety of there being no natural meeting point for arrivals, but baggage collection would be the obvious point to look for her name board and she had readied herself for that. It meant she almost collided with the cream linen suit that stepped into her path soon after she emerged from the jetty.

"On time, well done."

"Alphonse!" and she dropped her bag to respond to his embrace. Oops, careful not to push her face onto the cream-coloured tee shirt. "How lovely, I hadn't expected a welcome like this."

"Why ever not, my love?" and he kissed her lightly, but on the lips, and then picked up her bag. "You look, as ever, enchanting. Do you mind me telling you?"

"As long as you don't do it more than four times a day."

"Then I shall endeavour to restrain myself. Did you eat on the plane? Peter was hoping we might eat on board."

"I had a small snack, but I've got room for something. It will be lovely to catch up. And you're not getting away entirely with your enchanting comment, mister. You have to put up with me saying you look gorgeous. I hope that embarrasses you."

"Not the slightest, tiniest bit" and they both laughed quite loudly.

Alphonse was not driving. They stood briefly with her suitcase on the kerb outside the terminal and the long, black town car slid up. Alphonse opened the door for her while the driver took her bags to the trunk. She amused herself with her newly acquired American vocabulary but in truth it didn't go far beyond sidewalk, gas station and hood.

It was cool, almost too cool in the car as it drove off silently. She shivered slightly and Alphonse adjusted the dials on the a/c.

"It'll be an informal meal. We're expecting two more guests, so we'll just graze on what Hannes has prepared."

"Hannes is here?"

"Yes, Andreas too. He's gone to the other airport to pick up Andy and Jen."

"The other airport?"

"Yes, they're coming in their own plane. They don't fly into here."

Claudia was attempting to process too many thoughts at once: the roles of Hannes and Andreas; who were Andy and Jen; did everyone fly by private plane?

"I should probably tell you a little more about Andy."

"Well, I was just thinking that I'd like to know a little more about a lot of things but that's a very good place to start, yes please."

"You remember I told you about Peter's first area of business interests the group of twenty-odd companies in which he has large stakes?" She nodded. "Well, it's twenty-four to be exact. If we get you off the ground, that would be twenty-five."

"Woah, mister, that's going a little fast for me."

He smiled. "Sorry, we only want an open mind. I was a little nonplussed when Peter first propositioned me to build a property division, but he surprised me by how much he'd already worked out. Anyway, Andy's was one of the first businesses Peter took an interest in after the two tech investments. He was into high-end audio; superb products that Peter loved but he was going nowhere for lack of funding. Well, that's not quite true. He was going bankrupt, but with Peter's money and contacts he managed to sort out development and distribution and it really took off. Well, again, not quite true. It grew rapidly but it took three years to make a profit. That was because they were investing heavily and Peter believed. The point of that story is, if he gets behind you, you really will succeed."

"Every time?"

Alphonse snorted slightly. "No, not every time even with Peter's magnificent people judgement we have lost a couple of businesses: one to cocaine addiction and one to an acrimonious divorce. He managed to salvage his investments, but he takes even more care with people judgement nowadays. And he likes people in stable relationships." He took her hands in his and looked into her eyes. "But you've seen, of course, that those relationships are more open than is usual — and he does see the irony in his own marital history not quite fitting the template." They both smiled at each other.

9

She saw the marina in the fading twilight after they had passed the huge cruise ships on their docks opposite the causeway. As they approached, the marina boats looked small after the ten-story edifices they had just seen but, by the time the car pulled up, her perspective had changed again. The boats near the main dock were of human dimensions, some like Jack's borrowed boat. But those on the outer pontoons now loomed huge and she could see, looking directly out from where they had parked, the boat she had identified from all the photos, Yvonne D, brightly lit and serene. Now she really had to work hard to project a sophisticated nonchalance.

Alphonse led her out along the pontoon. The driver came behind with the luggage. She saw Peter waving from an upper deck. The call she had noticed the driver make had no doubt informed him of their imminent arrival.

He was waiting at the end of the passarelle when they got to the boat. These things were flimsier than they needed to be, she thought, as Alphonse ushered her on. He took her shoulder bag, leaving her with a hand free to cling onto the rope guardrail and she walked along the narrow gangplank — *I'm sure I mustn't call it that, Jack gave it a name, it sounded French* — to the back of the boat — *the back's called something, is it the stern?* Peter took her free hand gently to allow her to step on board relatively elegantly, but the walk had made her nervous and slightly shaky — the sophisticated demeanour already threatened. She returned Peter's embrace almost as much out of relief as out of the genuine warmth she felt about seeing him again.

"Let me look at you." He took her hands and leaned back to appraise her fully. "It's true what Alphonse says, you have grown even lovelier. I thought it was just because he was in love with you, but his objectivity hasn't deserted him. You look truly wonderful," he beamed.

"And you are still the monster of my memories, but I will take the flattery thank you, even though I've been travelling for eight hours and I'm hoping you'll let me shower and change before I meet anyone else. You have some more guests coming, haven't you?"

"I do but they're half an hour away. Let me show you your cabin and let you do as you wish. We're in no hurry for anything." He turned to Alphonse, who had taken the baggage from the driver and moved past them. "Ah, I see you have… Let's just follow him."

He led them up the stairway that curved to the middle level of the boat, through a lounge of muted elegance barely twice the entire floor area of her house, her irony amused her, its surreal familiarity disturbing her — she had studied so many photos – and then down a stairway to the cabin level. He opened the second door on the right, — *second door, I must remember, these neutral shades everywhere are disorientating* — stood aside to let her in and then placed her bags beside the bed. He embraced her gently, kissed her lips again, said, "I'll see you upstairs when you're ready" and left them.

She had been in larger hotel rooms, but none more opulent. The sumptuous fabrics, the sensuous textures, the toning, muted colours following through, broken only by the dark red splashes of cushions on the bed, the armchair and the bench seat below the windows — *portholes?*

"I think everything is self-explanatory, although sometimes, in the bathroom for example, there are buttons where you're expecting taps but I'm sure you'll work that out. Please have a seat for a moment." He gestured to the armchair and seated himself on the stool in front of the dressing table — *a fucking dressing table! Stay sophisticated, Claudia, calm down!* "I probably owe you a rundown of what this is about. I really don't want it to seem as mysterious as it probably does to you now."

She smiled and nodded slowly. "That is a masterly understatement. I am thrilled to be here but I'm trying very hard to cover up my 'little girl lost' look. Just an outline of what's going to happen would help me."

He laughed. "I'm sorry. It's quite simple. I think you could branch out on your own. I have two hours scheduled for us at ten in the morning. Friday is still a working day for the boys. Well, it will be for Jen too, but I think she's taking the morning off to go into town with Yvonne. Sorry, but you miss out on that, working girl! Then we head south after lunch to a favourite anchorage of ours. The afternoon is still worktime if you have catching up to do."

She nodded. "Yes, it's piling up."

"But Saturday's all ours. We'll get the toys off the back and play around and sunbathe. You'll have time to get to know Andy and Jen. Then we have a leisurely cruise back on Sunday to give you plenty time to get you to your flight at seventeen fifteen. Are you impressed by my mastery of detail?"

"Yes, but I'm going to be very careful not to be equally impressed by your mastery of bullshit." He laughed loudly. "But I am very excited, potentially, so I'm delighted we get some serious time tomorrow to talk it through."

He pressed down on his knees and then stood up. "I could go on explaining things, but you'll want to change, however wonderful you look already."

"Bullshit, Peter" and they both smiled.

"There's a button by your bed if you need anything, just press. Hannes or his assistant will be here in an instant." He paused. "I can't tell you how delighted I am to have you here." They smiled at each other and he left.

That may have been bullshit, too, but she had wanted to savour the warm glow of his charm.

10

The breakfast things had been cleared away, enabling Peter to sit down with her at the outer dining table punctually at ten. That had happened by magic, it seemed. The others melted away to allow for Peter's unspoken schedule.

She'd got there at nine, thinking that would be the most sociable time, to find Peter and Alphonse silently studying electronic devices. They both lit up when she arrived and Alphonse moved a chair to enable her to sit between them, sliding it in perfectly to meet her as she sat. *But you have to re-enter real life on Monday, Claudia!*

"Is it a buffet?"

"No." Peter smiled. "Hannes will bring you whatever you wish." And in that instant Hannes appeared at her elbow, just as he had the previous evening whenever her glass got low. Fortunately, she had spotted the danger early and had managed her consumption well — no headache this morning and no embarrassments, she didn't think, last night. She'd relaxed quite quickly. Andy, extrovert, almost boisterous, had been easy to get to know and to warm to. Jen, quieter, more reserved, had been more difficult to read and Yvonne, speaking with her a lot, still made her feel uneasy. But, if she ever got close to feeling uncomfortable, Alphonse or Peter always seemed on hand to engage her.

"Claudia?" Hannes raised his eyebrows to prompt her to speak.

"Oh, orange juice, black coffee and fruit, please, and a croissant if you have one."

"Of course."

Andy soon joined them and there was banter about the political scene, but the girls didn't appear until later and were plainly dressed for town.

"Not joining us, my loves?" said Peter.

"No, we're going for lattes on South Beach at that place with the gorgeous waiters."

"I thought all the waiters on South Beach were gorgeous," said Peter, with just a very faint edge, Claudia thought.

"Yes, my darling, but I'm not talking about the ones that appeal to Andreas and Hannes." This, from Yvonne, seemed a little barbed and she hoped Hannes couldn't hear but it did confirm her thoughts about their preferences. That had struck her more forcefully the previous evening when she noted that Hannes's assistant was one of the most exquisite creatures she had ever seen. Dark skin, probably Cuban, black hair, piercing green eyes, slim and with the finest features and a faintly camp lisp. But he had been smiley and very attentive and didn't appear at all self-obsessed.

The girls left the boat. Later, Andy and Alphonse moved to different spaces. Alphonse pressed on her shoulders and kissed her forehead as he left. "See you later," he said softly. Hannes cleared the table away quickly.

"Are you comfortable talking here?" asked Peter. It was exactly ten o'clock.

She looked over the other boats, over the palms fringing the marina and on to the sky-scraper skyline and then out to the surrounding water. "I can hardly think of any office more perfect."

"Good. Down to business then" and his tone, still warm, had changed slightly.

"Alphonse has told you about my activities, I think." She nodded. "It's the Group I'd like to talk about this morning. I can talk about Funds and Properties - that's Alphonse — as well if you wish." He raised his eyebrows.

"No, no, I'd rather stay focused."

"Excellent. Well, the Group is currently twenty-four businesses whose only real common thread is the type of person leading them. I like innovators who are driven but who can nevertheless lean across and give and take with others. We get together twice a year; I call those my Gatherings and I like to just sit back and watch them interact. We keep the time pretty unstructured, but the format seems to work. I tend to just make mental notes and follow up on an individual basis if I can see problems or missed opportunities. And it's these problems and opportunities that bring you and me together today."

She looked at him quizzically.

"I know a little bit more than you think about what you do. You've had the two meetings with Alphonse, I know, but we have some contacts in your corporation who have also helped me form a picture. I know Collins doesn't let out much information but there are always people who talk."

She smiled and nodded.

"Well, the people who run the Group businesses are, as I said, innovators, but they innovate with product, with marketing, with distribution, and sometimes, the really good ones, with all three, but almost none of them innovates with people and some of them even recognise that. I have at least eight businesses that significantly underperform because they can't get all their people working in the right direction. And four of them, mostly larger ones, are already aware of that; they talk about it and they're looking for ways to improve. I think what you do is exactly what they need."

Hannes arrived with a pot of coffee and fresh cups.

"But I'm not going to spoon feed you any more. I'm going to let you explain what you do."

She laughed. He looked quizzically at her. "I'm sorry. You just reminded me about something Alphonse said about selling: listen carefully to what they want and then persuade them that what you have is exactly what they need. That's what you're avoiding. You're not letting me listen to what you think they want."

He laughed very loudly. "Well, the approach has certainly made him very successful."

"It's even helped him sell boats to ladies, he said." *Was that too much, too forward? Important to push, even with this man, especially with this man!*

He laughed again, more ruefully this time. "I'm not sure I like my secrets being discussed like that but when you work with bright people and encourage them to stay connected, that's a price you have to be willing to pay. OK, madam, you have me on the back foot but now the spotlight is back on you. Tell me what you do."

"Well, you do have to start with a very clear picture of what the business is trying to do. At the highest level, what its strategy is and what it prides itself on. You're going to have to share that with everyone, even the cleaners, because you want them all working towards the same things. Then you're looking for ideas — and actions, that's the most important bit — that they work on to take the business where you want it to go. Then you pick the best ideas and reward them, remembering that recognition is a major reward for most people, especially if you publicise their achievements widely.

Oddly enough, getting a business to be clear about its strategy and real objectives is often the hard part. It surprises me how many senior guys are quite woolly thinkers. OK so far?"

"Very OK so far," he nodded. He really was going to let her talk — and avoid another pet hate she had of senior people she encountered: the insistence on too much, usually irrelevant, airtime — and it often went with woolly thinking, she found.

So, she poured more coffee, drew breath, and talked about how the programme worked through the different regions of the world; how it got focus and energy and pride into the businesses.

"OK, all good so far. Now tell me about the pitfalls."

She laughed quietly, and shrugged. "Yes, there are plenty of those, but the main three are: managers resenting the changed priorities, especially driven by their underlings, as the weak ones see their people; a lot of petty jealousies and turf wars if one set of changes impacts another area — and they can be very destructive; and people stealing each other's ideas or claiming credit where it's not due. So, it's not a universal panacea and it has to be applied carefully, but overall, in my experience, it does get businesses more focused and more energised."

She waited, she had said enough, she didn't want to fall into the trap of feeling the space had to be filled and she guessed, looking at him sat there, elbows on the chair's arms, his lips pursed, his fingers making an 'A' against them, that he was waiting for her to make that mistake.

He held the silence for an unnervingly long time but then slowly smiled.

"I like what you're saying very much, especially your honesty about where problems arise. That's something I can really understand."

She smiled too and began to relax a little.

"What I'd like to do now is talk about a couple of the businesses I mentioned earlier and then discuss how we should approach them. I'm not saying we're going to shoehorn your programme in but it's probably going to be a major element in improving things. But you're too smart to be a one-trick pony anyway, that's very clear, so I want us to talk about the total people plan for these businesses."

She nodded – and made a mental note to avoid that trap at Giddings. *I'm not going there to sell my programme. I'm going there to solve a problem — keep that thought uppermost.*

But now she focused on Peter as he began to talk about his businesses and she was delighted to see how much enthusiasm and commitment he had to them, and how much knowledge and understanding he had of them, dealing easily with any question she asked.

This was not Peter the party sybarite. This was a very serious man who, maybe, had an unusual gift for partitioning his life.

"I'm impressed," he said, sitting back in his chair as if closing the discussion. "You've grasped those businesses very quickly, as I thought you would. I wouldn't make the decision to use you for them myself, of course, that's up to the business heads, but I'm very confident you could have four clients quickly."

"Four? That would be too much, I would need staff. And where are these businesses?"

"Well, two are here, I admit, but two are in Europe. I know what you're thinking: how do I manage my family? I want you to help all four; there are common elements which would make your work more efficient. But I appreciate you need to think hard about how to make your whole life work and, if you can do that, I'll give you all the support you need: money; time; facilities to get you up and running independently. Will you think about it? Will you come back in four weeks with a proposition for starting up Brodie Associates?"

"Help! Can you give me five? I've just picked up a big project at Collins, well, not Collins, it's Giddings."

"The logistics people?"

"Yes, it's through a Collins connection. I've been asked by the chairman..."

"Arthur Gunter?"

"Yes," her brow furrowed, "am I allowed to be impressed by how much you know?" He smiled. "Well, I'm due to report there in four weeks. I couldn't do justice to either activity if I try to do both at the same time and the dates clash anyway."

He chuckled. "Yes, and I can understand their urgency. From what I read their needs are somewhat greater than ours. OK, five weeks then. I think I'm in the UK, which will make reporting back a little easier. One of our other companies is a recruitment consultancy, they're London based. Alphonse will put you in touch with Sandy Nicholls. It's his company, and he'll give you a quick primer on setting up a consultancy business. Is that OK?"

"OK? That would be a godsend, thank you."

"Oh, don't thank me. I have a very powerful incentive to make this work for my Group. I think you could do a lot for them so I'm just being selfish. But I do think it could be very good for you too in a number of ways. So, London in five weeks?"

"London in five weeks."

"Good, that just leaves me a few minutes to give you a little background on Andy and Jen."

"I wondered. I'm realising that all things have a reason for you."

"Oh, don't think badly of me. I do like to arrange for people to support and reinforce each other."

"I'm sorry if I sounded cynical. I am very intrigued to hear about them."

"Andy's is one of the businesses I've been talking about. Molloy have you heard of them?"

She shook her head. "Only what Alphonse told me briefly yesterday."

"Well, you might want to talk to Andy about it. He's knows why you're here, so he'll be expecting it. In fact, he'll probably approach you himself. Jen has her own business, it's called Jen, that's her label, but it's not in my network."

"Yet?"

"No, no, it just wouldn't quite fit. No point in forcing these things. I think she's lovely and she's very successful, but she does like to do things her own way, so there wouldn't be the interconnections I'd be looking for. But she may have other things you can learn from. Let's just relax together and see where the chemistry takes us. The point I really should tell you is that they met at a party."

"One of your parties?"

"Yes, it sometimes happens. People meet and want to go beyond the sexual encounters, and they form a real bond. I love it, it's just the best thing." He paused, looked hard at her, and smiled. "Of course, I love it too when people discover more about themselves and free themselves up to enjoy life a little more. But the important point is that, very occasionally, couples still come. They're devoted to each other but they still give themselves a certain amount of freedom and have fun in their chosen ways. I just wanted to reassure you that it can work. I expect you have occasional tensions with Jack?"

"Ha, definitely," and she nodded, remembering the conversation two days before, "and I suppose I'm letting him have fun in his chosen ways."

"Well, it's never going to be easy and your situation, I admit, is more difficult than most but I thought that you should see that, with love and the right attitude, it can work for both partners." He looked a little pensive. "That's can, and not necessarily will." And she assumed he was thinking of Yvonne.

"Anyway, enjoy their company. I'm pretty sure you will. Now, if you'll forgive me, I must get on and it sounds like you need to do some work for poor Arthur Gunter." He stood up, she did too and took a step towards him. He put his hands on her shoulders. "I am so glad you've come and so glad to see you doing well. If it comes off for us, I'll be thrilled. If you decide you can't make it work, I'll still adore you," and he hugged her very warmly, turned and went into the boat, calling over his shoulder as he left, "Hannes will put lunch out at one, we sail at two. See you, my dear."

"See you," she muttered to his disappearing back. It was exactly twelve.

11

She found a quiet corner on the upper deck and tried to work through the Giddings papers that Lavinia had sent. It was hard to focus. Her mind swirled with thoughts of becoming independent — *my very own business* — having to travel even more and yet keep the kids close, spending more time with Jack, maybe, but this still didn't change his geography, only his apparent need for secrecy. And did he really need that, or was it merely an excuse to sustain a lifestyle he was exploiting and enjoying? What was his commitment? Was he ringing as often as he used to? Am I still the vital soulmate or have I become the dreaded inquisitor? And what to do about poor Arthur Gunter? She tried to come back to that but had to admit to herself that she was too distracted.

Just then Andy came in. "There you are, I've been looking for you," he hesitated, "but you look busy."

"Oh, don't worry, I'm struggling here, trying to think of too many things at once. My gender's talent for multi-tasking seems to be deserting me. Anyway, I wanted to talk to you. Peter's been telling me about your business."

He pulled an armchair round and sat facing her. He was about six feet tall but very powerfully built, his dark red hair neatly trimmed, just stopping it looking too curly, the pale skin was lightly freckled, his face smiley and fresh, looking under forty but probably just beyond that. "Well, he's been talking to me too, or rather I've been talking to him." He paused. "Our products are brilliant — let's start there; d'you know them?"

"Not really. I've just googled them. They look really impressive but they're so far out of my league."

He smiled. "Well, we do have very stylish designs on our high-end boxes in particular but it's the sound that's the thing and most of our stuff doesn't get seen anyway. It's hidden in ceilings and walls. I'll stop there though, I'm way too nerdy about that. I admit I obsess about getting that better and better. But maybe I don't spend enough time thinking about how the whole business works. Peter tells me that, well, so does Jen, so I guess it might be true. Start point is, we have no issues with product performance — it's stellar." He laughed. "In fact, there are very few people who fully appreciate how really astonishing we are. It's really only the very best musicians who do, but we miss delivery slots, we have sub-optimal installations, and we get product failures in the field and our turn round times on those failures are shit, so the whole package isn't really working. Does that sound like something you could fix, or at least help with?"

"Well, I do try to make the whole organisation work together. I wouldn't commit to anything without looking at your business much more closely but, in medieval terms, are your developers the nobility and the other departments the peasants?"

He guffawed. "Ha, I like that. I guess that might be true."

"And you're the king, surrounded only by your sycophantic courtiers?" He looked pensive. "I don't want to jump to any conclusions, I really don't, but if you can't tell me that everyone's a hero in your business, then you've got some opportunities."

He nodded and smiled. It was very sweet, very boyish, the deep grooves down his face must have been charming dimples once. "You have to come and see me, ma'am."

"Woah, Peter's had to give me five weeks to even think about it."

"But I'm curious to get an opinion. Well, no, I'm actually impatient and desperate. Can't you spare a day? When are you here again?"

She pondered. It would be useful to get a view of what Peter's projects might entail. "I'm in Atlanta Wednesday to Friday in four weeks. I could do the Tuesday with you."

"Done." He smiled again. "I don't know the date exactly without checking but I'll make sure we're free."

"Wait a minute, where are you? I have to get used to the distances here."

"We're in Boston, part of me has never left MIT, but don't worry about that. Give us the Tuesday and we'll fly you to Atlanta in the evening." She hesitated and she got the boyish smile again. "I don't really take a 'no' answer."

She laughed. "I guess we have a date."

He laughed too. "I guess we do. Shall we go see if there's lunch?" He stood and held his hand out to her. "And thank you, I'm very grateful."

Yvonne and Jen were already there. Hannes was pouring them white wine. The table, which could seat ten easily, was laid for seven, two threes around the ends and one setting, a little isolated, and with no wine glass she noted, in the middle.

Peter breezed in from the main lounge shortly after with Alphonse in tow. "Good people," he beamed. "Thank you so much for being punctual. Jen, my darling, could you join Claudia and me at this end?" Yvonne frowned briefly, as if irritated, but then smiled as Alphonse took her hand and kissed it and Andy sat in Jen's chair. Peter waited for Jen, took her hand, kissed it and motioned to the two ladies to take seats either side of him. Jen, opposite Claudia, smiled warmly, plainly relaxed about the move.

"Hannes will serve wine to those who wish and we'll wait for El Capitano to give us our briefing."

Claudia smiled to herself. Andreas appeared shortly after and took the middle chair. He had passed through the lounge a few times the previous evening, stopping the first time to embrace her and then continuing to hold her hand while he told her, with an intensity somewhat alien to his usual cool, that he was delighted to see her again and that he hoped something would come from the opportunity he knew she would be discussing. She had been taken aback but then he held her arms, smiled and air-kissed her and later, each time she caught his eye as he passed during the evening, he would smile again and nod.

He looked to Peter, who merely nodded.

"Ladies and gentlemen, I will keep this short and simple, but I must emphasise its importance. There are risks on any sea journey." Claudia smiled again to herself, remembering Jack's similar almost-pomposity when briefing her. "We will not be going far, a total of only fifteen miles — and the weather will remain calm for our journey and our stay. We will head south past Key Biscayne, turn into the bay and anchor off the state park. The journey will take a little over one hour. My principal concern, as ever, is of losing one of you. Raul will be watching you during the journey," *that must be the taller, well-muscled Cuban boy who was adjusting the lines earlier,* "but I will ask you, as usual, to buddy up so that each one always knows where the other is in the event that Raul or I can't see you. Alphonse, will you buddy with Claudia, please?" He waited for them both to nod. "The married couples will look after each other. Now I wish you a happy, but short, journey after lunch. Salut!" And he raised his glass of sparking water to them all.

"Thank you, Andreas." Peter raised his glass and returned the gesture. "Salut!"

Hannes and Fredo moved around them quickly with gazpacho. Smart, thought Claudia, you drink less wine with a soup.

The conversations fell into two groups, no doubt as Peter had intended. Andreas moved towards the other end. Peter began by holding court but subtly moved to posing gentle questions, prompting the two of them to talk more, first to him and then to each other. Occasionally Claudia would catch laughter from Yvonne in particular as the other group became louder. But her awareness of that faded as she became more wrapped up in Jen, who had seemed initially so reserved but was now becoming more animated and friendly. She was a tall, slender and very elegant woman, striking rather than beautiful, large eyes but a prominent nose, looks that appealed to Claudia in the land of plastic-surgeoned homogeneity. She'd been a model before starting her own fashion business. "I loved the clothes, still do, but the modelling work was so tedious. Anyway, I had a boyfriend at the time who was an IT nerd and we started selling through the internet and then on to social media almost before anyone else did." She looked round to Andy and smiled. "I seem to have a soft spot for nerds. Well, if I think about it, I'm probably a fashion nerd myself. I was the one that tried to look at where trends were going and picked what I wanted to sell. I still spend ridiculous amounts of time trying to spot what's new or, if I'm on a roll, what's coming next. So, fashion nerd! I would never have specified nerd if I'd ever tried to write a dating profile. I don't suppose anybody ever asks for an obsessive. Have you ever done that, written a profile? Of course you haven't, silly question. You already have two men here who adore you. And Andy now seems very struck — but he does have a soft spot for anyone pretty. Still, it's an impressive hit rate." Then she laughed. "Peter, stop that man pouring me wine, I'm starting to sound silly," and they laughed with her, "but how did you get involved with them? Is your story as embarrassing as mine?" And Claudia found it surprisingly easy to respond about the party that old friends had taken her to, glad that Peter had let her know that Jen knew of the parties, so no details were necessary and it was easy to move back to clothes for a while until Jen started asking more about what Claudia did and why Andy wanted to work with her. Claudia was guarded initially until it quickly became obvious that Jen wanted to know about the business and wasn't probing to see if Claudia had any particular interest in Andy.

"I've told him, all he talks about is his products. I have to listen to all the latest things at home and, I love music, I really do, but it's been ages since I've been able to spot any difference in his latest great leap forward. I know he doesn't pay enough attention to the rest of his business. I mean, I know I'm very clothes focused but when I lost my first nerd, I knew I had to replace him with someone who could look after that side of things for me and my new guy's even better, especially on using the new media. If I'm honest, that's what gives us the key difference. Lots of people spot trends but nobody gets them in the market quicker than we do, and that's mostly our IT nerdery, but we also have a very good buying woman. She's ruthless and very organised, so I can still pretend to be a bit ditzy. I'm sorry, I'm rambling so much," and there was her charming, self-deprecating laugh again, so at odds with the cool presence of yesterday evening.

As she was finishing coffee, she became aware of a distant rumble of engines and the boat began to move, almost imperceptibly at first. She looked to Peter, "We're leaving?"

He nodded. "It's two o'clock. Andreas's deutsche Pünktlichkeit means we always leave on time."

"Do you mind if I look at what they do? I had to learn myself on a much smaller boat a few weeks ago. I'd love to see it done properly."

He smiled and nodded. "Of course."

Jen stood up. "I have to get going too, I have plenty of work I must deal with and some calls to make." She looked to Claudia. "I'll catch up with you later, OK?"

"That would be lovely."

Then she moved to the side to see Raul and Hannes, both with earpieces and small mikes, smoothly pulling in the lines and plainly communicating with the invisible Andreas, somewhere above them on the helm. *Helm, I remembered that.* When the boat was clearly free of the dock, the huge fenders — *fenders, well done Claudia,* were pulled in and stowed neatly away, a right place for everything on board here. It was all accomplished with minimum fuss and drama and no raised voices. When Jack had called out, "Quickly Claudia!" as she had pulled on a line, she'd laughed and muttered, "Fuck you, Jack." OK, there had been a little bump, but hadn't he said that was what the fenders were for?

Soon they were making a stately passage between South Pointe and Fisher Island and then turned south. She felt an odd thrill as the land retreated and then, from the port side, she could see nothing but sea and the vast sky. Moving across the boat there was what she assumed was Key Biscayne in the middle distance. Yes, it wouldn't be a long passage.

She returned to the upper deck where she'd left her laptop and managed to settle, this time, into some focused work and was almost surprised by the distant sound of a chain being freed. They were obviously anchoring. This process too was very different from the three attempts they'd had on the smaller boat before Jack had felt confident they wouldn't come adrift.

It was perhaps half an hour later when Alphonse came by. He put his hand gently on her shoulder. "We have the bathing platform down, are you coming swimming?"

"Oh, that's a lovely idea. I'll just finish this and I'll join you."

He bent forward to kiss her forehead again but this time she raised her face to let her lips meet his. They lingered briefly before he straightened and smiled, patted her gently on the shoulder and said, "Don't be too long."

12

It was an hour before she made it to the back deck, an enormous fluffy white robe covering her bikini. The whole huge door between the stairways curving up from the landing platform to the main deck had unfolded flat out into the water, revealing a vast storage space which plainly held the small boats and toys and a variety of chairs and tables for what was now the swimming platform. Jen and Yvonne were relaxing in two easy chairs, basking in the late afternoon sun, two colourful drinks on the table between them. Claudia draped her robe over the back of the third chair and settled down to join them. The bikini had been the right choice.

"Hannes will be here in a moment," said Yvonne, "he makes splendid mocktails."

"Perfect. And where are the boys?"

Jen harrumphed and, smiling, pointed to two noisy jet skis apparently racing in the distance. "I really don't know when they grow up. My father's nearly seventy and he has one. I can't get him off it when we visit his boat."

Hannes appeared as silently as ever. "Oh, Hannes, lovely, they've been recommending your mocktails. What should I try?"

"I'm recommending my watermelon margarita or my mango mule," he smiled, "mostly because those are my best fruits today."

She laughed lightly. "Is the margarita the pink one?" He nodded. "I'd love to try that, please."

She settled back in her chair. The girls were quiet, Yvonne leafing slowly through a magazine, Jen on an iPad. Claudia, who'd been working intensely, was more than content to relax and let her mind go blank. After a few minutes she felt a light touch on her arm. Jen was leaning towards her with a tube of factor twenty. "Have you?"

"No, I haven't. Thank you." She took the tube. "I should have done."

"It's more intense than you think, even with the sun going down. We northern girls need to be more careful. Yvonne's more Mediterranean she gets away with it and goes that beautiful bronze on her first day in the sun. I hate her."

Yvonne snorted good-humouredly, raised her glass and said, "Cheers" as Hannes handed Claudia her drink.

"Thank you — and cheers!" She turned back to Jen, "Northern?"

"Andy and I are proud Americans, of course, but we both have Irish roots, and you're Scottish? I hope I haven't embarrassed myself, it's a very light accent. It's very attractive but quite distinctive. I am right, aren't I?"

"One hundred percent. We can't even trace the last foreign intrusion in the family tree before me. I'm afraid I'm the first sinner in recorded memory to have bred across the border."

Claudia smoothed the sun cream in and settled back to do nothing apart from taking an occasional sip of her drink. Slowly the fever pitch of the last four days began to subside as she let the sun's warmth sink in. Everything that needed doing could actually retreat for the moment, everything would keep until... well, Monday actually, apart from ringing Pat and the kids — too late now — that could be done tomorrow. Then came the irritating crescendo of the two jet skis, engines cutting just before they reached the platform; two men with the faces of smiling children. Alphonse tied off and clambered aboard.

"Andy, aren't you going to take me for a spin?" asked Yvonne, and, if he felt put upon, Andy's puppy face gave nothing away as he nodded. Alphonse took Yvonne's hand to help her on to the rear seat.

"Take it easy, she has no life vest," said Alphonse.

"Of course," said Andy, and roared away laughing with Yvonne clinging tightly to him.

Alphonse took off his vest and hung it in the garage, "You two not swimming?"

They looked at each other and shook their heads.

"Cowards." He laughed and dived in.

Jen looked at the fast-disappearing jet ski, turned to Claudia and shrugged enigmatically. It was a gesture that didn't seem to want a question. Claudia settled back in her chair again and closed her eyes.

The distant sound of the jet ski returning was making itself heard some time later just as Alphonse climbed up the bathing ladder and back onto the boat. He removed his trunks and stood under the transom shower. She first looked away from his nakedness, which was not strictly in her eyeline, but then decided she could match his unselfconsciousness and turned to look at him. He, seeing her, smiled and waved. It was a body she knew but had never had a chance to study from a distance. The skin was tanned, even where the trunks had been. He was tall and sinewy, a lovely body she thought as he turned round, rinsing himself. Jen stayed focused on her iPad, showing no curiosity at all.

The jet ski returned as he was towelling down, quite unabashed, in no hurry to conceal himself. He stepped towards Yvonne to help her off the ski. She looked windswept but still glamorous. She smiled at him, looked him up and down. "This is a nice welcome home. Thank you, good sir. I think I'll go to my cabin to shower. I'm sure the master will want drinks at six thirty"

Alphonse put on a robe and took Yvonne's seat. Andy stepped under the shower, his body very different, Claudia now felt obliged to observe. He was slightly shorter, pale, more heavily muscled but when he turned it was his cock that struck her. Had she been waiting for that? For a man who'd been exercising in cold water it was surprising in all dimensions, hanging thick and low in front of him. She turned back to Alphonse who'd been watching her. He smiled. Maybe she blushed a little but then she smiled back.

She looked at her watch. "Gosh, six thirty's not long. Maybe I'll go and shower. What do we wear, Jen?"

Jen looked up. "Very simple, really, shorts and top. It's absolutely wrong on a boat to be glam or elaborate." She laughed. "Well, those are my rules. Yvonne might appear in something stunning." She leaned closer and whispered, "She likes to outshine the rest, of course, but in a small group like this I think she'll follow the style guru. If I can't make my life a little easier among friends, then why the fuck do I bother?" And again, her little self-deprecating laugh. "Let's go then, no point in letting the boys think we're impressed by the sights."

She got back to her cabin and the suitcase was waiting accusingly on the bench beneath the portholes. So far, she'd only taken out her clothes for last night and the bikini. *That was dumb, Claudia, most things will be creased.* When she opened it, she was surprised to see it nearly empty. She had packed with her boat clothes on top but they and many other things had disappeared. What remained was her travel gear for Sunday, some warm clothes and her work shoes. She opened the wardrobe and there, neatly hung and stacked, all freshly ironed, was everything she would need, but as she flipped through she found some alien hangers: two printed Chloe shorts and two plain, matching halter tops, all still with labels, all in her size. Puzzled, she looked around the cabin for an explanation and leaning against the dressing table mirror was a letter to her:

'If you're wondering about the dress code, what's in the wardrobe will be perfect for evenings. Alphonse XXX'.

She was slightly shocked. It was so alien to have a man choose clothes for her, parts of her felt a little challenged, almost offended. Was he saying that what she'd worn so far was inappropriate? *Claudia, you're more than completely stupid, he must have organised this well before you arrived!* No harm in seeing how they look, but shower first.

She never thought of herself as vain but, having chosen the blue combination, she felt really pleased with herself as she twirled in front of the mirror. Blue because her blue flip-flops were her least embarrassing footwear. Tomorrow, with the apricot, it might well be bare feet. No time to dwell on that, even Yvonne seemed obedient to Peter's timetable — and, at five minutes late, Claudia was the last to arrive. The first to greet her was Jen, with a beaming smile, a big hug and "Bitch!"

whispered in her ear. They both laughed. "Seriously, there's shorts and tops and there's shorts and tops; you look amazing."

"You look wonderful, my dear," said Yvonne, cheek to cheek with her, with perhaps incomplete sincerity. But Claudia's "You look stunning" was well meant. And Yvonne did, as usual, even observing a shorts and top dress code. Jen was dressed the simplest but, Claudia thought, she had a figure that would look wonderful wearing a dishcloth.

The gentlemen kissed their welcomes. Last was Alphonse with a slightly sheepish smile.

"I thought about being cross with you," she said, "but when I saw how fucking good I looked, I forgave you" and they laughed together and she took a glass of champagne from Fredo. Hannes, she assumed, would be looking after the food.

The back deck faced west. The sun, huge and red, was sinking towards South Miami, ten miles away, she guessed. Below them Raul was washing down the boys' toys and making sure they were well tethered, although the evening had an almost eerie stillness. Alphonse joined her at the rail, they clinked glasses.

"Thank you," she said quietly. He looked puzzled; she twirled around.

"Oh, yes. If I chose the clothes, am I still allowed to say you look wonderful?"

"You most certainly are. I'm the one that's looking wonderful in them and I'll welcome all compliments. But seriously, they're gorgeous, thank you."

"Seeing you now, it really is my pleasure."

Jen joined them. "Do you know the story of these?" Claudia asked.

"A little. I recommended a label, but he did the rest," she turned to Alphonse, "and you did very well, sir. She looks wonderful." He nodded with something like modesty.

Hannes and Fredo, behind them, were putting the starters on the table. It was laid differently this evening three seats on each side.

"May I seat you, dearest gentles," boomed Peter suddenly. "I will sit facing west opposite my beloved, with Claudia on my left and Jen on my right, Andy to Yvonne's right, opposite Claudia please and Alphonse the sinister, appropriately on my wife's left."

They settled easily, the evening amiably warm and the candles in their jars undisturbed by any wind. The conversation never really flagged but, if it slowed, it was prodded by Peter in some new direction and became ever more scurrilous as the evening progressed with Yvonne, ultimately, telling stories of some of their party visitors in England; some almost famous names that Claudia recognised, with peculiar tastes. Peter encouraged her but guided her away from too many specifics. If there was tension between them, as Claudia thought she had sensed earlier, she now had a picture of two people who tuned into each other and enjoyed similar situations.

It was dark in the distance when the coffee was served, some bright stars clearly visible through the warm, humid air.

"Shall we adjourn, dearest ones, and let the boys clear all this away?" asked Peter, standing and gesturing toward the main lounge, where a horseshoe of leather sofa surrounded a flat leather circle that looked as if it must double as a very large coffee table or additional seating. There was gentle music playing as Peter guided her to the head of the horseshoe and sat down beside her. Claudia was a little mystified as the others paired off, Yvonne sitting close to Andy, opposite Jen and Alphonse. Hannes moved around them and took silent refusals for drinks and then returned with water that he placed on the small tables behind the sofa. Peter held Claudia's hand as she was transfixed by Yvonne and Andy who began to kiss quite passionately. She looked to Peter, who merely smiled at her and nodded and guided her gaze back to Yvonne who was now rubbing her hand up and down the front of Andy's shorts. He was leaning back but still kissing her deeply. Claudia turned to see Jen's reaction but she was already kissing Alphonse.

Andy helped Yvonne as she fumbled with the front of his shorts but suddenly, he was free, revealing the largest cock Claudia had ever seen but the view was soon obscured as Yvonne's hands and mouth took charge. In that surreal moment Claudia found herself wondering how it could fit into a mouth, but Yvonne's head was bobbing slowly. Andy's eyes were closed and he was moaning gently.

She felt Peter's arm move around her shoulder and she let herself be pulled into him. It somehow felt better not to have to observe this alone. Jen and Alphonse at least were still contenting themselves with kissing.

But Yvonne obviously wanted more. "I want you in me, Andy," she whispered loudly, "come, lie on the table."

They stripped very quickly and Andy lay on his back on the circle directly in front of them, Claudia getting a close up of the enormous cock. She was strangely fascinated as Andy held it and waited for the now-naked Yvonne to lower herself onto it. She slid slowly down, somewhat carefully, Claudia thought, weirdly fascinated by the scene directly in front of her that she had only seen this way in films. Yvonne's perfect bottom moved up and down in a steady rhythm, never quite fully descending, probably designed to sustain pleasure for both of them.

Looking across, Claudia could see that Jen and Alphonse were now absorbed by what was happening in front of them, although Jen's hand had moved to the front of Alphonse's shorts and he was obviously responding.

Peter stayed still, watching intently, cuddling Claudia to him and rubbing her arm gently.

"Come on Jen, join us," said Andy. "Sit on me."

Jen turned to Alphonse and kissed him, then stood up and dropped both shorts and pants in one gesture and stepped out of them. She kneeled astride Andy's face and lowered herself onto his mouth, her hips gyrating slowly while she embraced Yvonne and began kissing her. Now Yvonne began to push down fully on Andy and Jen's hand moved towards her clit. Yvonne's movements became more violent and her groan became louder while Andy and Jen sustained their steady motions, only intent on provoking Yvonne's climax, which soon came with some loud screams and a huge sigh. "Oh, Andy!" She fell into Jen's arms but settled back into her slow movements up and down on Andy's cock. The women embraced, apparently calmly now, but Jen's gyrations became more pronounced, she seemed about to come too but then slowly lifted her hips to take her clit away from Andy's face. She turned to her left and said, "Please, Alphonse."

He rose slowly from the sofa and stripped completely, his cock standing stiff and Claudia's memories came back to her. He was a lot less thick than Andy but just as long. He knelt on the circle directly behind Jen, positioned himself and slid slowly into her

— always gentle, Alphonse, smooth and wonderful but was there passion? Where was the animal? Even when he came it was restrained — he held her hips and pushed deeply. Claudia looked at his closed eyes and slight smile but found herself drawn to Andy, who was observing his wife's penetration from not much more than six inches below! He seemed to be gripping Yvonne's hips harder and pushing more deeply into her.

"Easy baby." Jen's instruction was to Alphonse but it seemed to slow them all down and bring them back from a brink. "I want Yvonne to lick me," and they moved like dancers to leave the men standing while Jen lay back, opening herself fully to Yvonne, who buried her face into Jen while presenting her arse to Andy, now standing behind her. The girls were absorbed with each other for a while, with the men simply watching and holding themselves but then Jen gestured to Alphonse, who put one knee on the circle and placed his cock by her lips. He arched over her, putting one hand down to support himself, letting her guide his cock into her mouth. Andy stood watching, holding himself, sustaining that huge erection quite close to where Claudia was sitting so she could study its troubling enormity while he watched his wife take an improbable length of Alphonse's cock into her throat. Alphonse pulled back with an 'Easy baby', clearly struggling to avoid coming. Now Yvonne's wiggling arse brought Andy's attention back to her desires but before he knelt behind her, he reached over the sofa to where Hannes had placed the water but picked up what was obviously a tube of lube. He knelt behind Yvonne, pushed halfway into her and then squirted a large dollop of lube between her arse cheeks, a thought of fascinated horror flitted through Claudia's mind — *surely not* — but Andy's thumb began working the lube around and into her anus. She wiggled appreciatively and he squirted more. This time he moved out and knelt to one side of her, allowing Peter and Claudia a very clear view of his attempt to make Yvonne relax as far as possible. He pushed two of his thick fingers into her, all the time playing with her clit, allowing her time to relax around him. When she began to push back and move faster, he used yet more lube — *it's really going to happen, he's going to put all of that thing into her arse* — and slowly slid three fingers in, giving her time once more to relax around him. Jen meanwhile, being kept on edge by Yvonne's licking, was pulling Alphonse deeper into her mouth again and some detached part of Claudia's mind thought 'that's impossible' and 'maybe that's the sort of blowjob Jack gets' but then the fascination with Andy and Yvonne captured her again as Andy positioned himself behind her giving them, Peter and Claudia, unwittingly or not, the perfect view as he placed the head of the huge cock at her anus. She wiggled once more, to signal readiness, Claudia assumed, and then slowly he began to push. Loud animal noises came from

Yvonne. He eased back. "No, give me more, keep going for fuck's sake!" and he pushed again. There was a scream from Yvonne but she buried her face once more into Jen's pussy. Andy was halfway in and found a rhythm at that point, holding Yvonne's hips and studying his cock stretching her arse. She was still making loud noises with each push but her fingers had moved to her own clit and were brushing Andy's balls, he took this as a signal to push even deeper but now the noises were coming from Alphonse. He was clearly starting to come in Jen's mouth. He had pulled back slightly but she held him in one hand, controlling his depth, keen, it seemed, to savour everything before she swallowed and then, as Yvonne buried her face deeper, Jen came herself. Alphonse, spent, slid down onto the circle and wrapped his arms around her. Now everyone was focused on Andy and Yvonne. He, grabbing her hips firmly and pushing harder and faster, she moving her fingers more violently against herself and almost screaming until they both reached their climax together. It seemed to take ages to subside, Andy plainly enjoying still being inside her, Jen smiling at him, seemingly encouraging him to stay there, Yvonne sighing deeply.

Claudia couldn't resist looking when Andy finally pulled out. Yvonne's large gaping hole closed only slowly then the actors on their stage seemed to collapse into a random pile of limbs. The human montage was a memorable image for Claudia, although they began to unfurl quite soon. Yvonne stepped off first and leaned over, kissing Peter with real affection, affection he returned. "I'm showering, darling, can Hannes bring champagne?"

"Of course." He smiled. "I think he knows to bring it now things are quiet." She laughed.

Jen and Andy, their arms around each other, walked off naked to their cabin with their clothes in their hands.

Alphonse, gathering his things, smiled sheepishly at them. "I'll be back after a shower."

Claudia detached herself from Peter. "Is that what you were expecting?"

"Oh, I never know quite what to expect." He smiled. "Is it what you were expecting?"

"Well, I wondered what you wanted me to see."

"Come here," he said, opening an arm to invite her back into his embrace. She fell against him, happy to have his arm around her again. "I really never know what's going to happen, but I knew they all liked each other and people have these feelings and urges. It's obviously happened before in different ways and Andy and Jen are still devoted to each other. It's only something for you to think about. The most important thing about the weekend is not what just happened. It's about you taking a big step in your life — but I'm not pushing you on that. You have five weeks."

"And if I don't?"

"As I said, I will still adore you — and I also admire, by the way, your stoical and, well, inquisitive attitude to what has just unfolded. I think you were curious — but I didn't think anything that could happen here would faze you anyway."

"Well, I admit I was curious, and I think there's little that could faze me after what you put me through before" and they laughed gently with each other.

"Ah, Hannes, thank you, just there." And Hannes placed the large tray with the Taittinger in a bucket and six flutes on the circle in front of them. "Could you pour two just now?"

"But if you don't, to return to your question, I will carry on looking. It's something the group needs, I'm convinced, so Sandy Nicholls has the brief to find someone if you turn me down. I'd love it to be you, I think you'd do so well, but I'll still have a business to run."

They sat quietly for a while until Claudia had an urge to look at stars. She detached herself again and went out into the warm evening. There was no wind to make the water slap against the boat, the only noises the quiet music from inside and the distant, almost inaudible hum of the generator somewhere keeping the boat brightly lit. The boat had turned with the tide and she was now looking out over the dark expanse of parkland to the empty sea beyond and above it a few bright stars competed with the moon rising, high enough now to lay its golden carpet on the calm water.

"I've always had a fantasy about walking along the moon's path." It was Alphonse, a few metres from her, a glass of champagne in his hand. "You OK?" he asked, when she turned to him. He looked slightly nervous and concerned.

"Yes, I'm fine," she paused, "really I am. Are you worried I might be shocked?"

"No, no, not that, I don't think. I just wondered if you might be…" He hesitated.

"Upset? Disappointed? Surprised?"

"Well, any of those things, I suppose."

"Would it matter?" and she stepped towards him and let herself smile.

He seemed visibly relieved. "Ah, you're beginning to tease me, I think."

"You know, for a man, you can be quite sensitive sometimes," and here she moved right up to him and raised her glass. He clinked with her and smiled. "I'm having an extraordinary time at the moment. There's much more happening around me and to me than has happened for years, if ever. I think I'll go with the flow and hope I don't miss any important turnings but, deep down, I mainly need just to be sure the kids are OK and that I'm doing things that will keep them that way, and if I'm lucky those things will satisfy me."

"And Jack?"

She thought for a moment. "I'd love that to work out. I've lived with that idea for two years now, and maybe I had a fantasy for a few years before that without admitting it to myself, but some big things have to change to allow that to happen and I have more moments now when I'm prepared to admit they're unlikely." She moved in close to him. He put his arm around her shoulder, now, leaning against the rail; they were looking back into the boat where Yvonne had rejoined Peter on the sofa and they were laughing quite happily. "But I think he might like a relationship more like theirs and I'm not sure I could manage that. But what about you? Are you always enigmatic and uncommitted, or are you looking for something else?"

"Enigmatic and uncommitted, that will do" and he raised his glass.

She drank with him. "Secretive, is all I'm hearing" but then she laughed to herself. "It's funny, I've slept with you twice and it's been lovely and it's also been, for me, a big step of discovery but I've always assumed that, for you, it didn't matter that much. Oh, I think you enjoyed it" and they laughed together.

"Oh, I surely did that."

"But you always seemed so cool and self-possessed that I didn't give a thought about your feelings. That's not good, is it? But I'm pretty sure I didn't do any damage. And if I ask you if I did, it's only to show some belated concern. I'm not looking for some vanity-driven validation."

"But you knew I fell in love with you, I told you" and he looked momentarily serious.

She hesitated. Then, slowly, they smiled at each other. "Alphonse, you're a bastard!" and they both laughed. "So now I have absolutely no conscience about asking you to come and sleep with me now."

"Asking me?"

"No, telling you. Come to my cabin. I'm happy if you haven't recovered and you need to fall asleep, but I will insist that you fuck me in the morning."

"I remain, madam, your obedient servant" and, arms around each other, they moved to her cabin, bidding Peter and Yvonne goodnight as they passed.

13

"I want some time in your arms, Alphonse." She stood, enjoying his embrace, her arms wrapped around him. She looked up and they kissed. "I know we don't often share beds with anyone." She put her face to his chest. "Well, I don't actually know that, I know I don't. I just assume you live alone."

His kissed the top of her head. "I live alone. I have done for a long time."

"Hmm, that's a story you can tell me more about tomorrow. Anyway, we may not be comfortable sleeping next to someone but give me a few hours, please."

"I'll stay as long as you want, but you must tell me if you become uncomfortable."

"But I also have some needs and curiosities. I meant what I said."

"We don't have to wait until morning" and the bulge pressing against her belly told her that was true.

She looked up and kissed him again. "Lie on the bed for me, let me enjoy your body."

Their clothes dropped off easily but she smiled to herself as she carefully draped her new garments on the armchair. She couldn't disrespect a gift.

He lay full-length, his cock half erect. She stood beside the bed, taking him all in. *Alphonse the passionless*. She needed his body, for sex and for comfort, she could make him happy later, so she straddled his face and pushed herself down on to his mouth. His hands moved to her hips to hold her on him and his mouth and tongue began to move around her. Her emotions had brought her here but now she could feel her urges taking over.

Her hands were on his thighs to keep her steady as she moved herself on his face. His cock was stiffening; that she could deal with in a short while. Just for now she would focus on her own pleasure. His tongue moved easily over her clit and inside her, not allowing her to rise too high, and she held herself, not pressing too heavily on him. She found a plateau, it would be easy to come when she wanted to and he seemed to understand and move with her, just as she wanted; and some detached impulse in her allowed her to think 'he does this very well'. She felt sure her pussy could bide its time. Now she could focus on his cock. She moved one hand to it. She heard him sigh but his mouth's attention to her was unbroken. Now she could take him in her mouth. Yes, she would make him come later, but she had more to explore and learn first. She lay down on him, leaving her hands free to hold his shaft and stroke his balls. She licked its head and could tell from the way his fingers dug into her hips that his excitement was rising. She took the head into her mouth and ran her tongue around it and listened to him moaning quietly. Now she sat up a little, still holding him, finding his rhythm as she wanked him, enjoying the sight of him, all stiff and shiny, then leaning to take its head in her mouth again until he seemed to be getting too close. Her pussy feeling very warm and contented on his face, and very wet but not yet driven to urgency, she focused again on his cock. She held firm to its base and took him more deeply but pulled back sharply as it hit the back of her throat. Mmm, that would be difficult. She still had the width of her hand on his cock; surely taking the whole thing would be impossible but that is what Jen had appeared to manage. No matter, she had time to play and beautiful Alphonse had self-control. She knew she could have leisurely attempts to take him more deeply but she found it hard, however she tried, to get her lips down to her hand and he seemed to tense when she did and then, when she eased back and just sucked hard on its head he seemed to grow stiffer again and, when she stroked his balls at the same time, she could feel his tempo rising — *forget deep throat, Claudia, end of the lesson, let's just make the poor man come* — she moved her head back and forth in time with him but felt his tongue pushing harder on her clit, his hands pulling her more firmly down on to him. She couldn't stop this now. She felt him coming from a long way away, just as she was, and then suddenly, just as her own feelings overwhelmed her, she felt his cock spurting its blobs in her mouth. She wanked him harder to make more come as her pussy continued to push on his mouth until the moment came when she fell like a ragdoll on to him and she eased herself to one side and squeezed his last drops on to his belly.

Then, mischievously, she turned around quickly to embrace him and kiss him and let some of his own drops fall into his mouth. She could feel a laugh in his stomach but his lips stayed sensually on hers, taking the fluids until she pulled back and they both just laughed spontaneously at each other.

He made to speak. She put her finger on his lips.

"Mm, mm, my rules, now you cuddle me. If you're still here in the morning, you'll be sent for some lube. You've just done all that for me, that was my agenda — and you've endured it manfully, I have to say. But I want some time just to make you happy in the morning," and she nestled into him, spoon-like and enjoyed his body and limbs surrounding her in the minutes before sleep overtook her.

She was late for breakfast, but all the others were still at the table. She went round and kissed them all, it seemed entirely natural, and then sat down beside Alphonse, who smiled conspiratorially at her. She wriggled to sit comfortably, getting a strange enjoyment from the discomforts in her lower body. She had slept deeply, only being awakened by the click of the door as he left the cabin. Dawn was just filtering through the portholes. The space beside her was still warm; her thoughts drifted through the night before, she smiled to herself, she'd had him, she truly had, he'd come as she had wanted when she'd learned all she could about his cock — and her own talents, or not, at blowjobs. But she'd put him to sleep happy — and felt very contented herself. But she'd meant her sleepy-time remarks. She'd wanted him to enjoy her as he wished but, as the minutes ticked by, she'd thought he might not return. Twenty minutes later, though, he'd let himself back in, wearing only shorts, clearly freshly showered and brandishing a tube of lube and a wicked smile.

"I think you made a promise," he'd said.

Smiling back as wickedly as she could, "I meant every word," she'd told him.

But he'd rushed nothing. There was lots of sensual touching, his cock feeling reassuringly firm as she bent to kiss it lightly again, taking only his head in her mouth for a little while until, oddly, she'd begun to get impatient before he did. She'd turned and lifted her arse, making her invitation very plain. He smiled as he moved behind her. "It's almost as beautiful as the view from the front."

He'd slid himself slowly into her. She touched herself but soon moved her fingers away. Feeling him slide in so deeply was exciting enough, she could make herself come easily later on when he did. But then he'd pulled out and she'd expected the lube but instead she felt his mouth on her arse and his fingers were massaging her clit. "Easy," she'd said, "Don't make it too nice yet. Just lick me, I love it." And she did. It wasn't mere encouragement, she loved his hands spreading her cheeks, his tongue tickling and exploring and then the lube and some fingers.

"Are you ready?" he'd asked.

"You know I am," she'd said, and she'd been thrilled to feel him push slowly into her. She'd heard him breathing heavily, then easing out a little, controlling himself, but then pushing deeper again.

He'd already felt very deep when she reached back to touch him and wow, he still wasn't fully in. Then, as she'd reached to stroke his balls, she felt the thick ridge of the ring. "It's a cock ring, madam," he'd said, "You offered yourself to me, now you must take all the consequences. I will be thicker and longer and slower, I promise you" and he'd given a gentle, wicked laugh.

That had been true. Now she sat beside him, feeling sore and with a pain in her stomach where he'd seemed to get so deep, but she'd had a strange enjoyment out of the discomfort at the time. And he had been slow even as she'd reached back to stroke his balls until he'd finally said, "I think it's time now" and she'd moved her fingers to her clit as his hands gripped her hips more firmly and he'd begun to push harder and even slightly deeper, staying there as he burst into her, feeling her coming with him.

They'd had more time in each other's arms, she'd enjoyed his skin against hers. "Should we be moving?" she'd been the one to ask.

"There's no rush unless you've things to do, but it's meant to be a relaxing day."

"It's a day when I can ring the kids."

"Of course," he'd said, kissed her tenderly. "I'll leave you in peace, breakfast won't be before nine." And he'd left.

Now she was here beside him and Hannes was placing orange juice and fruit in front of her.

The kids had been fine, which is what they always said on the phone, Abbi impatient to go out to meet her friends, Jonah a little more communicative: Gran was taking him and Damian to the cinema that afternoon and then Damian was staying. Dad had wanted to take them out for an Italian that night with his girlfriend, but they already had plans. Claudia knew that feeling good about that was unworthy, but a little schadenfreude was always understandable. She'd then spent a long time talking to Pat. If her life was to change, then Pat would become even more important. Pat had seemed both excited and concerned, able to see the plusses of her being her own boss but feeling anxiety about the lack of security. The conversation helped Claudia get things more in perspective. How truly valuable was Peter's support? How much real work was in the pipeline? Could she work with smaller organisations? She resolved nothing but at least felt that, in Pat, she had a rock to stand on. 'You know I'd do anything for the three of you, Claudie' and that was one commitment, probably the only one, she felt she really could trust.

Not like Jack! She'd seen the email but left it unopened. Yes, she was now late for breakfast so she had to leave it anyway but, in truth, she knew she couldn't face it yet. It would have been hard after last night! She looked at Alphonse. No, not after last night, not really. It had been lovely and her body was acutely aware of its reminders but no emotional hooks were grabbing her. She knew that real life would go on elsewhere and it was just very, very pleasant to feel temporarily so detached.

Yet Jack, just possibly, might be real life. She knew she would have to deal with that later.

She and Alphonse lingered over coffee at the table. The others dispersed, she assumed to other sunbathing points, but soon noises below told her that someone was going jet skiing and soon after she saw Jen and Andy driving out into the bay.

She put her hand on his arm. "I have to go write some emails."

"Difficult ones?"

"Maybe, but if you keep asking questions like that, I shall start to think you care."

His brow furrowed.

"Oh, Alphonse, please don't worry. I'm finding I'm a surprisingly big girl. And don't feel threatened either. I do love fucking you and I hope we'll do it again, but I think we know where we stand." She stood up, kissed him and went back to the cabin.

She collected her things. She'd grown to like the corner she'd found on the upper level and felt sure it would be peaceful there, all windows and doors open to the very gentle breeze and almost the whole horizon of sea and distant shore open to view.

Darling Claudie,

Emails are seldom good for us. If they're not simple information, then they're usually about trying to rectify something.

I don't suppose this is any different. I always expect topics like the other evening (your morning, sorry) to be difficult but, because of your insistence on openness, I try my best and I think we've been managing very well.

As I've always said, it's not really my natural style so I approach conversations like that with trepidation, which probably sets you on edge anyway and makes it harder for you just to listen and harder to avoid drawing unwarranted conclusions.

It is very hard living like this. You were always important to me, even before I moved here, as the one person I could be open with and rely on. That's even more true now; I do feel more isolated. My boys, and I did used to spend some time with them when I was UK based, are now very much focused on their own lives so I'm not much more than an exotic place to visit and show off to their girlfriends — although it's only been one visit each, as you know.

I maybe don't feel guilty enough about the other evening. I know from how we finished the conversation that you were unhappy. But I also know that when I have tried 'hermit phases' that they haven't really worked for me. But two things remain true:

You are the only one with whom I have ever had such a bond — and this is principally emotional, although the physical has become astonishingly rich;

I desperately want to be much closer to you, to live with or near you and spend much more time with you.

I am hoping very much that something comes out of the opportunities that seem to be opening for you. You so deserve them and I have great faith that you could be very successful moving on to something much bigger.

And I need to give more thought to moving on from here myself. I am finding the work stretching and thrilling but our lives, yours and mine, are not growing together in the way I, and I hope you, want them to.

I will want to spend loads of time fucking you in four weeks (ever the romantic!) but I want us also to spend time thinking about <u>our</u> future.

I wish you all the very best for your conversations on the boat.

I am missing you terribly.
All my love,
Jack.

She read it many times. It seemed so sincere and yet… But was it her own feelings she was starting to doubt, and not his? And she couldn't even begin to think about how to reply.

She looked at the other emails. Nothing urgent. Important? Yes, very. Two more from Lavinia, with attachments but noises from the back deck called her away. There was time for Giddings later; days like this would be unique in her life. She closed the laptop and left it.

"There you are!" said Jen, as she stepped down onto the bathing platform. "I was just coming to look for you. There's a bar in the bay up the coast so we thought we'd go slumming in the tender. You up for it?"

"Yes, of course. Are we all going?"

"Yes, even Peter," said Jen, with a look that indicated this was rare.

"Am I alright like this?"

She got a cold eye from Jen. "Don't start that again, madam, you can have another chance to outshine us at dinner tonight. Your slummy shorts are just fine for the bar" and they laughed with each other.

Peter sauntered down, looking almost overdressed in a crisp blue linen shirt, quite formal cream shorts and blue deck shoes. But that was pure Peter. It was strappy tops and tee shirts for the rest, including Andreas, who also sported a jaunty captain's hat.

The big RIB jetted off, with Andreas abandoning the pompous formality of his control of the big boat to send them skimming quickly over the calm water with plenty of spray cooling them down but he slowed as he came to the bay entrance and then chugged around to the southern end, past a few moored sailboats, and eased them smoothly up to the dock by the bar, where Andy and Alphonse stepped easily ashore to tie lines to bollards.

After the sophistication of service on board it was fun to order beers and potato wedges. Even Yvonne seemed completely at home although Peter ordered a chardonnay. The conversation relaxed with a good deal of gender-based teasing and stories of previous passengers who had not adapted well to boat life. But some of Andreas's bad weather stories had Claudia wondering if she would have been so stoical in those situations. After two hours the party was merry; even Andreas was entirely tuned in, in spite of his commitment to sparkling water. Claudia knew that a sunpad would claim her for the afternoon. Company would be nice but non-essential.

The toys were out, ready when they returned. "Do you want to try a jet ski?" asked Alphonse.

"I would, but maybe later. I think it's siesta time. I was awake quite early this morning." She smiled at him.

She went below, changed into a bikini, smeared herself all over with factor twenty, grabbed a towel and a book and made her way to the upper front deck without the slightest intention of reading a page.

When she awoke, Jen was lying on the sunpad next to her.

"I wasn't disturbing you, was I?"

"No, of course not. I just wanted to catch up on sleep, I didn't want to be antisocial."

"We slept like logs but that's sea air and…" she shrugged in what seemed like mild embarrassment "well, we had fun."

Claudia laughed lightly. "Well, I did too, in a funny way. I had a broad education at Peter's the first time but it's different when you know everybody."

"How well do you know Alphonse? Is that serious?"

"Oh, good Lord no." Claudia guffawed. "Oh, I'm sorry. That probably seems rude. I realise I've been mooning around after him all day and he was very good to me last night." They both smiled. "He's been an absolute dear, but I don't feel I know him in the slightest."

Jen nodded. "I can see what you mean. He's always been so cool and charming, but I never feel I get inside his skin," she paused, "but when you're getting carried away it just doesn't seem to matter, does it? But you do have somebody, don't you? Peter said something to Andy."

"Ha, well I think I do but I'm taking a few days to make sure I'm sure. Does that make sense?"

"Oh, completely, don't we all have those phases? But, if you're far apart most of the time, I guess it's hard to work these things through."

Claudia shrugged ruefully. "Well, this is one of those phases where it's better not to think. But you guys seem to manage very well."

"Hmm, we're in a good place right now but we have had our moments. We've both done the 'behind the back' thing and it's so destructive. But, when things were really bad, Peter and Yvonne asked us to join them for a weekend and we had some good conversations. Yvonne was very helpful actually." She saw Claudia's look. "I know, I know, I was a little surprised too, but she talked to me a lot and she talked a lot of sense. It wasn't just a question of letting Andy fuck himself to a standstill with her, although I think she got quite a lot out of that too," they both smiled, "but she talked to me a lot about coping with Peter, or about him coping with her. It was good. Andy and I have been much more open with each other since and it's been better. Much better."

"That's strange, I was sure being open with Jack would help, well, about him being open with me really. I wasn't expecting to do anything myself, I never had. But I thought being open would be the only way to sustain it, but I have to admit now to finding that hard sometimes. Still, he's here in four weeks and we'll get some time together. And thank you."

"Thank me?"

"Yes, I can get so wrapped up in myself that it's good to hear about other people having similar problems."

"Oh, you're very welcome and I wish you the best of luck. But on a vastly more important topic," she took a deep breath, "what's Alphonse bought you to wear tonight? I don't want to be so totally outshone again." They laughed together.

"Well, it's a similar combination but orange apricot rather than blue."

"Oh, thank God you said." Jen looked horrified.

"Really? Were you…?" Claudia was worried.

Jen burst into peals of laughter. "No, but I just couldn't resist it — and your face. I'm sorry a picture!"

Claudia laughed. "Bitch!"

"I'm sure you'll look wonderful again but how about coming down now for a swim?"

"Great idea, I'm getting sticky," and she stood up and gathered her things.

When they got to the back deck the men were in the water and Raul was wiping down the jet skis. "Have you tried them?" asked Jen.

"No." Claudia felt dubious.

"Come on, they're much easier than they look and they're huge fun."

And ten minutes later, after some rudimentary instructions in Raul's rudimentary English, she found herself pottering out into the bay with Jen driving much faster in circles around her, encouraging her to speed up, which she did a little but still felt nervous. Her mood wasn't helped when Jen, having turned several doughnuts at high speed, finally flipped off her ski while attempting a figure of eight manoeuvre. Claudia was momentarily panicked but the ski stopped immediately ('thees ees thee keell cord, eet stop you straidaway eef you fall off') and Jen waved to her, very obviously unharmed and clearly laughing as Claudia approached her. She clambered easily back on to the ski, reattached the cord, restarted the engine and was off again. Claudia kept going slowly but began, at least, to try turning circles.

Jen eased up beside her. "Give some doughnuts a go. You can't say you've done it until you've fallen off!"

And Claudia began to experiment. First speeding up, it began to feel thrilling and very fast until Jen still sped by her. But the ski, she realised, did seem very stable. So she tried some wide turns at a higher speed. It was working, you leaned into it and the thing swung round easily. Yes, this was fun. She tried speeding up in a straight line. She'd seen the gauge on the dash and she'd been up to twenty. Could she do twenty-five? That couldn't be miles an hour, surely, it felt so fast! But again, Jen sped past her. No, twenty-five was enough, thank you. And the circles were more fun anyway, so she slowed a little and tried tighter and tighter turns, yes, now they were real doughnuts, wow, until, trying to come out of one, she flipped over the other way and pitched herself into the water.

Jen was soon near her. She found herself laughing and waving an arm to show she was OK.

"No harm done?"

"Only my dignity."

"Fuck that! Can you get back on?"

"I think we're about to find out." But it was easier than she thought. There were footholds and grab handles and the ski stayed surprisingly stable even as she got up one side. Jen had moved away to give her space. The thing restarted easily and Claudia pointed back to the big boat and they headed that way.

Raul took the line when she got back. Alphonse was on hand to help her off. He embraced her warmly, "You did it!"

"What?"

"Fell off. You can say you've done it now."

"What, abandoned my dignity?"

"No, bollocks to that! I mean you've pushed yourself. Admit it, you've had fun."

"All right, I admit it." She wrapped her arms tightly around his waist. "Yes, I've had fun!"

"Now, come on, you must try a swim."

She handed her vest to Raul and dived in after Alphonse. Jen soon followed. Alphonse set out along the side of the boat and, lacking her own plan, she swam after him. The boat towered above them and there was something weird, almost menacing about swimming close to it, as if it might suddenly pull her under. She moved further away from the side and immediately felt more comfortable — but going all the way round the thing, giving it that wide a berth, was enough exercise for her and she stayed by the stern and flapped around while the others set out for a second lap. No point in waiting; she could clear the shower before they got back, so she climbed up on to the deck. It seemed entirely natural to stand naked under the drenching water. Raul, in the garage now, glanced at her — *but he's not going to be interested anyway* — and Andy seemed to be asleep in one of the chairs although, as she began to towel down, she saw his head turn towards her and a smile spread on his face under his sunglasses, turning away again once she'd pulled her robe on.

The other two were soon back and Alphonse ushered Jen to the shower first. Claudia was slightly relieved to see her follow the naked convention.

She picked up her phone, five thirty, no point in settling down now, better to enjoy a more leisurely preparation. "See you guys at half six," she called.

14

It didn't seem that leisurely in the end. Her hair needed attention, obviously, and, having discarded the deck shoes she'd brought as too shabby, she had to pay a lot of attention to her toenails so she could arrive barefoot.

But the clothes looked wonderful again and she'd picked up enough colour not to look washed out in the paler shades. She twirled twice in front of the mirror and was still impressed. She smiled at herself, she felt unusually content, almost light-hearted, as the week's worries receded.

She was there on time. Yvonne could have her diva entry later. Jen had been effusive about her outfit again but, Claudia noted, she had definitely made a bigger effort herself. The clothes were still simple but she looked stunning. She'd also paid more attention to make-up this evening.

Yvonne had taken no chances. She wore a short print silk dress and an indecent amount of jewellery. But Claudia could only smile. She did look dazzling but, after the first appreciative glances, the men, in particular, seemed unmoved. Andy had shown far more interest as she'd emerged from the shower that afternoon.

"Opposite sides tonight," boomed Peter. "The others shall see the sunset." And this seemed fair. She might have preferred to be opposite Alphonse, but maybe she'd be seeing him later. Then she stopped, slightly shocked at herself for thinking that way. Had she stepped out of reality for these few days? Would she really welcome him again? She looked across at him, smiling at Jen and talking more animatedly than was usual, and thought yes, I would, I will, it will bring no more guilt than a dream, and have no more consequences. But she feared, somewhere in the back of her mind, that she might be kidding herself. But she also knew she wouldn't stop herself should the situation arise. Reality could wait until Monday. She turned to Andy.

"You weren't asleep!"

He smiled. "You're not going to blame me for peeping, surely? You're a very beautiful woman. Botticelli couldn't have captured that and now, here it is in my memory. I'm afraid it's photographic," he tapped the side of his forehead, "your beautiful naked body locked in here forever."

I have a similar memory of your cock, my boy, but I'm not publicising that. "It's not what I normally do but it's very easy to relax here. I seem to have stepped outside of reality."

"I think we all do that except Peter."

"What's that, my love?" At the mention of his name, Peter had tuned in to the conversation.

"We're just saying," said Andy, "we come on board for a few days and leave the world behind us but you disappear between mealtimes and connect with everything else going on."

"Damn, rumbled." He laughed. "I work so hard to cultivate this effortless dilettante persona and you spy on me when I retreat to my cave." He touched Claudia's hand and turned to her. "It's the major problem of working with smart people; they see right through you, dammit," he narrowed his eyes, "and I have a nasty feeling you could be worse than any of them. I may have to reconsider that offer. But I jest, I jest," he added hastily, "I can't ask you to do what I'm asking unless you can see through people like this," pointing his glass at Andy.

"Oh, she sussed me right away, accused me of lording a development aristocracy and ignoring my peasants."

"Ha," exploded Peter, and slapped the table with his free hand. He turned to her again. "That is so true. It's brilliant, in fact. I hadn't seen it that way before, but it does explain so much. My dear, you have to come with us, there are others who need you even more than he does. Of course, I balk at him qualifying as an aristocrat. You're going to see him, I gather."

"I thought it made sense to get some sort of picture of the problems in your businesses before I try to put any thoughts together."

He nodded slowly. "Well, I'm just impressed, I really am, I think that's an excellent idea."

"Of course, popping in to Boston on my way to Atlanta is a very surreal thought for little old me but I am starting to get used to that sort of idea."

"That's one of the attractions of this boat for me. We're very spread out geographically but it's not too hard to get them to come and see me, so I don't have to travel. I'd stay here all the time, but Alphonse insists I block time for charters. He says he needs to keep the resale price up for when Yvonne divorces me and a good charter book will help that."

Yvonne, who was half tuned in, looked at Claudia, shaking her head and smiling indulgently, like the mother of a charming but difficult child.

The conversation widened and the whole table began to participate. Claudia occasionally met Alphonse's eyes and they smiled at each other but even he, normally so reserved, had his fund of stories about difficult houses and difficult boats or, more accurately, the eccentrics who bought and sold them.

They may have sat later than yesterday. She had rather lost track, but there seemed no urgency to move. Neither had there been the previous night; none that she'd observed but, when she reflected, the surprising pairings did seem to be pursuing a preordained commitment.

The surprise when it came tonight was no smaller. Peter stood and, taking Jen's hand said, "Come, my loves" and led her to his central station.

Andy smiled at her and, with Alphonse moving off with Yvonne, she knew where she would be sitting but assumed the evening would be quieter.

The other couples nestled comfortably into each other and began quiet conversations which the music made inaudible. She felt Andy's arm around her shoulder and she shuddered slightly, reacting to a sense of coercion, but as he kissed her head gently, she felt the stirrings of curiosity mingling with her detachment from reality. Why not let it unfold like a dream?

She tried to convince herself, when she remembered the evening later, that she and Andy had begun kissing, but her obdurate and honest inner self would always remind her that, after his first gentle kiss on her head, she had moved her hand to the front of his shorts. It was unlike anything she had ever felt and, of course, it grew as she moved her hand slowly up and down.

Now they did kiss, both her selves were sure of that, but where the fantasist said passionate, the obdurate said perfunctory. She wanted to touch this strange object and the button and zip needed her full attention as the beast was trying to escape on its own. She pulled it free, laying her head on his chest to view it closely. Andy relaxed but was breathing heavily. The beast had grown to what she hoped was its full size.

"Come on Andy," she found herself whispering, "let's lose the shorts."

If he'd seemed in a world of his own while she held him, he was nevertheless quite quick to respond and his shorts and pants disappeared and he resumed his relaxed pose on the sofa, the beast, now vertical, commanding its due attention. She took two hands to it; it obviously felt thick, but it even felt heavy. She felt his hand touching her back gently, not making any attempt to push her. Maybe he was used to women being made curious by this challenge. She began licking its head, oblivious to anything else that might have been going on around her. She could fit the head in her mouth, just, but would have to be careful with her teeth. It was too thick to allow her lips to play their usual role. But it fascinated her and he seemed able to sustain himself, not letting the small bobbing she was able to achieve drive his excitement higher. Now she pulled her head back but kept her hands moving it was a fascinating sight. It was also intensely exciting and, huge as it was, her cunt would be very stretched but, she was sure, quite capable, although she had a moment's doubt when she remembered that the black friend in her bedside drawer felt really enormous but was nowhere near as big as Andy. Even Yvonne, she thought, had hesitated. Never mind, this had to be tried. "I think it's time, Andy" and she stood up and stripped completely. He looked up and smiled, stripped off his tee shirt and lay on his back in the centre of the circle. He was doubtless quite comfortable, she thought, with the lady having to manage the process, and do it carefully. As she straddled him the serious expression had left his face and he was smiling at her. "Take your time, Claudie," he whispered. "He'll wait for you."

She had one hand on his chest and the other had hold of his cock. Her cunt, with her hand's help, found the head easily but now she needed to go very slowly, carefully but, remarkably, her body adjusted. She knew now she wanted all of this but, if she moved too many millimetres at once, it got very uncomfortable, as if it were threatening to tear something but, going very slowly, she was taking everything. Andy's smile had left him and she was confronted with an expression of fierce concentration. Good, she thought, thrilling though this immense fullness was, it was not going to push her or him over the edge. This was something to be savoured. She needed him to stay calm, she wanted to move gently up and down and enjoy this extraordinary feeling. She lowered herself onto his chest and focused all her movements on her hips. She felt she had almost all, if not all of him. Certainly, she felt completely full, much more than she had ever been and she spent minutes just enjoying that, oblivious to all else.

It came as a mild shock to feel a hand on her back. She looked round. It was Alphonse with that wicked grin again — *surely not* — then she felt the lube on her arse — *no* — and somehow his finger was finding a way in — *not possible, surely* — but more lube and two fingers and a feeling of yet more extraordinary fullness. If this worked, and she remembered times with Jack and the big black one, her clit did not need to engage. With two of them in her she would fly very high. So now, if Alphonse succeeded, and she felt his cock pushing at her arse, it would make her scream in ecstasy. Now he pushed in; her whole lower body felt swollen but only with discomfort and the tingling from where he'd fucked her arse that morning. But this was so much more. She could feel the men's rising excitement even as her own began mounting. This would be so big. She felt Alphonse slowly start to come, then Andy began bucking his hips and suddenly it hit her, she was pushing her hips down and screaming, "Amazing, amazing, amazing," and still Andy thrust and still Alphonse pushed. She felt Alphonse stroking her back and kissing her, gradually more gently, and then slowly he began to pull out and then subsided to lie beside them, now smiling up at her. Andy slowed and softened slightly, still pulsing, but she felt a strange reluctance to let him go. Eventually she eased herself up to free him and suddenly felt hugely empty inside. She rolled to the side and squeezed herself between them, suddenly conscious of their audience.

Peter was sat facing her, his arms around Jen and Yvonne on either side. He looked mock stern but the ladies were smiling.

"Ladies, what do we think of this Jezebel? Stealing your men right in front of your eyes, behaving like a disgraceful harlot, is it not outrageous?"

"Outrageous, outrageous," they both said, still smiling.

"And should she be punished?"

"Of course, she must be punished."

This was clearly a game, but she had no idea where it was going.

"And these weak and feeble men she has seduced to serve her?"

"Punished, punished."

"And your recommendation?"

"Twenty lashes!" delivered simultaneously. It was obviously planned, confirmed when Peter turned and took a tawse from the table behind him.

"Very well, and the men's punishment is that they shall remain blind to this ordeal, however much its sounds may tantalise, excite and inflame them." Claudia looked to them, they looked as mystified as she felt. "You men shall lie back and look to the ceiling."

They hesitated, looked to each other with puzzled faces, but then lay back; obviously a new game for them, but not their first game under Peter's direction.

"Ladies, blind them if you will."

The two stood up, still smiling, in contrast to Peter's continuing stern face. Each took one of Claudia's hands and helped her stand.

"Jezebel, you shall place yourself across my knees" and he gestured by widening his arms that she should lie across him. Claudia was numb, wanting to retreat but somehow caught up in this strange ritual. She turned to watch Jen and Yvonne straddle the faces of Alphonse and Andy and, with their hands on the men's knees, look towards Peter.

"Jezebel, I am waiting, twenty can only become worse" and then the stern face softened into an almost-smile and he nodded to her gently — *he thinks he's doing this for me* — and in that moment she wanted to give herself to the experience. How would this be? Was this for just Jack, or was she uncovering something inside her that pre-existed, unsuspected — but then she remembered her childhood fascination with her friend's stories of being punished by the father's belt and the knickers pulled down in the bedroom to prove Claudia's doubts wrong. The hideous red marks had left feelings other than fear and revulsion in Claudia's memory; an odd fascination with how that might feel, not just the pain, which must be obvious, but the ritual, the exposure, the shame and somehow the welcoming of being controlled. She lay herself across Peter. She felt his hand smoothly brush her cheeks, not lustfully, more tenderly.

"You will count for me, Jezebel, count so that all may hear, even those who are blinded" and she looked to the four on the circle, the women already gyrating their hips on the men's faces. The men obviously eating them and, from their resurrecting erections, plainly enjoying the experience.

"We shall begin" and the loud crack was followed by a searing pain that made her gasp loudly. It wasn't quite Jack's cane, but it was close.

"I'm waiting."

"Oh, one, thank you."

Another stroke, just below the first, more painful this time because she knew what to expect.

"Two, thank you."

He smoothed his hand over her cheeks and whispered, "Well done."

But there was no let-up in his vigour.

"Agh, three, thank you." He left long pauses between the strokes, the heat built up and the pain spread slowly all through her, but she felt herself pushing her arse higher to welcome the next stroke. In the pauses she looked to the women, whose smiles had disappeared, who were quite clearly now focusing on her fiery arse, finding the unfolding scene exciting and pushing themselves faster and faster onto their men's faces.

At fifteen the pain was intense and universal but, somewhere at the edge of her awareness, she dimly perceived the screams of Yvonne's climax.

And later, "Eighteen, thank you" and she heard Jen now screaming and could see that Yvonne had now bent down to take Andy in her mouth.

Twenty was the fiercest one and she screamed when it came. "Twenty, thank you" and she was breathing very heavily, her heart rate soaring and her pussy drenched with excitement. She collapsed across Peter's knee and watched as Andy began to come in Yvonne's mouth, spraying her face as she pulled back, making her laugh.

Jen was still sucking Alphonse.

"Prisoner number two will be released for other duties." Jen slowly relinquished Alphonse's cock but still seemed to enjoy sitting on his face.

"Stand up, Jezebel." Claudia stood. "Ladies, return to your stations" and they both nestled into Peter. "Jezebel, assume the appropriate position on the circle in front of us. On your elbows and knees, please. Prisoner two, you will now service her until you are done. Jezebel, you are permitted to touch yourself while being serviced."

She would have had to anyway. She was amazed at how much this bizarre experience had excited her. Now her cunt welcomed his long penis deep into her, and the experience had plainly excited him. She felt the tight grip of his hands on her hips, felt him push with steadily increasing intensity. She touched herself lightly, wanted to feel him come first and savoured his slow build-up, but when he did come, loud and almost violent, she quickly followed, then collapsed on the circle with his arms around her.

She lay there with her eyes closed and his hands stroking her, unmoved by the sounds of people moving around her. Finally, when silence had descended, he murmured, "We should go? We're the last."

"Will you come with me?"

"You want me to?"

"I want your arms around me to fall asleep in. You don't have to stay, just take me to dreamland."

"I want to come with you" and they moved off, embracing, not even bothering with the discarded clothes.

15

She had wrapped herself around him. She was the outer spoon, her arse staying too tender to risk him rubbing against it, and they slept deeply, flitting threats of wakefulness banished by an enveloping embrace or his hand reaching back to stroke her.

She woke first as daylight began to seep in. As soon as he stirred, she moved her hand to his cock and began stroking him lightly. It grew pleasantly slowly and she enjoyed the playtime with him barely moving. And he was still barely awake ten minutes later when he was coming inside her as she ground down on him, taking herself to another orgasm as, propped by her hands on his shoulders, she enjoyed the changing expressions on his face as he had come with her.

They lay face to face, their breathing slowing.

"Thank you," she said. "I wanted to take away one sweet vanilla memory."

"Boring girl." He smiled at her.

"Is that bad?"

"Nothing's bad, don't be silly. I think that describes us on this boat: nothing's bad."

"But we step outside reality when we come here. That's what Andy and I were saying. But it must be different for you, you're here more often. The boat is business for you."

"Yes, but like this it is just the same for me too. It's a step outside reality while we're on board together with each other. Only Peter keeps all his links open to the real world. He has to, or it all might vanish. He's the ever-running engine that keeps pumping so this magic ball stays inflated."

"Is it magic for you?" He hesitated. "Don't worry. You're not going to upset me. I'm not trying to attach myself, although that must be a hazard for you."

"Ha, my life is much less wild and precarious than you think. I, too, have a business to run. It keeps me very busy all the time I'm not here."

"But apart from that, your life isn't complicated by commitments."

He was silent for a while. She wondered if she'd touched a nerve.

"No, it isn't, and I don't think I'd want that."

"Is there sometimes a risk?"

"Of course. I fell in love with you, remember?"

"Ah, I see the shutters coming down. I'm being too nosey. But there must have been something once. You said, once you weren't alone. What happened?"

He seemed to consider his response for a long time. "It finished. I didn't want it to but it did. It was very painful."

"What happened?"

"Someone else came between us. Ever since then, I've just found it easier not to commit. But I'm not just teasing you with the 'falling in love with you' line. I enjoy being with you very much and I think you get a lot out of me, and I don't just mean my semen." They both laughed. "I think this is becoming something very special but it's what I can call a real friendship. I think that's the same for both of us, isn't it? Please tell me if I'm wrong."

She nodded. "I feel that too, very much. But I've no idea how that will work in the real world."

"I wouldn't worry. Friends work that out for each other. They're the only relationships I need."

"So, no danger of anything deeper becoming permanent?"

"No, I couldn't bear to feel again what I felt when I lost him."

She felt stunned and completely disorientated, but she wrapped her arms around him and pulled him to her. That's what friends did.

16

They'd cuddled in silence for a long time, until she felt the tension in him relax. Then they'd managed some mundane, real world conversation. He knew when she was leaving. He had business in Florida, boats and apartments, deals in the offing, then back to London at the end of the week — she'd assumed London, but she hadn't known. And he would take her to Sandy Nicholls. She could make that an office base if she got started — and he very much hoped she would.

"And will you still fuck me?"

"Of course, I'll still fuck you. I'm still in love with you, remember!"

"Well, I don't know how I'd manage that in the real world."

"Friends work that out."

She'd kissed him. "Deal! Friends work that out!"

Now he'd left an empty space. It was her cabin but, after two nights, she'd begun to think of it as theirs. Now all she had left was the cock ring she'd hidden when he'd left the previous day. A peculiar souvenir, she thought, and smiled to herself.

She felt unaccountably sad for him but safe in herself. He had become a friend, especially now, knowing what he'd just revealed — and friendship was safe.

Pack now? Yes, there was time before breakfast. But she had to recover the clothes left on the main deck the previous evening. She put on her robe but, opening the door, there was a hanger and a bag. Shorts, top and pants, all laundered. Hannes clearly had cleaning and laundry staff somewhere in the boat who never appeared. She really had been detached from reality, then she chuckled. The role of the invisible provider was one she still played for the kids, although Abbi was now beginning to understand that clean clothes did not appear by magic.

She should catch them in the morning if her flight was on time. Then she would need a longer talk with Pat. Brodie Associates still sounded unreal, but it would remain so unless she could get to grips with the really important things: Abbi, Jonah, and Pat herself. It could maybe be made to work if Pat couldn't commit — *just how ambitious are you Claudia?* — but it would make the world of difference if Pat was really behind it.

But now, packing! She disliked empty mornings before travelling. The time never seemed well-used. She would, of course, have plenty time to write to Jack but she knew she should get home and re-immerse in real life to get a perspective on these three days before she could even attempt a first draft —. She wondered how many attempts his email had taken him. She felt very alive, and all that had happened had seemed very real and vivid — and memorable. She was sure it would be that but she had a sense of slowly waking from a wonderful dream.

Quarter to nine, hmm, maybe it would be best to go early and greet people one by one as they came. She didn't think she was nervous about them discussing last night in her absence. After all, yesterday had brought not a single mention of the previous evening, but, nevertheless… And she headed up to the main deck.

Peter was there alone, scanning a tablet. She leaned down and kissed him, then sat beside him. He closed its flap and turned to her, obviously happy to talk.

"Scanning the news? I'm embarrassed at how detached I've become."

"The UK is still afloat, my dear, there will be a landing strip available for you tomorrow. Anything else you can deal with then. We'll be heading back at around eleven, probably at exactly at eleven, if I know Andreas. If you want one last swim in warm water, you will have time, but I think Raul's put the toys away. You enjoyed that, I gather?" He smiled.

"Much more than I thought I would, I admit." She paused. "Peter," she put her hand on his, "I can't thank you enough for these few days. They've obviously been remarkable."

"I know," he nodded, smiling, "but don't go away thinking it was all orchestrated and choreographed. OK,

I may have prompted one or two situations, but most things were truly spontaneous and depended, as they almost always do, on people's imaginations and how they interact and stimulate each other. I just enjoy the luxury of being with," he paused, seeking a word, "well, people with warm blood in their veins who give themselves some freedom to enjoy life." He shook his head. "I'm not happy, really, with how I've put that."

"Oh, I think I get the idea, though."

"Well, they should be people you'll see again. I think you'll definitely see Andy and Alphonse in the next four weeks unless you get cold feet when you get home tomorrow. And you have an appointment with me in five weeks. I've checked, I am in London. Can we say the Friday?"

"I'm pretty sure I can."

"Well, let's say ten a.m., and please keep yourself free for lunch in the event that we get the outcome I'm hoping for."

"Well, I still have raging uncertainties, but I'm thrilled to be able to think about it."

This time he took her hand. "It won't happen unless it's right for you, my dear, but if it is right for you, then it will also be right for me."

Alphonse joined them, he kissed her cheek and sat down. "It's Thursday week for Sandy Nicholls. Can you manage that? I've set it for five p.m. so you can get a day's work done first. I'm conscious that you have a day job."

"It's Sunday morning! How've you done that?"

"Don't tell me you haven't checked your emails. Anyway, it's already Sunday afternoon for him."

"I haven't checked actually, but I admit that's because I wanted to get here early. I will succumb later. There's some Giddings stuff I want to read through and if I can have my corner on the top deck again, it won't feel like work at all. I'm not keen on mornings before travel anyway, it's nice to fill them with something useful."

Jen was next to arrive. She put a business card in front of Claudia. "All the contact details, can you email me yours?"

"Of course, I wanted to do that anyway."

"If you get into Boston early enough the night before you see Andy, I'd love to hook up with you. Just two girls, is that an idea?"

"That's a wonderful idea. I need to give some thought to how I want to structure the day in the business, but it wouldn't involve me letting Andy feed me his side of the story the night before, not now I've alerted him to his position as high priest and monarch."

Peter chuckled. "You are one smart lady, my dear."

Andy joined them, nodded to the men, kissed Claudia and saw Jen's card in front of her. "Good idea. I must give you mine."

"Yes, please. I'll put my details in an email. My card has just my corporate stuff. We shouldn't use that."

No-one mentioned the girls' rendezvous.

The upper lounge was her exclusive domain again. As she waited on the laptop's logging in routine, she took in the view again: the flat, green parkland out to the East, the water sparkling in the sunlight between boat and land; the more distant shore to the West, with the city presumably enjoying the quieter tempo of coming to life on a Sunday morning. The screen was now waiting for a password; time to get down to work. Her first task was to delete over one hundred emails she considered unnecessary, that was satisfying. There was nothing she saw as urgent so she quickly moved to Lavinia's messages. Both had been sent after seven p.m. on Friday, which impressed her — and made her wonder briefly about Lavinia's priorities. But the woman had performed an impressive edit on what must have been a lot of material. She had focused on two areas, assembling minutes from an 'HR Steering Team' where a group, ostensibly representing all levels and divisions of the business, met monthly to review a range of issues — and monthly quality reports which reviewed service performance levels across all markets and sectors:

'I thought, from your enquiries, that these would be the most interesting areas for you. There is further material

should you wish to pursue a different line. I am obviously not competent to offer a view on the issues raised but two aspects did stand out for me:

there are very few points raised in the second group of reports (quality issues) that appear to impact, in any way, the concerns of the wider group's discussions;

the long-term trend of data considered by the second group does appear to be deteriorating.

I doubt whether similar observations could be made at Collins.'

Claudia wanted to be cautious and keep an open mind. It would be too easy to be swayed into jumping to conclusions, but she was impressed by the points Lavinia had made. She nevertheless wanted to guard against being too strongly influenced by them. There may be even more powerful underlying causes of poor performance, but it did underline for her the importance of looking to solve a problem, rather than selling a programme.

She remained engrossed for over an hour until her concentration was broken by the distinctive noise of the anchor chain being lifted and the quiet murmur of the engines became more audible.

Fredo appeared with a pot of coffee and the exquisite monogrammed china which made such a contrast to the much more practical melamine and plastic of everything she'd seen on the boat Jack had borrowed.

"We weell have lunch at one, ma'am, Meester Hannes ask me to say, and your car weell be at two for airoport." She smiled and thanked him and allowed herself a few moments to dwell on her boat experiences. It wasn't difficult to be distracted since she was still sitting uncomfortably from the effects of the previous evening. The experience made a strange bridge between the two events but, as she began to drift off into thoughts about her peculiar sexuality — *am I beginning to understand Martha?* — she brought herself back to the more mundane but more urgent concerns of the Giddings reports.

When the boat turned an hour later to make its return passage between Fisher Island and South Pointe, she stopped working. She wanted to watch this. She felt an unaccountable thrill about returning to port; it had struck her on the smaller boat too, and she wanted to watch an expert crew managing docking smoothly without the tetchy shouted commands and the jarring bumps of her first experience: 'Have we actually damaged anything? Didn't those thingummys', 'Fenders', 'Yes, thingummys, fenders, don't they protect us?', 'Not the point', he had harrumphed. She nevertheless smiled at the memory, just as they had both been smiling as soon as the lines were tidied and the first drink had been poured.

She went out to the open deck to be able to lean out and watch the work at the lower level. When Hannes and Raul leaned out, she saw the headgear in place again. As they approached the empty space on the dock, two men appeared in blue uniforms and positioned themselves near bollards.

The boat slowed to a standstill, level with them, and, with a noise of churning water, easily moved itself sideways into the dock, where the men hooked the dangling lines ashore and dropped them onto the bollards. More lines appeared and were angled to different positions and then tensioned, presumably by winches — *winches, how did I know that? We didn't even have them on the little boat* — that Hannes and Raul must have been controlling. The sound of silence as the engines were shut down told her they were securely back.

17

They were all on the back deck to see her off. Even Yvonne gave her a huge hug. Peter had been unusually matter-of-fact. "Silly if we get emotional. You'll be seeing most of us in the next few weeks." But the warmth and length of his embrace suggested slightly different feelings.

Alphonse had offered to come with her to the airport. She had hugged him last. "This is a nicer place to say goodbye," but he'd helped her with her luggage to the car and hugged her again. She felt a little teary, then sniffed and dabbed an eye. "WTF! I'll see you in less than two weeks. Just kiss me!" and he gently brushed her lips then opened the door for her. The closing of the door was like stepping into a different world; all the feelings and sensations of the last three days were behind her. She didn't want to dwell on whether she could walk back in there again. She was now back in real life. She hadn't even upgraded the return flight although she'd been given ample funds to do so. She could sleep perfectly well in premium economy and that's all she would want to do. Now she was thinking about the kids and Pat and how everyday life could be made to work, but she had to admit to herself that she had only the vaguest idea of what running her own business would look like. That would need some clear thinking and a few helpful conversations. But who to turn to? Jack was obvious but... and, while she was pleased to feel that she'd somehow put Martha behind her, she realised that taking Jack through the past few days was almost impossible to contemplate. Yet who had insisted on the commitment to openness? A large lump of anxiety would have to be parked for a while and she wasn't sure if she could. She knew that, even at an unconscious level, it would continue to disturb her. Would it even make her question her relationship with Jack? That was a thought she rejected very quickly but she couldn't dismiss the notion that Jack himself might question it.

Her intense preoccupation at least numbed her a little to the awful airport processes and she found herself in the lounge — *thank God for the BA card* — with a small snack, a very large G&T and a blank screen on her laptop on which she intended to try to organise her thoughts.

By the time the G&T was empty she had only the list she'd compiled in the first three minutes:

Kids; Pat; Jack; own office; contracts — how many, how secure; locations of projects; home vs travel — fifty max; security; pension, fuck! funding; partners? staff.

As she kept staring at the screen, she found her thoughts revolving around two points in particular: home vs travel time — how would it work? She couldn't envisage spending more than fifty percent of her time away; that needed to be a fixed rule — if it can't work with that, it's not going to work; and Jack — and she had to admit that she wasn't parking that issue at all well. She was dreading the conversation, or would it be an email? — but she was at least relieved to find that, as the last few days occasionally intruded into her thoughts, she was merely emotionally elated and wasn't detecting any feelings like those of falling in love. She'd had wonderful nights with Alphonse but there was not the ache to rush back — just a warm sense of having something very special between them. She smiled to herself — *or maybe you're just a tart who likes kinky sex, Claudia* — that was a thought she could easily park, and she almost looked forward to time to herself to ponder on where she truly was on that one. Was she developing a sneaking and inappropriate admiration for her uninhibited self?

This isn't getting a consultancy business set up, you dozy bitch. Focus!

And she realised she should and would make a foundation of her fifty percent rule. First, she needed to convince herself that she could work that way. Any business she worked with would have to set up its own team. She would not be replicating her corporate role herself. She would need to identify, in each business, someone to fill that position so that she could work through them remotely. It made sense. And she would take on no contract unless she found not just an enthusiastic CEO, but a talented and energetic manager who could see the need for the programme and was desperate to run it.

Then she needed Peter to understand her rules.

And Pat to embrace them.

"I've been thinking." Pat was pouring tea. There was toast on the table but Pat was not going to distract herself with eggs this morning. Claudia had a sinking feeling this was obviously going to be a serious conversation.

She'd had a little time with the kids, told them something about the boat but she'd deliberately taken no pictures. Best let them think it was maybe impressive but not absurdly overwhelming. They had already made her promise a Chinese evening — *twelve-year-old boys can think that way at breakfast time* — but she would need to check it was open on a Monday (she did, it was).

But now Pat had been thinking. "This could work very well, you know."

Claudia was stunned, delighted, perplexed.

"We could run it from here in the early days. OK, you might want a posh address as a front but you link the phone line into here and I can handle all the admin."

Pat had worked in offices all her life, but Claudia had never given any thought to what she actually did.

"You'd do that? What about George?"

"So, George has to do a little more shopping and cleaning, that won't do him any harm."

"But are you comfy with technology nowadays?"

"Cheeky. It's not that long since I retired and your two keep me on the ball. I've got accounts on everything: Facebook, Instagram, Twitter, WhatsApp, so I can always keep in touch with them and watch what they're doing — and I'd challenge you any day on his Playstation" and she smiled. "Look, Claudie, you're obviously excited by the idea and I've always thought you were capable of doing so much better — better than my Dave, too, I'm ashamed to say — but I'd love it to work out for you. And one thing you mustn't forget…"

"What?"

"It'll say Brodie Associates on the letterheads. I know it's entirely your business, my dear, but I'd be working with my name at the top of the page, too." She had a beaming smile on her face. "Even George will be tickled, so I won't expect any complaints about him running errands."

Claudia was still a little stunned — *if it seems too good to be true, it probably is* — but there would be so many positives, especially in the start-up phase: someone she could trust completely; someone who would have the same priorities; someone who could lift lots of worries. Whatever her limitations, and the Playstation argument wasn't truly convincing, Pat was a bright and capable woman who would work immensely hard to make this a success.

"Pat, I don't know what to say — apart from yes, definitely, please and thank you very, very much. You've just removed about fifty percent of my worries, thank you!"

"The other fifty percent?"

"Oh, where do I start?" But start she had to. If Pat was going to fill that role, she would have to know everything, so she went down her list of concerns. She started with the time commitment — she'd been pleased with that; she must have a programme head in any business she contracted to — if she couldn't have that, someone she approved of, it would be doomed anyway so she wouldn't take the contract. Pat was nodding vigorously, plainly relieved to have one of her main concerns, time at home, addressed.

Pat was more sceptical when she talked about Peter's project pipeline and his financial support. "I'm worried too, but he's running twenty-four businesses and only had two failures."

"Well, nothing's going to be risk-free, is it?"

They'd spent half the morning talking things through and Claudia was feeling excited. It could work. When Pat stood to go. She gave her a huge hug. "Will you and George come with us to the Chinese tonight? I'm excited we should tell them all together."

"Are you sure? There's a few more things to put in place first."

Claudia hugged her again. "You're right. One of us has to stay down to earth."

Pat smiled. "That'll be me then. I'll see you Wednesday."

"Wednesday?"

Pat raised her eyebrows but smiled again. "You're in Brussels, early flight."

"Oh, shit, yes, thank you, see you by six then, sorry. That's my first job this morning: work through the diary."

But maybe it wasn't her first job: three missed calls, all from Jack.

18

"I'm sorry. I've had Pat here all morning, talking about this business thing."

"Pat? Business?"

"Yes. If she's not fully on board, I don't see how it can work. Anyway, she's very enthusiastic and keen to do something for it."

"What can she do, apart from looking after the kids?"

She'd expected grumpy, and the hour spent thinking about the call hadn't made the prospect any easier. But, actually, grumpy was good — well, better than the alternatives, *let's try and defer those.*

"She's worked in an office all her life so she can manage basic admin while I'm out and about."

"She's over sixty or something, isn't she?"

"Not being ageist, surely?"

A grumpy sigh. "You know what I mean." *So, not ready to be jollied into humour yet.*

"She's very up to date; the kids see to that. She does more social media than I do and she and I use internet all the time to make sure we don't drop one on the kids' timings. I've yet to catch her making a mistake — not a level of performance I can achieve. I'd forgotten about Brussels this week until she reminded me."

"And it takes you over three hours to return a phone call, apparently."

"Well, I'm sure Pat will answer you quicker." *Oops, no, that wasn't good.* "I'm sorry, Jack, I've got very enthusiastic about this, but I need her and I need you to be fully behind it."

"Well, I'm not giving you top marks for winning me over yet, so you'd better tell me more. It's obviously got you very excited."

"It has, it has. Have you got time now to listen?"

"Of course. We've not talked for days and that wasn't one of our best. I've kept the evening free. I wanted some account of life on your hedonistic pinnacle." *Oh, fuck!*

"It was utterly spectacular. I'll tell you all about that later," *if I can't get out of it*, "but can we do the job thing first? I really need your advice and then, I hope, your blessing."

"My blessing?"

"I don't like sounding pathetic but if you don't believe, I'll have a hard time trusting my own judgement. I love your body, my wonderful man, but you've also got a pretty sharp mind and my plans would have to get past that to get me feeling confident."

And she went through her conversation with Peter, his business structure, his funding plans, the project pipeline, with Jack slowly asking more questions. By the end he was sounding quite animated.

"So, you'll be seeing the consultancy guy in two weeks about how to set up a business, you see the audio guy in Boston in three weeks as a check on Peter's project pipeline and we're together the weekend after that — and you also get a chance, in the meantime, to get a detailed look at another corporation to see how it might work somewhere else. Sounds ideal — and I think your list of the questions you want answered is very good. Funny, isn't it, in three minutes you can dump everything that really matters into a list. I'm pretty sure you won't add much to that as the next few weeks unfold. Anyway, tell me about the boat and what you've been up to. A little bigger than the Motley Fisher, I guess."

"Is that what ours was called?"

"Yes, but James hates fishing so he threw all the rods and brackets away when he bought it. What was yours called?"

"Mine? I wish. Yvonne."

"Yvonne?"

"Well, Yvonne D. Yes, it's his wife's name. Don't ask. Anyway, it was huge."

"I'm googling it now."

"You might find two. If you do, it's the bigger one, the one with the D."

"Jesus Christ! Well, that answers one question."

"Which?"

"Well, this guy is seriously successful. Maybe you've ticked one box already if he's fully behind the project. So, who else did he have on board?"

"Well, his wife, of course Yvonne; Andy the audio man it's his business in Boston; Jen, his wife she has her own fashion business I really got on well with her. I'm seeing her when I go to Boston, probably, if the flights work out okay. And Alphonse I've told you about him he's the one that Peter asked to keep in touch with me."

"Is that the smoothie Mr Monochrome."

"Yes, that's him."

"Is he gay?"

"Funny you should say that. He is actually."

And she was off the hook with Jack, but a terrible hole opened up inside her. One little remark and she'd let down two people terribly, two people who meant so much to her. She was desperate for Jack to hang up. She daren't do that herself.

"Well, it sounds like you've had an amazing time, but it also sounds like it might work. Even I'm getting excited about it."

"Thank you, I'm ever so pleased, obviously, and thank you for helping me think it through."

"You're very welcome. Now is it time to talk dirty?"

"I would love to Jack, but it won't be long before they're home and my suitcase is still in the hall. Can we talk again tomorrow, maybe teatime — I like you a bit drunk and naughty."

"OK, but make sure the kids can't hear you."

"I will, my love, talk to you then." And she couldn't remember ever feeling worse.

19

The Nicholls office was on the second floor of an older building near Berkeley Square. Sandy, short for Alexander she assumed, had not enough evidence left on his head to decide if the name had referred to a hair colour. He was shortish, bespectacled, smiley and radiated energy.

"Claudia, I've been dying to meet you. Peter has sent me a spec of what he thinks he wants in the event that you don't take this on and, frankly, that person doesn't exist. It would be unusual for the Nobel peace prize to be awarded in the same year to the recipient of the economics prize."

"Oh, Lord, what has he written?"

"Well, I co-authored it," said Alphonse, sat beside her on the sofa, smiling, "and Sandy is exaggerating."

"Only slightly, I assure you, but to be fair, the right points are being made. We're getting more and more enquiries from companies looking for skills to help them enhance total workforce performance. I would have thought a consultancy acting in that area would find lots of business. If you start this thing up, I could envisage us directing a lot of people your way because frankly, just now, there aren't many suitable people we can put in front of our clients. They sometimes push but we usually find ourselves apologising for a mismatch and we have quite a low success rate. Frankly, if you want another job and you're half of what these guys say you are, there are some positions where you could command 150k plus, but I digress. The only point I'm trying to make — and this is from me, not from Peter — is that it's a very good area to set yourself up in."

Claudia nodded slowly, distracted by the thought that she could almost double her money by switching jobs — *forget that, just focus*.

"So how did you start?"

"I worked in recruitment in a much bigger consultancy, but I always found it inefficient and unsatisfying. I'd done some work for a couple of Peter's companies. I took a different approach to search, I started using new media and hired a friend who developed some algorithms which were better success predictors than the old 'who does well at interview' technique. We back-tested against all my old firm's data, so I can't, hand on heart, plead that it was entirely ethical since I didn't really share what I was doing, but we were trying to move the science of recruitment forward and there were lots of sceptics where I was.

Anyway, the guys I worked with mentioned what we'd done to Peter and he asked to meet me. Then I got into the phase that I guess you're in now and I think I probably had the same fears as you do: how do I start up; will I get enough business; am I good enough to make it work?" She was nodding. "Well, I'm ashamed to say, it was almost too easy. He'd said his businesses needed to recruit better talent and even if people like me found the right people, it took much too long, so he thought my approach was promising — and for over a year I worked almost exclusively for his companies — so his pipeline was underestimated, if anything, and he had less than half the number of companies then, but I worked my arse off. I don't think I saw daylight for eighteen months. I don't recommend doing it that way. I didn't even know if I was making money. It was only when the accountants he'd recommended told me I'd earned three times what I'd ever earned before in a single year that I began to sit back and plan a bit more sensibly. Now I have eight guys actively recruiting and the same number on admin and development. I still use the same accountants. They still tell me I'm earning big money, but I do keep my own tame finance woman so I can personally keep a close eye on the money situation. Well, I'm wrong to call her tame. If Penelope doesn't like an expense claim, I hear about it very quickly.

"Now, I'm going to listen to what you want to do but you can start from the premise that I'm going to help. But I'm also going to set your mind at rest, up front, by reassuring you that there is absolutely no shred of altruism in my position." He smiled warmly. "We can provide a front office and London address for you; we will let you use an office when you need it, given notice, of course; we can manage the accountancy function for you through the same people we use, plus Penelope here in this office; but we will bill you handsomely for those services on a cost plus basis. For me, though, I also expect to work synergistically with you. I like the area you're working in. I think we'll end up being a great to help each other. Well," he smiled, "you might be doing much more for me than vice versa. But all that's on the assumption, I promise I'm going to pause for breath now, that what you tell me now impresses me at least half as much as it has obviously impressed these guys, Alphonse and Peter, I mean."

She took a deep breath and smiled. "Wow, bit of a whirlwind." Alphonse laughed. Sandy, after a moment, smiled.

"Just between us," he said, "I'm terrible at my job. I just get carried away with enthusiasm and don't let people speak when I'm supposed to be listening and assessing them. I had to get the business big enough so I could pull myself from the front line and let other people do the real work" and they all laughed. "But, OK, spotlight on you now."

Claudia, with her major concerns addressed — *London office address, accounts management, client pipeline, wow* — found it easy to talk about how she managed the current programme and how she planned to manage her model in the future — *committed CEO's plus passionate advocates or no deal.* Sandy, contrary to his earlier self-critical observation, kept mostly quiet but posed only the occasional, but always very sharp, question. She'd started by liking him but, over the next hour, she also developed a real appreciation of a very incisive mind.

"I'm impressed," said Sandy. "I respect these two guys immensely but I'm aware of... how should I put this?" He paused. "Aware of their susceptibility to pulchritude so, among friends now and off the record and without prejudice, when I saw how lovely you are, I thought, uh, oh! But you've just given the best exposition of how an organisation should get all of its people focused on the right things that I've ever heard. That was really well done." He was smiling and nodding.

"Thank you. And amongst friends now, etcetera, etcetera, I was terrified" and they all laughed even louder this time.

Sandy suddenly looked a little serious and said slowly, "I don't think I'm being premature, but I think you've made a decision, haven't you?"

She smiled. "In principle, yes, but I do have a little time to ease some of my other concerns so I can be clearer about how it's all going to work, although you have taken a great weight off my mind today, thank you. It's beginning to feel like it might become real."

"There's a little bar around the corner. I don't think it's too early for a bottle of Bolly."

"She's a Taittinger girl, I think." Alphonse looked at her with raised eyebrows, she nodded slightly.

"My treat, my Bolly, let's go."

She walked the short distance on Alphonse's arm, unable to quite believe what she seemed to be committing to; it was both completely unreal but really, really exciting.

It was a haunt of Sandy's, 'any big deal, we come here' and the Bolly was on the table quickly. There were big smiles to accompany the 'Cheers' — *am I committed? Oh, fuck, I suppose I am now, cheers!* — and the men fell for a while into banter about Alphonse's people, who'd clearly all been recruited though Sandy but two of whom, from what she could gather, had not been overwhelming successes — but they were sources of humour and not recrimination. Their banter gave her a little time to collect her thoughts and the realistic prospect of a consultancy business was firming up in her mind. She was still distracted when Sandy stood up. "I have to go. I'd promised to be home for dinner, but there's another bottle coming. I thought you two would have some things to discuss. It's been wonderful to meet you, Claudia. I didn't think it would be possible for anyone to live up to the billing they'd given you but, honestly, you have done. I really hope we'll be working with each other." They all stood, he hugged her and kissed her cheek, went to the bar, signed a bill and waved them goodbye.

"Well, that went rather well, I'd say," said Alphonse, smiling, "has it taken you over the edge?"

"Oh, now I really, really want it to work. But I do have a few nagging doubts that I want to get clear about before I talk to Peter."

"But that's not all, is it?" He looked straight at her. "Do you want to tell me what else is on your mind?"

"No, I don't really." She was looking down into her glass. "It's something I'm very ashamed of."

There was a long pause. "I'm not going to push you. If you want someone to talk to, you know I'm here. If you want to battle on alone, I'll understand. After all," he took her hand, "it's what I usually do."

She leaned towards him and put her head on his shoulder. "I think I've let two people down very badly but the odd thing is, neither of them knows." She sat up again and raised her glass. "Well done, Claudia, really well done."

He looked quizzically at her. "I don't have to be home for dinner. I'm here if you want to talk."

"Well, one of those people is you and, in a way, I feel worse about that but it's probably easier to talk to you about it…"

"Than to talk to Jack?"

"Yes, how did you…?"

He smiled. "Easy, you wouldn't ever let your kids down, so he was the only option and it's not hard to guess that you're experiencing complications after the boat weekend. So, first of all, tell me where your feelings are, are you fairly clear about that?" She sniffed and dabbed her eyes. "I haven't complicated anything, have I?"

She took his hand in hers and looked in his eyes, "No, no." She paused. "Well, I am finding our relationship very strange and unexpected. I feel very close to you and I get immense enjoyment about the time we have together — and you have enough tact not to make me spell that out in a public bar." They smiled at each other and he nodded. "I've quite shocked myself at how much pleasure it's given me — and," squeezing his hand, "how much I'm looking forward to the next time." She dabbed her eye again, snorted and had to pay attention to her nose. "Well, not now obviously, you're not going to be asked to pleasure a snotty-nosed, guilt-ridden weepy woman, but if we do Coworth again, I'll be looking forward even more to the afternoon than I will be to lunch."

He was smiling. "But somehow you think you've let me down. I'm going to be surprised if this is as big a burden to me as it obviously is to you, but it sounds like something that friends should talk about." She sniffed again and nodded. "So, what happened? Deep breath now, and tell me all about it."

"Well, when Jack moved away, I made him commit to being open. I thought I'd handle a long-distance relationship better if I knew what he was doing. It's been two years now and, in the main, it's worked. I've struggled sometimes with some of the things he's done and I worry about some of his relationships becoming serious. I've had to tell him about one or two things in my life — I never expected there would be anything — and he's struggled quite a lot with the party, although I think he's had a lot of enjoyment from me losing my inhibitions and discovering that some quite strange things excite me. Anyway, I'd convinced myself that openness was worth it and I think he's managed to observe it, even though he says it's not natural for him."

"Hmm, I don't know that it's natural for most people." She looked at him and he lowered his eyes. "I've felt I've had to live a life of some discretion" and he shrugged. "I think you know what I mean."

She nodded. "That goes to the heart of my current problem. I knew I was struggling with what I would have to tell Jack about the boat — and before I say any more, I have to say that I don't have a single regret," she squeezed his hand again, "and our time together was absolutely wonderful. I'm slightly embarrassed by some of the other memories but they were thrilling at the time and a bit of me is quite proud of myself for being so adventurous — but nothing changed my feelings for Jack — except for the nervousness about what to tell him. In my mind I thought that telling him about you would be enough. There are some people he sees regularly and, although it upsets me a bit, I do believe his reassurances that they don't disturb his feelings for me. So, I was primed to talk about you…"

"And?"

"I had told him a little about you before. I'd said how handsome and stylish you were, always impeccable, but sensitive and considerate, so, talking about the boat, when I mentioned you again and he asked: 'Is he gay?', I just said yes." She welled up again, put her face on his shoulder and said, "I'm sorry, Alphonse, I'm so sorry. That was such a stupid and dishonest way of getting out of a situation I was afraid to confront. I'm very ashamed of myself."

His arm was round her shoulder. "What did you want to say? What do you think you should have said?"

"That you're a very real and important friend and we have a very rich relationship which I want to build into my future life. And that you have a very interesting sexuality. To let that be described and dismissed by one silly word is stupid beyond belief."

"And how would he have taken that? How will he take it now? Especially since you've kept it a secret." Now he was holding her hand.

"I've made it worse, haven't I? I knew that instantly. I'd made him commit to honesty and you and I had agreed on friendship and I let both of you down."

"I'm glad you've told me — and I understand why you feel you've let me down — but I also understand what you're dealing with. But, deep down, I think your convictions are right. I think, looking back to that time in my life that I don't like looking back to, I would have got through it better if there'd been more openness. Having said that," he smiled a little, "I wouldn't say now that I was an open person. I would tell you now honestly, as a special friend, anything you wanted to know about me, but you'd have to ask some pretty specific questions."

"So, where does that leave me? Where does it leave us?"

"For a start, we're still friends. You're suffering much more than I am, but I would have been hurt if I'd found out about this any other way. I don't really identify with that label. I just enjoy the company of certain people and what we do together," he was still holding her hand, "but your big challenge was always going to be Jack."

"I know, I know, but I felt worse about letting you be described that way, not the word itself but the dismissiveness, as if you couldn't matter..."

"Or threaten?"

"Or threaten, yes. But if he is threatened by it, and heaven knows he gives me enough opportunities to feel threatened, then he and I can't get to the sort of relationship that we both probably need." She laughed to herself. "I thought I was targeting becoming a 'little woman', but I appear to enjoy a more complex life than that — but I still do love him."

"So, you do have to talk to him, don't you?" She nodded. "And soon." She nodded again, leaned across and kissed him. "Thank you. I love you too — a little bit." And they laughed together.

20

Can we talk? I had a brilliant meeting with the recruitment consultant yesterday.

I would be very happy to. But I would have been equally happy to have talked dirty to you on Tuesday last week. Is this call really going to happen?

She hadn't been able to face a conversation until she could start with a major distraction. She was expecting a reaction in spite of the good news, but it could have been much worse.

Of course, but you have to be there when I ring. When suits you?

She'd managed, much to her relief, to contrive two missed calls to him by picking times when she thought he'd be tied up. There had been four calls from him she just had not accepted.

I'm committed until five, but I'd rather talk from home at six. Then I'm out at seven, back by eleven. So, eleven UK or four UK, what suits you?

Four please. I'll still be at the office, but it'll be quiet by then. If I try to dash home, I might hit the Friday traffic and I'll certainly have kids around. And I don't even know how many.

OK, I'll call you at four.

She could have insisted that she would ring him, but she might have hesitated and delayed. Better to let him call, then she was inescapably committed, but fortunately, this time, she had the big news about the Nicholls visit *but don't use that to wiggle out of the boat story, Claudia!*

When he called (punctually) she almost asked 'where were you tonight?' but stopped herself in time. Talking about the Nicolls meeting was a much better distraction than a query about his Friday evening — and she did need his advice and his reactions.

"So, are you going to tell me about your meeting? It sounds like you're very excited."

"Oh, Jack, I am. I can't tell you how much my worries were shrunk — and he seemed so positive about the prospects for the business. When he started up, he got loads of help from Peter. He said the amount of work he got from Peter's businesses alone kept him completely busy for the first eighteen months, so he thinks Peter's pipelines are immensely helpful. And he offered me a London address and office space whenever I need it."

"Really?"

"Well, that was quite funny, I thought. He reassured me he was doing nothing altruistic: he would charge properly for services; and he thinks the area I'm planning to work in will attract lots of new business and that will benefit him too. He took us for a bottle of Bolly at his local bar, or maybe it was a club. Anyway, it was a cosy joint around the corner."

"Us?"

"Yes, Alphonse and me. I told you Alphonse had set the thing up."

"You didn't, actually, but I get the picture. I know he's been a bit of a go-between for Peter. But I thought you said he specialised in property."

"Did I? That's right but I don't remember saying that. Anyway, I get on with him very well and it's useful to be able to listen to someone who understands how Peter works. He was also set up by Peter and his business works well, too. But Nicholls was so effusive about the help Peter had given him, the funding, the contacts, the setting up in a London office. I'm almost there, Jack, I want to do this thing."

"When will you fully commit?"

"I'm seeing Peter three weeks today. He's got to put up the money to get me started and keep me going, so I have to convince him I'm going about it the right way — and there's one element in how I set it up that he has to understand and agree on."

"You're making it sound a bit dramatic."

"Am I? Sorry. It struck me the other day and it's so fundamental. I can't go into these businesses and do what I do now at Collins. I have to find, in addition to a CEO who's committed, someone in each business who wants to do my role. Someone who believes and who's powerful enough to make it happen. I'm not saying I'm powerful in our place but the system was up and running when I took it over, it's driven more by people like you."

"I wouldn't underestimate what you give it. There's been much more focus and enthusiasm since you took it over from Johan — that was his name, wasn't it?"

"Yes, but you see what I do very closely. I don't think you ever spoke to him."

"It's not just that, it's what other people say. I can't think Henderson would have asked Johan to talk to Giddings."

"Maybe not, but he wouldn't have tried to hold his hand at dinner, either."

"Oh, is there a problem?"

She laughed. "No, Jack, it's just what we have to deal with a lot of the time. Anyway, I might be wrong but I think I need to be careful."

"I suppose I should be grateful that your main contact for your consultancy seems to be that gay guy."

"Jack..." This was the point at which you tip yourself into a conversation and it becomes irreversible, she thought. One of those tiny moments after which you know, or think you know, that everything will now be different. "Jack, that's just too simple a label."

There was a long silence — but she'd said it now — and felt hugely relieved.

"I think you're telling me that more happened on the boat than I'd assumed."

"Yes, Jack."

"And it's taken the high priestess of openness ten days to come out and tell me. That says I should be worried."

"No, Jack, it's telling you that I am now realising why you have struggled being open with me, admit it."

"Oh, I can admit it, but you give me such a hard time when I tell you anything. Anyway, rather than me giving you a hard time, you'd better tell me a bit more about it. Is he gay or not? And I'm now assuming you fucked him."

He was obviously tetchy and upset. She needed to stay very calm even though his comments stung. "I want to tell you Jack; are you OK listening to it?"

"Claudie, I'm a bit cross and I'm a bit grumpy, I admit it. I've had to get over feeling bad when I open up to you on a number of occasions, but I think, in the main, it's served us well. I assume I'll get over my annoyance at your hypocrisy, or this nasty sensation in my gut that feels awfully like jealousy. The more important point is whether your feelings have changed."

"No, they haven't Jack. I know that for certain. I love you and I love what we have — it's much richer than anything I could have imagined. But I think that's been helped by me discovering things about myself that I never suspected. I think you've enjoyed a lot of that, lots of it initiated by you, but I have made one or two little discoveries by myself — but only because I want to bring them to our relationship."

"That's true. I even have to admit that I've told you about my fantasies of you being fucked by other men but, of course, it's very different when it really happens."

"Well, I'm not going to say you brought it on yourself. I obviously didn't do it for you. He's a lovely man; he's bi, if you want to give him a simple label, but that's probably just as daft as calling him gay. He's turning into a friend who's giving me lots of support. He's certainly not looking for more than friendship — and very obviously neither am I, my wonderful man, but," and here she paused, undecided about what to say next, but it came out quickly, "I enjoyed fucking him. There, I've said it. That's not something I ever thought I would say in my life. But I did. I've spent two years learning from you that it's possible to do that. If you tell me that you're seriously upset, then it won't happen again."

There was a long silence. She steeled herself, she knew she had to let him speak.

"I know you're right, intellectually that is, but, as you've always shown me, there are feelings involved in one's reactions and they're in turmoil right now."

"I know, and right now all I want to do is lie naked next to you, cuddle you and show you everything is all right, but seven thousand miles is making that difficult. I'm going to say it, Jack. I edge around this because I don't want you to feel trapped or too committed, but I do want more. I want time with you. I want us to be a couple. There, I've said it now. I've spent two years avoiding saying it, not putting any pressure on you — but if it hasn't been blatantly fucking obvious to you then you're a much more stupid man than I thought. Now don't say anything. I don't want an 'I do too', and I certainly don't want a 'nah, that's a stupid idea'. I will go on living with this situation while we have to and while you want to but, if you get based back in Europe again, then you can expect some serious questions, my man."

"Finished?"

She breathed out heavily and smiled to herself. "Yes, finished. I feel good about that."

"Stunning performance. You ring me to confess to fucking another man and I end up feeling guilty."

There was a silence for a while. "I think, I hope, I'm sensing a little Jack tease and a little Jack smile. I am right, aren't I?"

"You're right, and if you're also picking up a serious Jack desire to put you over my knee, pull your knickers down and thrash your bum, you'd be right on that as well."

"Not the bench?"

"That will have its time again but right now I want my hand on your bare skin, followed by my cock in your pussy."

"Jack, you know I would love all that. I want my bare arse over your knee and I want you to spank me as hard as you can. Then I shall want him everywhere. Hah, I'm looking out into an empty office and just thinking about fucking you. If you were here, I'd be bending over the nearest desk for you and telling you to spank me and fuck me senseless. It's two weeks until I see you it seems so desperately long. When I get to bed tonight the big boy is in for a very busy time."

"Ring me when he's fucking you."

"What? That'll be…"

"Around six my time, probably. I will want to masturbate while I listen to you fucking. I'm going to come with you."

"We have a date. I love you."

"I love you."

21

It would have been more sensible to work from home in the morning and go from there to get the fifteen twenty but, taking so much time out of the business this week, it seemed better to be seen behind a desk for a little while. If Davis rang at least she'd be there, or just have left, and she had a plausible story about the Boston day tomorrow. Atlanta was a Henderson directive; Davis couldn't say a word against that, even though she suspected it grated. Still, maybe she only had two more weeks of subterfuge, her conviction was growing.

There were no calls. Davis rarely troubled her; he had too many fires to fight and the programme was a rare and trouble-free plus for the HR division, so she settled back in the car and began to think about the days ahead.

But she also reflected on Pat's visit to London the previous week. When she'd come to the house after her day at Nicholls, she was glowing. She swanned into the kitchen and Claudia was almost bowled over, first by the smart suit and then by the hair, which must have had some serious attention the previous day — not really a different style but trimmed and coloured and highlighted like Claudia had last seen on the day she'd married Dave.

She even got a "Wow, Gran!" from Abbi.

"Don't be cheeky!" was said with the usual smile.

She'd met Nicholls briefly but then spent a lot of time with the infamous Penelope, with whom she seemed to have struck up a real bond. Penelope was much more than merely the expenses tyrant. She was the node of all Nicholls activity and would be, as Pat saw it, an ideal role model for Pat in Brodie Associates. Claudia had misgivings about how much she could expect from Pat, but she would be a godsend in the early days, and establishing a clear link through to Penelope would be priceless; she sounded like a woman who could spot trouble early.

Jen had emailed. She would collect Claudia from the airport and take her to the hotel. She'd booked a restaurant just round the corner. She had told Andy — 'it's a girls' night' — he hadn't made much of a fuss because he preferred eating early. He would pick Claudia up from the hotel in the morning.

Coming into the arrivals hall soon after seven was as good as she could have wished, and Jen was there with a huge smile. They hugged like lost sisters.

"I can't believe you're here!"

"Well, I also absolutely can't believe I'm here, or what's happening, really."

"Tell me all!"

Claudia found herself going over the familiar ground in the car, but Jen was a new audience. She'd picked up a little from the boat conversations, but only enough to prompt Claudia with more questions if details were skipped or links weren't clear. She was a gratifyingly avid listener.

"I'm not big enough as an organisation to need your approach but I absolutely do get it. Peter thinks I'm a lone wolf, but I always try to get everyone to understand where we're going and I always ask my guys what they're doing to take us there. It makes so much sense to me, but Andy doesn't really understand, I don't think. He has one or two big problems but the last thing you need is to listen to my diagnosis of that." Claudia nodded and smiled as Jen turned to look at her. They were pulling in at the hotel. "Do you need to freshen up? Find something devastating to wear?" She laughed.

"No, I'm happy like this if you don't mind me scruffy. I think it suits us both if we go straight on out, doesn't it? I'll just sign in and let them deal with the luggage."

"Suits me. I'll let them look after the car. OK if I put it on your room? If I drink too much I can Uber home and pick it up in the morning. Actually, that's a decision!"

"You're very welcome. Andy's paying the bill anyway" and fifteen minutes later they were sat in a booth in the restaurant.

"So, it's really going to happen, you think? I'm very excited for you. Do you think you'll work with Andy? Hard to say, I suppose."

"It is, yes, but like I said in the car, I'd need to identify someone who really wants to run the programme in his business. If I can't find that person, or if I suspect there are too many blockers, I won't even start."

Jen looked thoughtful. "I'm glad you said that. It means I don't need to warn you. Anyway, that wasn't the point of a girlie night. No more talk about Andy, well not his business, anyway."

"Agreed, but when did you meet him?"

"It's nearly ten years now. I was working in London. I'd just finished a long relationship and some friends took me to one of Peter's parties. He'd been with Peter for a few years by then and was," she raised her eyebrows, "a bit of a feature at Peter's."

Claudia laughed, "Well, I admit it made me curious, as you saw."

"Yes, it still has that effect, but we live with it." She showed no disapproval. "I won't say it didn't have an impact on me but when he was tired later that evening we got talking and I thought he was funny — and we both had links to Boston, so we had a common interest.

I didn't get too committed at first. I thought that thing might lead him astray…"

"It's funny how they can blame their cocks for all their misdemeanours, isn't it? It seems almost universal with them."

"I know, but I was a fairly free spirit too, so it was manageable. It took us a couple of years before we decided we wanted to get a bit more serious. Once you do that the little adventures start to hurt. Do you get that?"

"Well, it's slightly different because he's so far away. I just ask him to be open. I think he has been, but he's struggled — but I've come to appreciate how hard it is to be open myself."

"So you've told him about the boat?"

"Not entirely, no. So I'm a hypocrite as well. I only got as far as telling him about Alphonse. That was hard enough. I don't know how I'd begin with our little scene." They were smiling and shaking their heads.

The waiter brought the lobster. "I'm sorry for bullying you into that. I always feel we have to get visitors to try it."

"Oh, I don't feel bullied I love it but I'll admit it's a rarity for me."

"Good, and the wine?"

"I'm slowly getting used to how much brilliant wine you have here. But I will go carefully, I'm planning a full-on day tomorrow — and this was one big martini!" She raised the glass to Jen, smiled. "Cheers again" and drained the rest of it.

"So how did he take the Alphonse thing? Do you mind me asking?"

"No, not at all. It's such a relief to be able to talk about it. He took it about as well, I imagine, as any man does who says he's been fantasising about you fucking other guys, i.e. he took it badly. This is very new to me. I'd been living a simple and perfectly normal British life: two wonderful kids and an abusive husband. But I just had to deal with him being drunk, never with him going with other women. Well, I don't know that for certain but by then I wasn't giving a shit anyway. And I certainly wasn't thinking about other men. Well, I suppose I'd had a crush on Jack for a long time, but I never expected anything to come of it. Now I love him, but I like my time with Alphonse as well. Although he is an enigma, isn't he? What do you make of him?"

"Enigma's a good word. I suppose I tune in to him because we both have a slightly unorthodox sexuality. You know about his past?"

"Enough, I think" and Claudia felt careful, as if too much gossip here would be another betrayal.

"Well, Andy's a little like your Jack, only he likes to fantasise about me with other women. But when it happens, he gets confused and troubled. He's got so used to that thing of his being worshipped, he thinks it's all we should want" and they were laughing.

"But you seem to be in a good place now, the two of you."

"Oh, I think we are, relatively. Of course, it's much easier on the boat; parties like that are fun and you know what's going on with each other, but it's when you want a bit of time with other people that it can get difficult. It's not too bad with Andy because most women just want a short-term relationship with his cock but sometimes signals can get crossed. But, like you say, we've found it best to be open; things seem to heal quicker that way. Of course, we could give up everything else completely, but neither of us has shown any ability to follow that path."

"It's funny. I would have said that was me, that's what I'd be aiming for, pure monogamy, but I don't get the impression Jack would have a talent for that and I'm slowly wondering whether I could ever go back into my shell. I've already told Alphonse I want to have him the next time I see him."

Jen smiled. "Yeah, me too, but in a good way." They both laughed although Claudia didn't find the thought an easy one to assimilate.

Andy was waiting when she came out of the hotel in the morning. He gave her a big hug, opened the door for her and then tipped the boy who put her suitcase in the back of the huge SUV. Claudia was glad, she knew she hadn't mastered tipping.

"You had a good night? Jen was only just waking when I left. That's how it usually is in the mornings."

"We had a wonderful time, thank you, although we may have got a bit loud but we had a booth, fortunately. We were tempted by a second bottle of wine, but we showed iron discipline. I need a clear head today. Thank you for all the stuff, by the way, it was a lot to get through, but I appreciated all of it. It's a very different business for me but I think I made some sense of it."

"I have everybody on standby. Do you know how you want to play it?"

"Well, if you could introduce me to the key people. I've got my list here, but you can correct that if you think it's necessary, then I can leave you in peace until mid-afternoon. I'd like to spend the morning talking to people and looking around, then have an hour to myself after lunch to put some thoughts together, then you and I should meet at around three and talk about what you might want to do. Does that work for you?"

"Sounds good." He nodded.

"Looking at your org chart, I think I should finish with Hank Rice over lunch. He's your COO, isn't he?"

"Yes, and my oldest buddy. We were at MIT together."

And the little whisper of doubt that had been hovering in the back of her mind became a murmur moving toward the middle.

"OK, and it looks like you get the VP's for buying, for manufacturing, for distribution and for service to report to him, while you look after development and sales and marketing. Is that right?"

"Spot on, smart lady. And I have Geoff on Finance."

"Well, I'd like half an hour with each of the six of them. I have a simple set of questions I want to ask them, and then I'll put the same questions to Hank but then try some ideas and observations out on him. I'll leave Finance out of the sequence, unless you think I should talk to him?" She raised her eyebrows at him. He shook his head. "But I'd like to start with a tour of the place. Only thing is, and this may be sacrilege, I need someone who can take me round in one hour max. I can imagine though, because this place looks fantastic from the pictures you sent, that your people would spend much longer than that talking about it."

"Ha! You're right about that but I'll get Eddie to take you round. He's the manufacturing VP and that will lead straight into your session with him. I've blocked the boardroom for you for the day, you can base yourself there."

"Excellent, thank you. And if you could give the guys a schedule and just ask them to step in at the appropriate time, that will help me close any conversations that threaten to overrun. Now, I'm going to have to admit that the COO role is not one I'm used to. Through our organisation the CEO's run everything in each business."

"It just seemed right for us. Hank and I started this thing and built the first products ourselves, literally in my garage."

"So, it's his business too?"

"Emotionally, yes. But financially he has only nine percent of it. I have fifty-one and Peter has forty."

"How did that split come about?"

"It's what we negotiated. Forty is quite common for Peter. I guess you still have to have that conversation with him, don't you?"

She laughed. "Ha, yes, you've made me feel very naïve, but I guess that'll be part of the meeting in two weeks. I suppose I should have asked Sandy Nicholls what he does."

"You've still got time for that. It's probably different for a consultancy. I tend to hang out with the guys who have 'making and selling' businesses when we have our group get-togethers. But, coming back to Molloy, Peter wanted me to have sixty, but I said I needed Hank and he deserved a share. Peter gave in but insisted I had control, so I ended up with fifty-one. Hank was the least happy, but it kept him on board. He's quite a wealthy man now and he's paid off most of the loan to Peter."

"Did you have a loan to pay off?"

"I tried to pay my dad back, but he wouldn't take anything. So, it's my business. I owned fifty-one percent the day we signed the papers."

Claudia nodded. There were some important messages in all of that. It would be interesting to hear Peter talk about it, but she thought already that she could make an accurate guess about his attitudes.

"Here we are. Molloy!"

"Wow!" They were a few miles out of the city and they swept into the wide drive of the Molloy campus, flanked by immaculate lawns, rising to a two-storey white building with a central portico. There were two industrial-looking units built back from each flank. A road with a car parking sign led off to the right. Andy swept up round the circle, parked under the portico and handed his keys to the waiting uniformed guard with the 'Molloy Security' patch on his shirt.

"Morning, Wayne. This is Claudia, she's with us today."

"Morning, Andy; nice to meet you ma'am."

Claudia smiled and nodded, *first names, nice.*

In the lobby the woman on reception smiled and handed a badge to Andy.

"Morning, Pris."

"Morning, Andy, this must be Claudia. Morning ma'am." The women smiled and nodded. "That's the badge you wanted."

"Do you mind?" He held it towards Claudia.

"Of course not" and she lowered her head to let him place the lanyard over it.

She'd been quite pleased with the five questions she'd developed They had evolved out of her experiences going round her own corporation and they were designed to tell her something about how communication worked, how people got involved, or not, whether the place performed, and how the divisions interacted — and she thought, from their responses, she'd get a feel for the attitudes of the main players. It worked better than she had hoped and by the time she sat down with Hank a clear picture was emerging.

She'd stayed in the boardroom. He'd wanted to take her to the office restaurant but she felt it would have been too easy to get distracted. They lost fifteen minutes at the start when he turned up late for his session.

He looked at the untouched sandwiches at the end of the table. "Oh, were you waiting for me? I ate already." Claudia felt cool enough to be glad of the insight and not be prompted to irritation.

"A misunderstanding." She smiled.

"The boys shown you all you want to see?"

"Oh, I couldn't possibly do it justice in a morning, but it's been a good start. Eddie covered a huge amount of ground for me. He seems a treasure."

"Yeah, he sure is, I guess" and he shrugged.

"You're not convinced?"

"Look, we design the world's best products here. We win awards. His job is to get the boxes out the door."

She nodded. This was the time to gather information. "Can I start by going through the same questions I put to the other guys? It will be different for you because you see the whole picture."

"Yeah, sure, but what are you trying to get at?"

"What's Andy told you?"

"I'm asking you, ma'am."

This was already becoming unpleasant but, she warned herself, it would be too easy to jump to conclusions. She was aware that she had an initial aversion to the man, always a dangerous start. If he had a smile, he was careful not to deploy it. He was Andy's height but had darker colouring, as if there were a Hispanic grandparent, at least. Where Andy was powerfully muscular, however, Hank was borderline obese.

"OK, well, I start from the position that organisations work best when everyone in them is working to the same goals."

"Yeah, sure."

"Then, when these are clearly understood, I try to get everyone to think what they can do to reach these goals better."

"So, my packing department can improve the world's best speakers?"

"Well, I would have thought they could ask themselves why two percent of the speakers don't work when they're taken out of the box at the customer's end."

"Bullshit!"

Interesting, let's take this slowly, time for a smile. "The two percent number is bullshit, or it's bullshit they can do anything about it? Do they know it's two percent?"

"It's in the reports, they can read them." The surliness had moved to hostility. It didn't serve her purpose to tell him that the real number was nearer three and had been getting worse. It was a number that Eddie, in particular, was evidently very concerned about.

She continued with her scripted questions and was not surprised that there was less communication either up or down or across divisions than she was used to seeing, but that had been a common theme in all the conversations. Now it was time to find out a little more about Hank.

"It's an impressive set-up here. I love the sense of space when you drive in. I live in a very crowded corner of England. There doesn't seem to be room for anything." *No response, I guess I need to make sure I formulate questions.* "When did you move in here?"

"Office and manufacturing and shipping five years ago. Development came two years later. We spent a long time getting the environment right for that. You probably saw. There's a lot of investment in getting the labs right. It's amazing how sensitive the best ears are so the interference must be absolutely minimised."

"And everything is built for the best ears?"

"Of course. It's how we started. It's how we built our reputation. Andy's a genius at product development but I had the perfect ears. Before we had all the high-tech labs, we just had my ears to make sure things were perfect." And, for the first time, he smiled slightly. "They were fun days."

"Is it less fun now?"

"It's different now" and he looked prickly again. "We needed the money-man, but things changed then. Did he send you?"

"No. He introduced me to Andy and Andy asked me to come and take a look. It's a fascinating business, even for someone without perfect ears. But now you've grown this big, what are your priorities? I presume you're way beyond product testing, personally."

He bristled. "I still listen to any new development. There's six of us who do that. You can have a lab full of dials and instruments, but you still have to convince the listener and, over the years, we've found a few guys with hearing as good as mine." He paused and nearly smiled. "Almost."

"OK, but on the operations side, what are you paying most attention to."

"I'm paying most attention to trying to get decent sales forecasts out of the marketing and planning people. Jesus, they get those wrong and I end up with no capacity or a full warehouse and everybody looks at me. Fucking useless, pardon me, ma'am" but it wasn't said with the hint of an apology.

"What about after sales service and support, that comes under you, doesn't it?" He nodded. "Do you have any particular concerns there?"

"Why would I have?"

"Are you happy with the data?"

He shrugged. "Look, I know they're not as good as we'd like 'em to be but we do put a lot of effort in there. Sometimes you wonder if people these days just don't get too dissatisfied too easily." She nodded. Not the time yet to reveal her true thoughts.

He left before two o'clock, giving her a little more time than she'd expected before she would meet Andy and it meant she had the first real break of the day. A chance to stare out of the window over the young trees whose leaves were just beginning to turn. There must be similar developments to Molloy out there, but more mature woodland kept them screened so all she could see was greenery and a friendly sky, a rich blue between the sheepy clouds. This was turning out to be a good day. She'd felt at the start like a little girl playing a grown up but, until Hank, they had all treated her with respect. They'd been guarded and cautious as they answered her questions, but they clearly assumed that her knowledge was well-grounded, so she was very pleased with the preparation she'd done and with the approach she'd developed, even though the day was feeling rushed. She would have a little more time in Giddings in the next couple of days, so she was feeling confident now about how she would play that. And then, Friday afternoon, Jack in Charleston. She smiled to herself. The week's major bonus. He'd booked a small villa on a seashore. It looked enchanting.

Andy came in on the dot at three. "Have you been upsetting Hank?" he asked, but he was smiling.

"He's talked to you, has he?"

He nodded. "He has, but I think I should let you feed back to me the way you think best. So, what's your verdict — are we hopeless?"

She smiled back. "Best audio in the world. That's a good place to start and, to be fair, it's where everybody does start in this business so I'm not even going to question that."

He nodded and seemed to relax. Then she went through her pre-work and the reactions from the VPs to her observations: a fair bit of agreement about issues but quite a lot of defensiveness and finger-pointing. "Pretty typical, I'm afraid."

"And your approach can fix that?"

"It could help."

"Could? But?"

"Andy, I've had less than a day. Well, I've put a lot of hours in on the stuff you'd sent me but actually sitting with some of your people for a little while means that anything I say has to be extremely tentative."

"I understand that."

"I think you'd need a different atmosphere among your VPs. I only met one who really seemed to want to look at things from a whole business point of view."

"Eddie."

"Yes, he'd be brilliant if you wanted someone with energy and enthusiasm to push the programme but…"

"But everyone else thinks he's a pain in the ass!" He laughed.

She smiled back. "I picked up a bit of that and if that attitude didn't change, I don't think you'd have a chance. This isn't about whether the programme would work or not; it's about a collective approach to solving problems and seizing opportunities. Sorry for the clichés. But there is a problem here, you know that."

He nodded slowly.

"And I think you know what the biggest problem is, don't you?"

"My oldest buddy? You're not the first person to tell me that." He was staring at her levelly.

"It doesn't look like, from the data, that you're addressing some real problems and it doesn't feel to me, from the responses I've got, that your guys want to get together to do that. Well, only Eddie. But he can't start that, that needs to come from you. It can only come from you, programme or no programme. And I honestly can't pretend I'm competent to advise you on your senior guys, but I would not like the prospect of trying to work with Hank."

"So, what would you do?"

"I'll offer an opinion but I'm very conscious that I've had a day or so looking at a very successful business you've spent nearly twenty years building. It seems to me that Hank is a square peg in a round hole. It just feels like the place has gone past him."

He drew a deep breath and slumped back in his chair as if resigned.

"I suppose I knew that. Peter felt it right from the start, that he wouldn't grow with us. Jen's always been against him. But you're coming up with data and insights that make the case inevitable."

"I'm sorry. This has to come with a health warning; I'm making a tentative observation."

"Nah, don't be sorry. I suppose I was hoping you might point to a different way forward but I'm afraid you're confronting me with the… how do you guys put it? With the bleeding obvious" and they laughed together. He was still slumped, but he looked relaxed. "Jesus, why am I worrying, he's still got several percent of the business!"

He walked to the window and looked out over the trees. "I like it here, don't get me wrong, but I miss the buzz of being in that old converted warehouse in the city. Maybe I haven't grown up enough to run this place."

"I don't get the impression that Peter puts his money in if he has doubts like that. That's supposed to be his skill — reading people."

"Well, ma'am, for what it's worth, I'm pretty certain he's backing the right person in getting you set up. Everyone here's impressed, especially me, and even Hank had a grudging admiration — 'how'd that bitch know about out of box failures?'" and he laughed again. "So, what about your project, am I a client?"

"If you're going to make the big change and if I can have Eddie as the major partner, I'd love to try and help. Do you want me to try to put a proposal together on that basis?"

"Yeah, I definitely do. I think we've been needing it for a while."

"I can't do it until I've agreed it with Peter. I don't know if I have a business yet."

He smiled slowly. "I don't think there's anyone that doubts that any more, is there?"

"Yes, there is," she laughed. "Me."

"I can remember feeling that way a few times. First when I took my dad's money to get started and then, big time, when Peter wanted to come in. Although that wasn't too hard a decision, going bust didn't look like an attractive alternative. Everyone else that wanted to help would have taken pretty much everything. OK, what say I drive you to the airfield and we get a beer there."

"Sure, when's my flight?"

"Your flight's when we get there, ma'am. You're on your own. Well, we gave them a window between five and six, that'll be fine. They've got a driver at the far end to take you to your hotel. All part of the service."

22

She had what felt like a serious dislocation from reality once the jet had taken off and the co-pilot came back to act as her steward. Andy had brought her to the airfield and staff had taken her luggage. There had been a small bar with two low tables and armchairs around them. They'd sat down together and a uniformed woman came to them.

"Good evening, Mr Molloy. Hi, Mrs Brodie, I'm Shirley. I'll get the paperwork completed momentarily but may I bring you something to drink first?"

"I'd love a white wine, but I'll take water with that too."

"Beer for me, Shirley, please."

"Certainly, and would you like anything to eat before take-off, Mrs Brodie? We will be serving hot food on your flight."

"No thank you, I can wait until we're airborne."

And none of that had felt too abnormal. The hug from Andy at the bottom of the steps was a big 'thank you' hug — there were no reverberations from the boat. The relationship now seemed entirely friendly and professional. She was more focused on trying to quell her nervousness about boarding a small plane for a long flight. Having to manoeuvre herself into the narrow confines of the cabin did not help that, although the feeling eased as she settled into the plush leather seat.

The take-off process was extraordinarily quick. The plane was moving moments after she'd settled herself. The briefing, "We wanna go through our safety procedures, Mrs Brodie, we just need a few minutes of your time," was barely complete at the end of the short taxi to the runway, where the plane seemed to pause for only a moment before the engines wound up and they were suddenly catapulted forward.

After the bumpiness of the first few hundred feet, the plane, still climbing, settled into the smoother passage of a normal flight. She began to relax and then the absurdity, as she saw it, overtook her and she almost laughed, but it was a few minutes later — when the plane was levelling out and the co-pilot came back to her, 'Hi, Mrs Brodie. I'm Jamie, your co-pilot'. 'Can you call me Claudia?' 'I'd be delighted to, Claudia' — then she realised she would have to reset where she was in her new life. Private jets were never going to be normal, whatever happened, but that it was happening at all would have been a completely alien idea even a month before.

But as she settled and reflected on the day while she waited for the food (mushroom risotto, best not take a chance with chicken) she realised there were stranger elements than being flown alone in a jet. She'd spent a day in a significant and successful company and undoubtedly been treated as someone of importance by the VPs, been treated almost as a threat by the COO (which, she thought, in the light of the subsequent conversation, she actually was) and been treated, effectively, as an equal by the owner/CEO. She recalled a conversation with Jack from the early days. They were lying in bed one morning, relaxed, still somewhat sweaty and with different blobs and smears drying on their skin, talking about how they'd got to be doing what they were doing.

"I've only ever known you as the boss. What was it like when you first took over a job like that?"

"It was very different from what I'd been doing. And I hadn't really expected it to be, which was pretty stupid. I mean, I'd seen people doing these jobs and didn't consider them better than me — *(that doesn't surprise me, Mr Stephens!)* — but suddenly you walk into a new place and you think nearly everyone is looking to you to make the right decisions and a few, maybe, are going to try to stop you making them, and you suddenly feel completely unprepared. So you wing it. Well, I did. It was like a game of pretend for the first six months. I felt like a boy in disguise, hoping no-one would catch me out, but then slowly you grow into it. After a year, if you've survived, the Old Man comes by on a regal visit — it's almost the only time you ever talk to the chairman — and he talks to you about the job and the business. Now that was memorable: 'Well, we've really fucked you now', 'Sir?', 'We give people these jobs and they never want to do anything else. Every one of my team in HQ would love to be back running a business unit'. So, in the end, it's you, it's your job, it's what you do and who you are, but at the start it feels so unreal."

And that described her feelings now. She'd had one day of wearing the grown-up suit and it seemed to have worked. Now she had three days of doing something similar and she had to make that work too. Gunter had invited her — that should help — but Giddings was a bigger, more complex organisation than Molloy. She doubted whether it would be so simple.

The food came, with a glass of red, and she was seeing herself as Claudia Brodie, head of Brodie Associates, international businesswoman – and trying not to find the idea ridiculous. There were five empty seats around her telling her it wasn't.

The co-pilot took the plates away and brought another glass of red — *why not* — and she was feeling more relaxed.

There had been another metamorphosis in the past year, from abused housewife to adulteress to rampant sex deviant. She smiled — that was a description that really did not fit but somehow her phrase amused her. But then she recalled the scenes of the past year or so. It had all started with Jack and what they had done together. Had she just been pleasing him, finding new levels of intimacy? Yes, that was definitely part of it. But she had brought curiosity to that. Where had that come from? It was a part of her that she didn't recognise. She'd married fairly young the first time and that had quickly gone sour. Then, coming south, there had been a romance with Dave. There really had been, she had to remind herself. They soon had Abbi and life was still sweet, but after Jonah they had never really re-established themselves as a couple and the idea of sex, with anyone, and certainly with Dave, became unthinkable. So she'd just focused on the kids and on her job and, barring the odd bout of Dave's drunken aggression, they got by.

She'd found Jack attractive from the first time she met him, but she was never moved to any fantasies about him. Even the mock-lustful comments of other women had never prompted any similar thoughts in her.

But now, even loving Jack, she could look forward to seeing Alphonse again. She could look back to the boat and only feel mild embarrassment about it: being curious about Andy; about encouraging him; about feeling excited when she felt Alphonse behind her; about wanting Peter to spank her. Had she really wanted that? She wasn't sure but she had to admit to curiosity. Even now, looking out into the darkening sky, with weeks between herself and those events, she wasn't feeling regret — except about the prospect of telling Jack.

But if they were to have more of a life together, maybe it would need to include similar experiences and she realised that she at least had an open mind.

And that surprised her more than anything.

23

They landed soon after eight thirty and she was delighted to find that disembarkation was even simpler. How could anyone ever put themselves through a big airport again after an experience like this? *It's hard to know who could possibly find that funny, Claudia!*

The town car cossetted her — too soft? too silent? *Nah, go with it!*

By nine thirty she was in her hotel room ordering a light snack and a half bottle of wine from room service. Nine thirty in the morning in Singapore, that was how her mind worked — but no, he was in DC already. She was going to text anyway; maybe he could even call.

Had a fantastic day — but missing you. Now in hotel. Can you call? XXXX

The reply came quickly:

I'll call in thirty, just finishing dinner XXX

Time to unpack and get comfortable. Staying three nights made it worth making the room a home.

Inevitably, he rang just as room service arrived.

"Don't worry, it's only a club sandwich. I'll munch while you're talking."

"But it sounds like you have more to tell me."

"Well, I will give you headlines. Obviously, I'm thrilled to have been flown by private jet but really it was the day in the business that was more extraordinary. I think I've agreed with Andy on two big people changes he has to make and he seems very keen for me to start working with him, subject, of course, to me agreeing to set my consultancy up. D'you like the way I said that? My consultancy. It really might happen."

"Well, that might be very handy for us both if it does."

"Why? What's happened?"

"I don't know, but Davis has asked if I can stop on to next week for some senior organisation discussions."

"Couldn't that be good news for you?"

"Good news usually comes as a complete surprise and I'm told that the Old Man normally tells you to go and talk to someone. It's his way of telling you you're being promoted and that he's already signed off on it. It's how it happened when I got asked to do Asia. I asked Davis what this was about and he just said he'd explain more on Monday, that he had some free time on Friday afternoon but he understood I was heading off early for the weekend."

"He knows where you're going?"

"Well, I don't book my own flights — and you don't book yours — if they want to dig into it, they'll know we're both heading for Charleston and they won't acccpt it's a coincidence."

"Are you worried?"

"Would it do any good?"

"I suppose not but I think I've just gone from ninety-eight to a hundred on my leaving probability. But would it hurt your career?"

"It depends who wants it to, I guess. I mean, Davis is a slimy shit, but he's still got to make good people available for the right positions. I don't like him, but I don't think I've upset him or crossed him. He can make life hard for his enemies. Anyway, that's next week, I'm not going to let it spoil my weekend. But you're the big thing, I want to know more about your day."

"Well, I'd decided on my approach, just a few simple questions for each VP and I'd studied the data so I could prompt them with that. They were mostly defensive but always treated me with respect. Except for the COO, Andy's old buddy."

"So you're getting him fired."

"Don't put it like that. The job has just way outgrown him. Andy knew that really; this just confirmed it. He's already holding up progress and we'd have no chance of improving the place if he stays in position."

"Do you feel that's going beyond your brief?"

"Yes and no. I told you, I need to be very disciplined about what I accept or I'll get overwhelmed. I have to feel the business itself can run the programme and that means enthusiastic senior support and a minimum of blockers."

"I heard you — and I completely support you. I think that's essential."

"It's given me a clear head and a more confident feeling about tomorrow."

"Are you there first thing?"

"Not exactly. I start with Arthur Gunter but that's not until ten. I hope he doesn't think that Southern belles can't function before then. But I'm looking forward to having more time than today. And I'm looking forward even more to that three o'clock plane on Friday afternoon."

"And I'm looking forward to catching you in my arms when you fly through the gate."

"And I'm looking forward to sitting on your cock within five minutes of getting in our villa."

"See, you're slowing down!"

24

"Mrs Brodie, we've been expecting you, ma'am, please take a seat for just one moment." Claudia delighted in the slow drawl of the pure South. Arthur's had been little more than a hint by comparison. This lady's voice was deep and gentle. She would have to be careful or she might slip into its cadences — a weakness of hers, wherever she travelled — and maybe give offence, but she found this so attractive that she knew she would love to ape it.

She'd barely settled on the leather Chesterfield when she heard Arthur's voice.

"Claudia, my dear, dear Claudia. I am so thrilled to be able to welcome you here." He took her hand in both of his, shook it gently and swept one arm towards the shallow curving stairs. "Please come this way."

The wide corridor on the first floor that led past panelled doors to his suite at the end was carpeted, old style plush, in complete contrast to Andy's high-tech building. He kept up a stream of solicitous questions all the way to his PA's office.

"Claudia, I would like you to meet Arabella." The woman stood and came round her desk to shake hands. She smiled warmly. A black woman in her mid-forties, or maybe older, but she presented herself very well, slim and very smartly dressed. "Absolutely anything you need in the next few days, Arabella will take care of."

Arabella, smiling again, said, "I will be delighted to help in any way, ma'am."

"Arabella, will you ask David to step through, please? Come this way, Claudia," and she was ushered into a large oak-panelled corner office with views to mature trees to the side and to a very large warehouse unit with a vast number of docking bays across the road to the front of the building. His desk, to one side, looked out directly towards the trees over a large table with eight seats. Behind the desk were two portraits, father and grandfather, she assumed.

He went to the table, pulled out a chair and gestured to her to sit down. He sat down next to her at the head. A younger man knocked and came in, well-groomed, tall, handsome and smiling.

"Claudia, this is David Wilkins. He will be your Man Friday for the next three days."

She stood to shake his hand. *Too firm young man, I'm not playing football – but very pleasant looking.*

"I'm delighted to meet you ma'am. I've heard a lot about you" — *I hope that's just politeness* — and took the seat opposite her once she'd sat down again.

"Now David runs planning, which is in the Finance division. I know you run your stuff out of HR, but I've asked him to help you for a few reasons. All our data gets pulled together in planning so all the information you've had was collated by David. Was that satisfactory?"

"It was excellent, thank you" and she smiled and nodded to David. "I think I have a very good overview and it did suggest some areas that I should look at more closely." In truth, what had come directly had duplicated much of what Lavinia had unearthed and David may well have been the source for both information streams, so alike were they, but she had been impressed by its presentation.

"Excellent, excellent. But the next point is that he's only in planning for a while. He's already worked in two other divisions. Two?" He looked to David.

"Well, three actually."

"Of course, of course. The point is, he knows the business thoroughly, so he can take you to all the right people. David's one of a few who we think will be running this place sometime, so we try to give them the broadest experience possible. Now, before I send you two off to get on with this, I'm just going to say very simply, so you both have the same message: I think we're falling behind. We're not growing like we should be and we're struggling to deal with margin pressure. Those things are easy to see and probably most people like me say the same thing about most businesses, but I just don't feel we're working together like we should be or that everybody's focusing on the right things. I'll be very interested to hear on Friday if you think you can help us do something about that. Is that clear?" They nodded. Now there was a look of seriousness on his face and she was glad of that. It made her feel that he thought this was a genuine option to improve the way they worked. "Now, I am around the next couple of days, so you can come to me if anyone isn't helping but there shouldn't be a problem. I've told people why you're here and that we want your help, OK?" They were nodding again. "Good. We should schedule lunch tomorrow so I can get an idea of your progress. Arabella will organise that. I'll see you then." And he stood up. It was still Southern courtesy, but only just, and she liked the fact that he had become so business-like. David led her to the door, opened it for her, and walked her past Arabella's desk to a door on the far side.

"We keep this office free so it's ideal for you for your time here." Before he entered, he turned to Arabella. "Everything links though Arabella. She'll show you how it all works once you and I have discussed what your plans are." Arabella nodded and smiled.

The big desk faced the door and had its back to the view of the trees. To its left was a low table with four large, comfortable chairs around it. Claudia tried to look cool. An office like this for herself would have been beyond her dreams.

Take control, girl. "Let's sit here for a while and go through how I think I'd like to proceed" and she gestured to the large chairs. David nodded and waited for her to sit first. "A few themes stuck out for me going through the package you sent. It was extremely helpful, by the way, I have to thank you very much. I hope you don't mind me complimenting you, but it seemed very well selected and very well sorted." He smiled and looked modest. *Trying to look modest? Another Yaley? Is that what they look like?* "I'm going to ask you later today where you think the biggest issues are, but I'd like to run though my approach first and see if you think it's appropriate. Mr Gunter has already made the point that you have growth and margin issues. You can probably give me a very good overview of that, but I would like to talk to the Operations, Sales and Finance heads tomorrow. Could you see if I can get an hour with each of them?" He nodded. "I also want time with your HR VP tomorrow but not until the afternoon, please. I want to be ready to try out some ideas on her — *the one woman on the team, is that typical?* — and if I haven't had some thoughts by then, well, you'd better book me an earlier flight and just apologise for me," she laughed. David tried to but looked awkward — *just testing you, boy, I wonder if this place is just too formal to move forward.*

"Today, I'd like to meet groups of people from the different divisions. Is that going to cause any problems?"

"No, of course not. Mr Gunter's been quite clear. You can have access to anything and anybody."

"Excellent. Well, working backwards, I'd like to finish the day with you but just before that I'd like to meet your quality people. There aren't many of them, are there?" She smiled. He looked a little nonplussed.

"I appreciate Sales is field-based but it has a central office function, doesn't it?" He nodded. "I'd like some time there and please tell them I want to keep today's sessions very informal. That goes for everyone today, of course." He nodded again. *Not sure you're understanding informal, David, but we'll persevere.*

"Now here's where I struggle, I have to admit. The operations and the IT department that supports it are so complex that I'm going to need a lot of help getting to grips with them. I don't know where that will lead but I would be very grateful if you can point me at some guys in each area who can explain all that to me." Here the smile looked a little smug. — *Comfortable now the little woman has admitted this is all too difficult for her?*

"But first I'd like to talk to some drivers and some warehouse guys."

"Drivers?" He looked shocked.

"Yes, I'm sure they have a canteen or a coffee bar in the warehouse over the road. I'd like to sit there for an hour and chat to people. Is that a problem?"

"Er, no, no, of course not. I'm just trying to think who I can get to take you over there and introduce you."

"That would be great, and maybe if I haven't made it back by one o'clock you could come and rescue me?"

"Of course."

"Then you can take me to lunch and let me know how the timetable's shaping up."

"Yes, yes, of course."

"OK, so why don't you think of who can take me over there and I'll get Arabella to take me through this intimidating technology," and she gestured to 'her' desk. "I'll wait until someone collects me."

"Yes, yes, I'll get on it straight away." *Play the game, Claudia, try and look the part, maybe you'll even get away with it.*

Arabella was easy and helpful. "Nine for me ma'am."

"Can you call me Claudia?" She looked slightly nervous. "Well, when it's just us then. I'll accept Mrs Brodie if there's company, that OK?"

Arabella relaxed, smiled and nodded. "OK, Claudia, nine for me and zero for an outside line and this button here's for speaker phone if you need it. Now let's get your laptop logged in." And that was easy, too.

David stood nervously just inside the coffee bar door, plainly visiting for the first time. He may have been standing there a few minutes before she noticed him. The population around her had fluctuated during the hour, never less than three and sometimes as many as eight. The conversation had been a little slow to start with but, as she'd guessed, an attractive woman in a public space, even here, was never short of male company for long and the truckers soon began to outdo each other with their tales from the road. There was the occasional surly and resentful comment, but most seemed to meet their fate with humorous good grace. The themes of poor communications, incorrect information, fractious and difficult warehouse managers and organisations claiming to be lean — 'they have no frickin' idea ma'am, they really don't, look good in their reports, I guess, but they never frickin' ready when we show up and we drive roun' sweatin' our asses off and missin' the next trip', 'yeah, an' usually the guy that's tellin' you he's lean is some fat motherfucker, oops, sorry ma'am', but that, like many other observations, was drowned in laughter — which helped bring more people into the conversation, but a glance at the clock or a nod from a warehousemen at the canteen door, had them moving away smartly as, she assumed, their loads were ready.

"Well, guys, it looks like I'm being rescued. Thank you ever so much for your time. I've learned a hell of a lot, but I've had fun too."

"You're very welcome, ma'am, you come again, you hear."

"You seemed to be a big hit." They were crossing the road when David spoke. A truck, turning at the corner, hooted and the driver waved a big tattooed arm out of the window. She gave a wave and a big smile back.

"Well, they were fun, but they seem to meet some common problems. I've got good data on scheduling inefficiencies from the information you sent me but it's good to get the human side of that."

"I guess so," said David, not yet convinced, it didn't seem.

She'd been right. It was Yale, and his uncle Rod had recommended him to Giddings. — *Surprise, surprise.* He'd had other offers — *of course you had, I entirely accept and expect that* — but Giddings seemed to offer the better long-term prospects. She was very happy to listen about Yale and the US job market for the elite (not his word, that was merely assumed). It was, for her, very educational but he surprised her, given that she was here to analyse and report on the organisation and its development, that he showed no reciprocal curiosity about her. *Perhaps a Southern gentleman would regard that as impolite.*

The hour with the truckers made it much easier to understand the schedulers and the warehouse managers, who seemed surprised and impressed by her observations and questions. In truth, she'd plucked a few items of interesting data, as she saw it, and remembered some of the pithier observations from the coffee bar, but it all helped her navigate her way through the session and understand the major problems.

IT was nevertheless mystifying. She could understand why it was utterly essential for operational efficiency, but she could not make the connections herself. The transport modelling seemed immensely sophisticated, but she wasn't convinced it fully integrated the real-world problems the drivers faced. "We have to be honest with you, ma'am, we're not happy with that either," said one of the two young guys who'd spent an hour with her in front of an array of big computer screens. "We know that's where we fall down."

She laughed, and they joined her. "Thank you so much for your honesty — and for your time. I'm not going to try to pretend that most of it hasn't gone over my head but I'm immensely impressed by how you go about it," she smiled again, "and for your appreciation of its limitations."

Sales had brought no great surprises. The three she spoke to: an older man who had spent years in the field (and had been, she suspected, retired into an office job where his knowledge could be valuable but his attitudes could no longer damage); an active salesman on a training period in head office; and a young man who was very systems focused and 'just want to give the guys better information and support, ma'am' — at least gave her an impression that the business was trying to cover all the bases. But she wondered how much the older man's approach of 'always needing to offer the best prices' was contributing to margin decline. It was a comment she'd often heard elsewhere from the less successful. The salesman on training at least showed some awareness that the chase to zero margins was suicidal.

She remembered Alphonse's comment. 'Find out what they really want and persuade them that's what you've got'. It was not designed to sell at the lowest price.

The 'Quality' interview was more interesting. She had tried to locate them only to be told that they had gone to 'her office'. OK, well that would be comfier than the rather dingy corner allocated to the Quality Department's desks. She found them waiting in Arabella's anteroom. "Hi, ma'am, I'm Gerry, this is Tania."

"Hi, I'm Claudia. I hope I haven't kept you. I must admit, I went to your department to find you but they said you'd come here. No harm done. Come on through.

Arabella, could you possibly organise some drinks for us? I would love a tea."

"Of course, ma'am. And for you two guys?"

"Diet Coke," for him — *inevitably* — "And tea for me too, please?"

She sat them in the comfy chairs. "I've left you until late in the day because this is, for me, the most important session, although I will say that the hour I had with the truckers this morning was probably the most informative."

"You were with the truckers?" asked Gerry, slightly incredulously. Tania merely looked impressed.

"Yes, I'd been given lots of very good data from David Wilkins, especially from your department, I have to say, but I find it comes alive more if I talk to people. Now, your data covers a range of activities."

"Not enough, in my opinion," interjected Tania. Gerry looked a little irritated.

"OK, so can you tell me first about the areas that worry you most in the data you already have and maybe tell me something about what you're worried about missing?"

Gerry sighed. "Maybe you want to go first, Tania." Her edge-of-seat readiness made the suggestion appear superfluous.

"Thank you" was at least said with a gracious smile and she talked with some passion about the hard data they collected on delays, missed schedules, damaged consignments and how these were, in many cases, trending badly.

"And no-one seems to react."

"Are you shouting loud enough?"

"Pardon, ma'am?"

"I had a boss once who, if I ever pointed out that I was repeating a difficult message, would just say: 'Well, you didn't shout loud enough the first time'."

Tania looked pensive. Gerry felt the need to speak. "We get the monthly reports out reliably and I give a debrief to the management team at their meetings."

"May I put a difficult question to you? I know that some teams hear what they want to hear and gloss over difficult stuff, so, do you ever get actions minuted in those meetings? Have you ever asked for changes to be made?"

"Sure!" and "No!" came simultaneously. Gerry looked irritated and Tania looked indignant. Then Tania retreated a little. "Sorry, Gerry, you're right, of course. We do get points minuted, ma'am, but I have never yet measured any changes in the subsequent data. That tells me that nothing's really done." Gerry looked a little mollified, his status and credibility restored. Claudia doubted, however, whether he truly questioned his own effectiveness.

"I guess I'm already seeing your point, Tania. Like you said earlier, the trends aren't good. But you also said you thought you were missing things. What sort of things?" Gerry sat back, arms folded, seeming resigned.

"We don't try and collect any soft data, we don't pull in anything on satisfaction levels; what our customers really think. We're probably in an environment of rising expectations. Even if our quality trends were flat, and they're not, as you've seen, but if they were, we might still find that our customers are getting less happy with us and we don't find out until they pick another logistics provider. I'm sure we should be doing more."

Claudia nodded. Gerry was looking out of the window.

"Gerry?"

"I've always tried to focus on facts, ma'am, see where the objective data is pointing. That other stuff can send you chasing wild geese." Now it was Tania's turn to look irritated.

"So how do you resolve this?"

"He's the boss."

"But are you shouting loud enough, though?" At least they both smiled with her.

Gerry softened. "Oh, she shouts loud, ma'am, nobody accused her of not doing that" and he smiled again.

Tania merely looked a little frustrated. "Maybe, but I don't feel I'm getting anywhere."

The drinks had been quietly brought in and left near the door. They took a break to serve themselves and then sat down again to let Gerry talk about company history and how his department had developed. It was all useful background for Claudia but it didn't give her the impression that she was listening to an agent for change.

That was an impression that persisted when she listened to David. He'd invited her into the boardroom where his company presentation was set up on a large screen. She sat in the middle of the long side of a table which seated about twenty. It meant that he was set up for a presentation, rather than a conversation and she was happy with that to start with. She wanted to imagine herself, for a while, in the position of a VP or a director. And besides, she would probably have to be standing where David was now on Friday. It wasn't a bad idea to get a sense of how the room worked.

It was a crisp overview of the company, its history and its current financial status. It was here where she started to ask questions and began to suspect that he would report coherently and cogently but wasn't pushing for changes to correct any trends.

Well, maybe his boss drew those conclusions during the meeting. Or maybe, with roles in three departments already, he wasn't about to provoke once and future friends.

Still, she was disappointed when a 'what would you change?' question produced only a few platitudes. Disappointed, but not surprised. She would also have been surprised had he invited her to dinner. She already had her excuses prepared but the danger passed anyway.

Arabella was still waiting but clearly ready to leave. "Oh, I hope I haven't kept you."

"That's fine, ma'am. I just had to make sure you're good for getting back to the hotel."

"Oh, thank you, that's wonderful. Yes, a car as soon as it's convenient, please."

It was six thirty. It had been a latish start but it was still a long day. A bath, room service and a book, a few peaceful hours, and maybe a call with Jack later.

25

Very interesting day. Can you call when you get back? I don't mind what time. XXXXX

She was awake when he rang but thought she'd probably dozed although it wasn't ten yet. She didn't have to worry about who he'd been with in DC — she didn't think.

"So how was it?"

"Well, I'm getting more time than at Molloy but it's a bigger business and the issues don't seem so clear-cut. I don't have any obvious conclusions yet. Probably a good thing at this stage, although some issues are emerging, but I'm feeling uncomfortable about whether I'll be able to help. How was your day? Any more from Davis?"

"We've all been on planning; no time for trivia like people and politics. But seriously, the day's quite intense and we wanted to get out and eat together without staff around the table. It's everybody's favourite Italian and I'm afraid we probably drank more Amarone than is good for us."

"Yes, you sound, well, relaxed is probably a good word."

"Yes, it's probably the only hour in these weeks when I can feel that way, the end of a wine-drenched dinner and the sleepy aftermath."

"So, are you sleepy?"

"A little, but I wouldn't be if you were here. What have you been up to?"

"Bath and room service this evening, that's all. I think this is the only chance I get to relax this week. It's dinner at Arthur's tomorrow and I'm also going to have to think of something to say on Friday morning. So, I'm just leaning back in my bathrobe waiting for you to tell me what you'd like to do to me."

"Well, I'm feeling, as you said, pretty relaxed, so, is there an armchair in the room?"

"Of course. It's the Four Seasons, you're about to have phone sex with Claudia Brodie, founder of Brodie Associates. You may no longer fuck her in any old Hilton."

"Oh, OK, so, I'm just leaning back in my big old chair. I don't even think that I am going to fuck her. I actually have some different plans. She's leaning back on the bed, isn't she?"

She moved some pillows against the bedhead, "She is now."

"Good, now she's opening the front of her robe, I can see the swell of her breasts and the sweetly shaven triangle."

"Can you?"

"In my mind's eye, yes, and let's pretend it's you who's just unzipped me on your way to reclining on the bed."

"Is he out and looking at me?"

"He is now and he's just beginning to rise to the occasion. He's getting more excited now he's thinking about you opening your legs a little wider and touching yourself to show me those sweet pink lips."

"I'm showing you now, are you going to come and kiss them?"

"No, I'm not, I'm just watching you touching yourself gently."

"I'm touching myself now — I'm a little wet already. Is he getting nice and big? Does he want to come and fuck me?"

"No, he wants to watch you. He's getting excited waiting for the knock on the door."

"Who's going to be knocking on the door?"

"It's a special room service I've ordered for you. You have to go and answer. I'm staying in the chair, watching you go to the door with your robe hanging open. It's a tall and handsome young man that I've organised for you. You'll check at the spyhole and he'll be holding up a single red rose for you, so you know it's him."

"How romantic!"

"Yes, but it's the last romantic thing that happens for the next hour. As soon as he comes in, he throws the rose to one side and pushes you back on to the bed. You're a little startled but when you look to me you can see that I'm just holding myself, enjoying watching you. I'm watching you knowing this is what you want. This will be a very rough fuck from a young stud and you are going to enjoy it."

"Am I?"

"Yes, you ignore me now and look at his cold, blue eyes. He's standing at the foot of the bed, unbuckling his belt and looking at your body and saying 'get that robe off, bitch'. You throw it to one side quickly and say 'let me help you there' and you slide off the bottom of the bed and kneel in front of him."

"Are you watching this?"

"I'm only a few feet away and you make him turn so that I can see everything from the side. You rub the front of his jeans and I can tell you're already impressed by the size. You turn to me and give a little half-smile."

"Then I start to unzip him. I do it slowly. I'm careful but he's commando, it's there in front of me straightaway and you're right, he is big. I am going to want this."

"That doesn't matter, this is now about what he wants. 'Suck it, sister', he says, and you wrap both your hands around it and there's still plenty for your mouth. For now, you just focus on the head. You give me the odd sideways glance, but you're mostly focused on licking all around it, especially the underside. That's where his breathing starts to get heavy, and then you take the head in your mouth again. Now here's where you feel his hand on the back of your head, 'you can do better than that, bitch', and he pushes to the back of your throat. That makes you choke but he doesn't care; you have to fight him off. 'You can take your time, miss, but you're gonna have to do better'. He's looking down into your eyes and you know you have to nod; this is a challenge for you; you lean back a little and look at him; he's the biggest you've seen." *He probably isn't any more, Jack, but I'm enjoying the story and I'm touching myself, Christ, I'm so wet, just keep talking, I'm going to get lots of this big dick in my mouth, aren't I?*

"But you've got to get lots of him in there. You take it slowly, no-one's been this far in your throat before, you know you won't be able to take it all but you know he won't stop easily. You gag a bit but you try and take more. He's huge, he completely fills your mouth but suddenly he pulls back, 'you have a fucking nice mouth bitch but I ain't coming until I've had everything' and he lifts you up quickly, throws you face down on the end of the bed, you know what's coming and you open your legs wide and he sticks all of his cock right up inside your cunt, while his hands press on your shoulders to keep you pinned down. You took him in easy." *Christ, yes, where's big boy? In my fucking suitcase.*

"Jack, stop, I've got big boy in my case, I want to get him."

"Go get him quickly, stick him in your cunt!"

She goes straight to it. She pulls the pillows down the bed, lies across them and feeds the huge dildo into her. "Jack, I'm on my belly now, I have a big cock in me, fucking me crazy,"

"Keep him there. Your boy is still fucking you, your cunt is so wet it's easy but he's bumping into something right up in your belly, my God, he's deep but you're loving it, even with the stomach ache, and he keeps that in-and-out going, he's found that place where he can keep going nice and slow. After a nice long while, he pulls back slowly and turns to look at me, looks down at you again and says, 'man, you said she had a beautiful ass' then back to you, 'up on your knees, bitch, let's take a look at this beautiful ass of yours' and you get up on your knees, turn to look at me and then wiggle your arse at him."

"I am doing, Jack, I've got my arse up higher right now and I'm wiggling it for him but I'm not letting go of big boy."

"Doesn't matter. He's rubbing his hands over your cheeks, stretching them apart. 'Man, that is one purty little asshole, I'm gonna have to stretch that real wide'. He's still kneeling on the floor, you push your arse on to his face and you feel his tongue licking you, licking all around you, seems he knows how you like to be tickled. Now you're moaning for him, you want his tongue in you, you can feel it, it's a big tongue, it's pushing right inside, you're loving it, 'man, that's beautiful,' and he turns to me, 'mister, you got some lube?' I nod. 'Good, gimme some or it's sure gonna be hard on your girlfriend here'. I hand him the tube of lube, he stands up and squirts a lot between your cheeks. At least he's calmer now, less rough for a while. He massages it in and around your hole, pushes it in slowly with a finger, obviously enjoying playing with you, squirts some more, uses two fingers this time, 'man, I am so gonna enjoy this ass', and you're wiggling, obviously enjoying every bit of it now, especially when his fingers tickle your clit. You're looking at me and smiling but then you do look a little bit uncertain when you feel him press hard on your lower back to get your bum the right height for his cock. You feel its head against your arsehole. But your smile returns when you feel him push the head in. You managed that, it stretched but you like that big discomfort. He's finding a rhythm now and inching himself in slowly. You're touching yourself and looking at me."

"I'm touching myself, Jack, are you holding your cock?"

"I certainly am, I'm feeling huge now, I love this, I love watching you being fucked, I want to see guys pushing their big cocks into you, I want to hear you scream, I want to hear you come. He's pushing that huge cock in deeper and deeper. You're gasping a bit, this is too much, too much, it's prodding somewhere deep in your belly, but you do so love being full, you slut, I know that, you want all this huge cock in your arse and he wants to push it all in. Now he's getting rough, his hands grab your hips, it's starting to hurt but you want it, you want it, he's starting to come."

"I'm coming, Jack, come with me!"

"He's coming now, coming so deep in your arse. I'm loving watching this, watching him fuck you as hard as he can. I can see him pushing that big dick right up inside you. I'm coming too, I'm coming."

And they can hear themselves breathing heavily for a few long moments until, gradually, the breathing subsides into sighs. They say nothing for a while.

"Wow, Jack, I think I've just had the best fuck I never had."

"Well, I have a pretty copious mess I have to clear up here. I'll have a quick shower, I think, and call you in fifteen."

"You don't have to call again."

"I'd rather send you off to sleep with a whispered 'I love you' in your ear than with a toy boy's cock still stuck inside you."

"Well, he's out now. You can just tell me that again."

"What?"

"Jack!"

He laughed, "I do love you, you, crazy cow. I hope you're tired and relaxed now. I know I am."

"I feel very dreamy, thank you and I do love you very much. Just one more thing though."

"Yes."

"The toy boy's number, what was it?"

"Goodnight sweetheart."

"Goodnight, Jack."

26

David had started her appointments at ten again, but she was in her office before eight thirty. Arabella was already busy but looked a little surprised to see her.

"You got everything you want?"

"Yes, thank you, but I just want to get my thoughts straight about today and I need to check in at home." Pat said the kids were fine *you always say that Pat, but I have to admit I've never caught you out.* She was very interested in Molloy, already thinking of it as the first client, and she'd been asking her new friend Penelope about the nature and structure of the business relationship of the Nicholls consultancy with Peter. *Have I talked to her about that?*

"Pat, you didn't!"

"Any reason why I shouldn't? You have to be sure that man doesn't own you."

"Well, I'm impressed, but be careful. You won't commit me to anything, will you?"

"Don't worry, Claudie, it's your business, you say what goes, I can't commit you to anything and I wouldn't anyway. Besides, Penelope wouldn't let you do anything silly. She's a smart woman."

"I'm beginning to think I've got one of those too. Thank you very much for that, you're right, it's important. Now I've got to get on here. This looks a bit more difficult."

"So, not a future client then?"

"Well, it's a corporate connection. We'll lose the link when we go on our own. Anyway, I need business nearer home, or it's not going to work."

Arabella had walked in with a memo from David detailing the day's appointments. She was about to close the door on leaving. "Arabella, could you leave it open, please? I'm not keen on closed doors."

"Of course, ma'am."

"Where do I find these people?"

"Well, I was going to take you. They're all along this main corridor backaways, the other side of the main stair."

"I guess I can find them myself then. It sounds simple; I don't want to put you to any trouble."

"It ain't trouble and it's best I introduce you."

"OK." Not what Claudia was used to at all, but best to go along with it and see how these rituals worked.

At the end of the morning, waiting to join Arthur for lunch, she had a Groundhog Day feeling of having gone through the same experience three times. In each case Arabella had taken her, through a closed door, into an ante-room with a smart PA, all women — *of course* —

but of different colours and ages — *thank God for that* — but all well-dressed and perfectly groomed. Each had then knocked on a door behind her and waited for 'Come in' before opening the door to announce, "Ms Brodie to see you, sir."

Each one of the three gentlemen — *I could hardly call them less* — in turn, had come round to shake her hand and then adjusted, unnecessarily, one of the chairs opposite his desk to allow her to sit and then resumed his position with his desk protecting him. Each room had the same arrangement of four comfortable chairs around a round table, as she had in her office, but in no case did that space look well-used.

The conversations, with Finance, with Operations, and with Sales, all had a similarly unreal quality. Claudia would ask questions that had been prompted by issues she'd noted in the data, needing only rarely to refer to her notes. The responses were all slow in coming and unfailingly polite, no question was treated as intrusive or offensive, but it was as if everything that happened was a result of some external ineluctable fate which was dictating how the business would evolve. The data deductions had surprised no-one. Each was very aware of the business situation in general and his division's situation in particular but in no case was Claudia made aware of any urgent desire to reverse an unwelcome trend and, even as she could feel herself becoming slightly strident — *be careful, girl* — nothing seemed to dent the wall of politeness that confronted her.

When she got back, Arabella took the three of them, Arthur, David and Claudia, to a room at the end of the long corridor arranged for small dining parties. The round, dark table could seat eight but was laid for three. Food was laid out on the credenza to the side but Arthur invited them to sit beside him at the table where small cards indicated the dining choices. A black man in a dark grey suit poured water for them.

"There is wine, if you'd like, Claudia."

"Oh, no thank you Arthur, not with lunch."

"I'm pleased to deduce that at least you'll be drinking at dinner." He smiled. "Ms Brodie's a champagne girl, David. I must see I don't disappoint her this evening. So, Claudia, how have we been treatin' y'all down he-ah?" He smiled.

"I do decla-ah, suh, I have nevah bin treated with such unfailin' curdesy" *not bad, girl,* Arthur laughed uproariously – *Thanks, Arthur, but it wasn't that good.*

"If only my grandma had learnt South like you already have, I might have learned a lot more in my childhood." He turned to David. "My grandmother was Scottish, David, like Claudia here, and she just thought I was stupid. Truth is, I never understood a single word she ever said" and he laughed again.

"But really, everyone's been really helpful, punctual and polite." She laughed gently. "It feels a little unreal, to be honest. And I must thank David very much; he's got everyone organised exactly as I asked; that's been brilliant." David lowered his head modestly *doing it again, aren't you?* and Claudia smiled.

"I think you rather took him aback with your request to see the truckers." He was smiling.

"Yes, he looked a little shocked," she smiled again, "but I found it very useful and, let's face it gentlemen, just amongst ourselves, it's not so difficult for a lady to get testosterone talking." Arthur laughed loud again but David looked embarrassed. "They had lots to say, which was very good. It made a lot of the data stand out and become real for me but one thing I do have to say, as soon as they got the nod that their loads were ready, they were off in an instant." Arthur smiled and nodded.

"I've got one or two more conversations to have and then I'll pull my thoughts together, so I won't risk too much in the way of premature observations, but I'm not finding much discontent. That could be a good thing but, as you said yourself, the business isn't trending how you want it to. I was expecting people to be a bit more challenging, like some of the truckers, but I've really only encountered that in a young woman in your Quality Department."

"And who was that, may I ask?"

"Her name was Tania." Arthur nodded slowly, David looked shocked.

"Please don't get me wrong. I thought she was really excellent. I think she's got the attitude you need more of and she made some very shrewd points."

"Well, are we ready to order something?" Arthur asked. Grey suit man was hovering.

"I'll have the chicken Caesar, please." And lunch lapsed into small talk with Claudia worrying she'd damaged a young woman's career — *but then the place would really be screwed.*

Arabella took her to Marybeth's office at three. The procedure and layout similar to the pre-lunch sessions but at least, this time, the doors were open and they sat at the round table. Claudia berated herself for her silent observation that Giddings had solved its diversity challenge all in one person at VP level — *that's a disrespectful thought, sister* — and she found herself warming to Marybeth quickly. She was a smart, sassy woman who was under no illusions about the dangers of the smooth complacency that seemed to infect the place.

"How did you get here?"

"Oh, they brought me in a couple of years ago. I was a consultant in logistics and transportation and I'd specialised in HR issues. No, it wouldn't take you long to see that there ain't no career ladder to VP here in Giddings for a woman of colour. But what's your story?"

Claudia was taken aback. It was the first time since arriving she'd been asked a question about herself. She talked about Collins and the programme and what she was trying to do with it.

"I can see why Mr Henderson's got Gunter looking at it. Do you think we could use it? I'm not questioning the programme, I think it sounds excellent, but whether we could implant it here?"

"That's exactly my concern and I have to admit, even after two days and a lot of pre-work, I'm not really anywhere near a conclusion."

Marybeth smiled. "I think that's a very healthy place to be. Can I work with you on this? I think we've got to set tomorrow morning up as a discussion rather than a presentation. That'll be hard, mind. D'you understand why I'm saying that?"

"I would guess they don't reach across." Marybeth was nodding vigorously. "They're too polite or too protective to comment on each other's areas so you don't get the big problems, the cross-divisional ones, highlighted or addressed."

"You and I see that the same way, girl, we can do something with this." She was obviously animated. "Tell me what you've got, and we'll see how we can set this up. We have a two-hour slot in the morning, don't we?"

And, for Claudia, it felt so good to have a 'we'.

27

The large gates swung open as her driver turned into the estate; she could call it no less. The drive led up to the imposing house with a large circle in front. Cars would park, she assumed, somewhere at the end of the road that led off the circle to the left through the banks of rhododendrons, now in their waxy, fat-leafed autumn green.

There was enough light left to enjoy the changing colours of the foliage, bright yellows and golds edging a few of the green leaves but most of the acers already turning to vibrant, almost luminous, crimson. The pines, further back, loomed darkly above them. One of the double doors at the top of the wide steps was open and out came…

"Tania?"

"I was thrilled when Daddy said you were coming, although he says you said bad things about me." She gave Claudia a big hug, which at least gave her a moment to regain some of her lost composure.

"I absolutely did not and if he says that," Arthur appeared, smiling, "if he really said I said bad things about you," she turned to him, "why, then, he ain't no true Southern gen'leman."

"I'm afraid my daughter is teasing you, Claudia, it's only one of her many bad habits. Please come through and meet Samantha." He led them into the long, wide hallway. "Samantha, my dear, our most important guest has arrived."

An elegant woman appeared from a door further down the hall, slim, proudly grey-haired and a still-beautiful face with plentiful smile wrinkles. "Hello Claudia, I'm delighted to meet you." They shook hands. "I've already heard a lot about you, not just from him but you made quite an impact on my daughter." Henderson emerged quietly at her side, evidently from the room she'd been in. "And I believe it's this old yankee reprobate that brought you here."

He extended his hand. "Claudia."

"Mr Henderson."

"Rod."

"Rod." She corrected herself reluctantly.

"Tania, my dear, why don't you take Claudia through the orangery and show her a little of the garden while there's still light."

Tania led on eagerly. Claudia noted the gesture from Samantha that curtailed Henderson's intent to follow.

A lofty glazed walkway led directly on from the hall into a huge glass conservatory — *oh, we call it an orangery here* — a glass dining table to one side, laid for six but with ample space for more, and, on the other side, four large sofas in a square around the biggest coffee table Claudia had ever seen. Potted palms, all more than head-high, were spread around but did not crowd the space.

"Let's walk down to the pond, it's paved, are your shoes OK?"

Claudia smiled. "I've learned to be practical. I always bring one pair of killer heels on my travels, but they usually stay in the case. Now, do I have a right to be cross with you?"

Tania smiled. "For not saying Arthur's my dad?" Claudia nodded, smiling. "Well, I wouldn't have said it anyway but he's the one you should be cross with. He didn't want you to know; he thought it might affect you."

"Mmm, it might have done, I admit that, but, if he's been honest with you, and I'm sure he has been, then you'll know I picked you out as one of the few bright sparks."

"You think my daddy might not be honest?" Claudia was fairly sure the girl — *oops, woman, sorry* — was teasing again but that wasn't going to make a difference.

"I'm pretty sure he's very honest. What he isn't, I don't think, is open, but that's a very different thing and you'd be silly to be too open in his position. Well, probably in any position, really."

They walked on, with Tania seeming to ponder on that point.

"What were the other sparks? Oh, I am so pleased that you singled me out, by the way. It's obviously hard to get honest feedback when you're Daddy's girl so it's like double strength when it's genuinely positive, so thank you — but I asked you a question."

"Yes, you did. Well,"—*is this a time for caution, nah, no point in starting now,* "I was really impressed with Marybeth. She's a very smart lady and I think we got on well. Apart from that, I liked the truckers."

"Yes, you shook Gerry up with that one, he couldn't really believe it. What did you think of David?"

Perhaps there was a time for caution. "He's a bright young man, well organised, very polite, and very pleasant."

Tania looked a little thoughtful. "Yes, that's what they tell me. Would you date him?"

"I'm married. No."

"You know what I mean. He's here for dinner tonight. He's tried to ask me out a couple of times." She looked at Claudia, expectant somehow. Claudia didn't know how to respond. Tania's refreshing spontaneity saved her. "I think you were going on to say 'very boring' weren't you?" They both laughed loudly.

"I might have been — but what have I just told you about being open?"

"As opposed to being honest?"

"Yes: honest always; open when it suits you." *Oh, Jack, for us do I mean 'open when it suits me'? I think I've just told Tania what I truly believe!*

"That's good. I'll remember that. So, this is the pond." She pointed out over the expanse of water.

"Hmm, I think I might have called this a lake, but it is very beautiful."

"Yes, we've always loved it here, we could get lost for hours in the gardens."

"Where are your sisters?"

"Both away at college, they're younger. I graduated two years ago."

"Did you want to join the family firm?"

"I was kinda interested, so, yes, I guess so; my parents didn't push me. I'll let Debs and Ange be the doctor and the lawyer. But now I'm in there it frustrates the fuck out of me." She paused and considered. "Now that's something a Southern lady shouldn't say."

"And you think a Scottish lady might give a fuck?" And they laughed again and turned to go back.

"I like to think I had something to do with Daddy asking you down here. I keep telling him that the place isn't changing, and it needs to, even I can see that. Anyway, he talked to his old buddy Rod. Are you close to him?"

"No, not at all."

"I don't like him," she said abruptly.

"Well, that's open as well as honest, I should say."

"Oh, shouldn't I have said it?" and she looked a little concerned.

"Oh, I absolutely value your frankness. I haven't known what to make of him. I've been wary, I must admit."

"Mama says he's a snake." It was said with such childlike vehemence that Claudia laughed loudly and Tania sniggered with her.

"Well, you young ladies seem to be hitting it off." It was Arthur calling from the orangery steps. "David's here, will you join us for a drink? I've had to order champagne in specially for Claudia."

"Daddy, you are one outrageous fibber — and here was Claudia saying she thought you were an honest man."

"But I am."

"Yo' mock injured innocence, mah good suh, don't fool no-one!"

"See, Daddy, she's rumbled you!"

"Dammit, I fear you're right. As if I didn't have enough trouble with all of you and your mother" and he ushered them in.

David and Henderson, on the sofas with Samantha, stood when the ladies arrived.

A young woman in a white blouse and black skirt offered a tray with a choice of champagne, water or orange. Claudia took a champagne glass, as did Tania. Samantha stood. "I'm going to see how they're doing in the kitchen, but I think Claudia might be interested in a little tour. Will you come with me?"

"I'd be delighted, thank you."

They walked into the room she had seen Samantha emerge from earlier. It was a huge kitchen with three staff busy with preparation. Samantha exchanged nods with the chef. "Twenty minutes?" He nodded again. "We'll go into the drawing room." She led Claudia through the main dining room, the table there would seat twenty. "Thanksgiving and Christmas!" and Samantha was shaking her head, then across the hall to a large panelled reception room.

"Tania seems very taken with you," said Samantha. She had a very warm smile.

"I was very impressed by her, I have to tell you. She was one of the few who seemed to want to challenge things."

"Ha, she's always been a little like that. It does mean that she wasn't an easy child. You have children?"

"Girl and boy, fourteen and twelve."

"Oh, well done, you! I drew the line when he wanted a fourth attempt. He didn't help his cause by saying that he'd like to finally get it right," they both laughed, "but Tania is his son, if you know what I mean. I suppose that's a very outdated idea now. Look at you, travelling the world, putting men in their place."

"I wish! I don't think we've come that far yet. But I would think Tania has a very good chance of going a long way. I'd encourage her."

"But how did you get to do what you're doing? You're still really at Collins, aren't you?"

"Oh, yes, I inherited a programme there. It was already working quite well but I like to think I've done a good deal to expand it and make it more effective. Anyway, Henderson seemed to think it's working very well and he told your husband about it."

"You call him Henderson? Not Rod?"

Their eyes held each other's. "No," she said carefully, "not if I can help it."

"You're a wise woman, Claudia" and nothing more was said.

Dinner was mostly an Arthur and Sam show, although they managed to bring the other four in on different topics. "Arthur wanted to visit Arbroath to find the place where his grannie was born but we never found it."

"No, when we got to Dundee we had to give up. We could no longer understand anything anyone was saying. It was just like being a child again. Can you do that accent?" he asked Claudia.

She tried to locate her best Dundee and raised the pitch of her voice to a nasal screech. "Ah kin try but we aw find them a wee bit duffucult tae understan' even in

Scotland, ut uz a verra awd aksaint." They looked suitably mystified.

"That's it, that sounds just like her. Now did you get a word of that, Sam?" Samantha shook her head. "But it was wonderful golf all around there. That's what I'd gone for really."

"But we had some time in, oh, I need to be careful here, I'm going to say Edinbruh, that's how I should pronounce it, isn't it?"

"Perfect," smiled Claudia.

"A Scottish grannie and two weeks in the country and I still couldn't cure him of Edinburrow. No wonder nobody in Dundee understood where we wanted to go. We had a wonderful time, though. Edinburgh is a lovely city."

"Yes, and I could understand what they were saying. Are you from there?"

"Not far, a small place, it's best to just say Edinburgh."

"You see, Edinburrow, that's what I said!"

"You said Edinburrow, dearest."

"Claudia, I appeal to you."

"I'm afraid Samantha's right, Arthur. I could say your way's cute — but I'd be lying" and they all laughed, even David and Henderson.

It was a lovely evening for her. Her nervousness at sitting next to Henderson was eased by the spaces being large, too large for any touches or conspiratorial whispers, and the hosts kept the conversation boisterous. Coffee was on the table before she even looked at her watch. Nine thirty. She leaned towards Arthur. "Arthur, I do hate to be a party pooper, but I have a big day tomorrow."

"I do understand, my dear, but Rod has a car organised to take you back to the Four Seasons. What time, Rod?"

"Whenever we're ready. He's waiting outside."

A little tremor of dread flitted through her and she caught Samantha's raised eyebrow. *For fuck's sake, Claudia, be a big girl, what's the worst? You slap his face? There will be more situations in the bigger world, get used to it.*

"Well, I hate to break up the party; it's been a wonderful evening."

"It's been really lovely having you here," said Samantha, "and I hope for his damn businesses' sake that it's not the last time we see you."

"My business, too," said Tania, coming round to give Claudia a very big hug. "Don't leave tomorrow without saying goodbye."

"I won't, I promise."

Samantha hugged her. "Look after yourself. I hope you'll come again, I mean it."

She shook hands with David. "I'll see you in the morning, I guess." He nodded.

"I'll see you in the morning, too," said Arthur, taking her hand.

"Yes, eight thirty in your office with Marybeth," said Claudia, allowing herself to sound slightly schoolmarmy.

He tried to look like a reluctant schoolboy but then smiled and hugged her to him. "Eight thirty, you'll have me. No HR here now." He kissed her forehead. "Goodnight, my dear."

The driver opened the nearside door for her and Henderson walked round the back of the car. They waved as the car pulled away. She settled back, squeezing herself into the corner of her seat as far as she could.

"We need to talk when we get back to the hotel."

"Mr Henderson, I really do have to get on with some preparation for tomorrow."

"This is about preparation for tomorrow, I assure you, and you are going to have to grow up and call me Rod. I won't tell you again."

The line was delivered calmly and quietly and his face looked quite relaxed, just a slight raising of the eyebrows. But that was a threat, undoubtedly it was a threat. She now felt even more uneasy.

After a silent five minutes he said quietly, "I'm sorry for not being more of a conversationalist but we need to talk privately" and he nodded towards the driver.

Now Claudia was mystified as well as uneasy and she found it hard to distract herself in the remaining ten minutes of the journey.

As they walked into the lobby she asked, "Are we going into the bar?"

"I said we need to be private" and, in a strange way, she relaxed a little. If this was a hit-on routine, it was unusual but, she admitted to herself, her experience was limited. She normally avoided dangerous situations. "We'll go to my suite."

That sounds like a dangerous situation. "OK."

In the elevator they were finally alone. He looked at her; she was watching him carefully now. "This isn't what you appear to be worried it is," he said softly.

They got to the room, two opposing sofas and a view of the city lights. They could have been anywhere.

"I'm having a whisky, will you join me?"

"No, thanks, just water."

"OK, please, sit down."

She took the sofa further from him, keeping him in view. He put the drinks down and sat opposite her.

"You're a beautiful woman, Claudia, and an interesting one. And we know you're not averse to unusual relationships," she was startled, and sure that she looked it, "and I'll admit I find you very attractive. Cheers!" He raised his glass. She drank some water and said 'cheers' but it felt silly. "But I'm not an insensitive man; I know I don't appeal to you, unfortunately," and he smiled in a way that looked almost human for the first time, she thought, "but we're here to talk work and this is serious." Her brow furrowed. "Don't worry, it's just serious, not dangerous. Do you know what I do?"

She was nonplussed. "As far as I know you're a director of Collins and Giddings, and a number of other companies, I assume, and you seem to specialise in HR areas. Is that right?"

"It's not wrong." He reached for his wallet from the jacket he'd draped on the sofa and pulled out a card. The dark grey card simply said 'Networks' and 'Rod Henderson' and gave a telephone number and an email address. "That's my company." He leaned back and paused.

"I do what you described, and I am very interested in the way companies work, so I do like your programme and how it works at Collins. I think they will want to try it at Giddings unless you fuck up royally tomorrow morning, and I'm pretty sure you're not going to do that."

"I have a full-time job at Collins. I've no idea how I could make that work here."

"Yes, you do" and he looked hard at her. She was frowning and shaking her head.

"Brodie Associates."

A punch in the stomach could not have left her more breathless. "How the…" He was smiling — now it looked a little more sinister. "I think this is where I let you do a little more talking," she said shakily.

He nodded and sipped a little more whisky. "That would be a smart move. Companies, as you may have assumed, worry about the problems their senior people can create for them. That's particularly the case in distant parts of the world or when they choose to employ more, shall we say, interesting people. If I tell you that you would not ordinarily come onto our radar, you shouldn't feel offended. We're talking about very senior people who are stationed abroad or whose behaviour moves into embarrassing areas i.e. we're talking potential blackmail threats."

"What do you call very senior?"

"If their removal would seriously harm a stock price or significantly disrupt business operations."

"So why on earth are you talking to me?"

"Initially, because your name occurred on two screens. That triggers an automatic query, but even that wouldn't have prompted a conversation like this. It's just that I was directly aware, wearing my other hat, of your work at Collins, so I took an interest."

"Is that job a front for you?" Claudia was feeling deeply uncomfortable but trying to remain cool. This was a time to try to stay unshockable and find out as much as she could.

"No, it's not a front. It's the part I enjoy more in fact," she wasn't convinced, "but it also does generate some useful connections. The other work grew out of it and it helped to have a background in military intelligence. I found myself dealing with a couple of situations in two different companies I was associated with and I decided that would give me the basis of a separate business, that's Networks. It's not a card you should ever show around. We try to remain extremely discreet and avoid interventions wherever we can. To help you understand, I'm going to describe a situation, without mentioning names, that may sound a little familiar to you. The Far East head of a major global business has a particular taste; some might call it deviant, but it's much more common than people realise. When that little pastime is indulged in amongst friends, or at least with basically trustworthy people, people who also would not like it publicised, then it's of no interest to us. If a link is made with a name or a situation that we could not give clearance to, then that triggers a query. If the query flags a concern on our system, that will trigger an intervention. Almost no-one is aware of us until that happens. Then either I, or one of my associates, makes a quiet phone call, explains our concerns and, in that case, suggests that the new contact be broken off. If there's a commitment to do that, it stops there. The information goes no further." *So Martha had a phone call and had to go back to Jack! I wonder who had been playing with her.*

"Who uses you?"

"Generally, it's only by direct contact with chairmen. Sometimes, in very large corporations, they share it with HR heads. And sometimes chairmen like us to share what we do with their key people. It might feel intrusive but, when they think about it, most people are reassured. I never tout for business, by the way, I only take on new assignments after word of mouth recommendations. I still have a business that's growing worryingly fast and it's needed a lot of IT investment as well as a network of private detectives. I have to be very careful to stay extremely discreet. Our methods are entirely legal. We rely mostly on people's ill-considered use of social and communication media. That does come under the public and media spotlight from time to time but there are many targets in the firing line ahead of us and, anyway, we're finding new ways of mining and examining information faster than avenues are closed off."

"I still have not the faintest idea why you're talking to me now."

"Peter Dickinson."

That was another blow to the stomach, even harder this time. She felt herself shaking and knew that the colour must have drained from her face.

"Now calm down and listen. It's very important that you understand that this conversation is happening because he cares a lot about you. He cares a lot about his businesses, of course, but in this instance there's also a personal concern."

"So, he cares enough to have me personally fucking spied on?"

He took another sip of whisky and looked calmly at her, plainly waiting for her to calm down.

"You're not being spied on. You're being protected" and he was speaking very calmly, as if he were genuinely concerned that she understood. "You're meeting with Peter on Friday next week." Once again, she was startled. "He wants you to understand that this protection is in place, but he didn't want the issue to get in the way of the bigger things you have to discuss."

"Bigger things?"

"Brodie Associates."

"That's a bigger thing?"

"Of course it is, for him and especially for you."

"But you're a director of Collins. How can you encourage Brodie Associates?"

"I like the programme, I want it to continue. I know that it didn't really work until you got hold of it. But now you can run it from outside and I'd encourage Davis to give you a consultancy contract. I think you could put a team in place to run it for you now. Giddings would be a bigger challenge. Can you think why?"

Clever, she thought, get me focused on something real. "I think the culture would be very resistant. They have silos for departments, they don't talk, and the hierarchy is quite rigid."

"You see, that's why people will want you. That's an accurate appraisal of the situation — and you're not going to have to take on contracts where you'd struggle to succeed. Arthur will want you, he likes you very much, they all do, but you need to think hard about taking that on."

"Why does Samantha dislike you?"

He almost laughed, then sipped whisky again, as if considering what to say. "Arthur fired his HR VP two years ago. Samantha had liked him — a lot. She thinks I had something to do with it."

"And did you?"

"Discretion. Anyway, you'll do much better at Molloy."

"Jesus Christ! Am I in a fucking goldfish bowl?"

"I appreciate there's a lot of new information coming at you here but when you calm down, you'll realise how much is being done to help you. Think of it as a safety net, not a cage."

"I'm struggling with that right now."

"I understand but I think I should go on and give you the full picture. Peter wants you to know." He let her think for a while. She wasn't comfortable, but it would be silly to break off the conversation now. "Peter, as you are aware, employs interesting people — very interesting people, some would say. He thinks that gives his businesses the right chemistry. But his fabled people judgement is backed up by some very good intelligence. We spotted the cocaine problem for him and he got out before that went south. So, he's very aware that interesting people can be vulnerable and he wants them protected — not spied on, as you put it. It's a very different perspective, I promise you. The Far East head is still doing the job but is no longer exposed to risk and is free to enjoy the favourite pastime again. You have some tastes that some would say were unusual but, in the company you keep, you are entirely safe."

"The company I keep?"

"I don't need to spell that out. You can carry on living your life as you are doing when you have the consultancy set up and you won't hear from me again, not in that context."

"So, my relationship with Jack?"

"Is not a problem, even under the current circumstances. Certainly not when you're independent."

"Do I talk to him about this?"

"Join the dots. I've told you enough. You're a smart woman. I can't stop you if you want to talk to him about this conversation. I am going to trust that you won't."

"I understand. I won't." *Openness, Claudia, where did that go?* "Has Arthur told Samantha what you do?"

"He probably has done, but that would have been against my advice. It will have helped no-one. It certainly hasn't helped her relationship with me. But at least the two of them seem settled now. The important point for me tonight is that you're quite clear: you can carry on living life to the full as you are doing — and you are starting to lead an exciting life, aren't you?" She nodded. "Well, enjoy it and don't worry. If we pick up any threats, you'll get a quiet phone call. Well, I hope you will, I can't pretend that we pick up everything. We didn't pick up the divorce that ruined one of Peter's businesses," he shrugged, "but those were early days."

"I'm not expecting secrets, but have you made many of your discreet phone calls in Peter's network?"

"Maybe a dozen, but we go back more than ten years and there are twenty some odd businesses now. Peter was an early adopter. He's very aware of the dangers that interesting people bring so it made sense to him straight away. Feeling a little calmer now?"

"I guess I feel like a boxer. I've taken some very heavy punches, but I haven't gone down and now I'm on the stool in the corner. I don't have to come out for another round, do I?"

"No, fight's over, kid. You may even have won on points."

He stood up and opened his arms. She moved gingerly towards him, let him hug her. "Thank you, Rod."

He let go. "Thank you, Claudia, and goodnight, guess you've still got work to do."

She smiled. "Bastard!"

He laughed, warmly for him.

28

She texted: *Getting frantic about prep for tomorrow. Fascinating day though. Tell you all about it after you've fucked me tomorrow. XXXX*

He replied: *Interesting here. Old Man wants to see me Monday. Tell you more after the second fuck tomorrow XXXX*

Jesus, well, at least it didn't sound bad.

She got ready for bed and sat in her bath robe, anxious to get her thoughts clear but acutely aware that it was impossible to focus. Had Rod's intervention really helped her to plan for tomorrow? She couldn't decide but it didn't matter, she just knew more than she'd known before, a lot more. Best just to rely now on her gift for falling asleep quickly, she thought. She set the alarm for five thirty in the almost certain knowledge that it would be superfluous.

She woke at five, quite pleased to have slept that long. Under the shower she found herself going over the conversation with Rod again. It now seemed completely surreal, as if it had been a dream. Then it began to take on a quality of her thought processes of dealing with

Jack: things happened, they appeared threatening, you thought through them, you thought around them, and you ended up, usually, in a better place. Unwelcome knowledge — but vastly preferable to unwelcome ignorance, that just allowed the fevered imagination to flourish.

Now she had a little time, but she recognised there was little she could do to prepare beyond familiarising herself once more with the issues which arose out of the data and the conversations. But the sessions would need participation, not presentation. They had to demonstrate that the answers were inside the people present and would emerge only when they engaged and interacted. She and Marybeth had agreed on their approach, but they needed Arthur to support them. Then all she could do was prompt more discussions with relevant facts. In that culture, she was aware, it could go spectacularly wrong.

When Arabella led them in, she was surprised to see Rod sat at the large table with Arthur. They said their good mornings. She, at least, said 'Good morning, Rod', and noted, with amusement, his discomfort when Marybeth said, 'Hi, Mr Henderson'. *That's his thing, is it? He wants pretty women to use his first name — powerful men displaying their universal petty vanities — but why's he here?*

"I've asked Rod to sit in while we discuss how we want to approach this. That's what this is about, isn't it?" The women both nodded. He laughed mirthlessly. "Well, it might be more accurate to say he's invited himself." Rod smiled at this and looked to Claudia. *Strange, he has no idea what I'm going to be proposing.*

"May I start?" asked Claudia, with no intention of taking no for an answer. Arthur nodded. "The problems that you think you have seem quite clear from the data, and you've identified them yourself: margins; growth; delivery performance etcetera. But I believe these are only the symptoms of the underlying problems, not the problems themselves. I don't have a programme that would solve the real problems for you because, to my mind, these are cultural and I accept that this is a gross over-simplification, but they are symbolised for me by your VPs sitting alone in their offices with their doors closed." Arthur looked sceptical; Rod was nodding. *Maybe I am glad you're here.*

"What we'd like to try," said Marybeth, "is a small session at ten with only the VPs." She looked to both of them. "That would not include you, Mr Henderson, it will hard enough to get them to open up."

Rod was nodding. "I understand — and I also agree, which is a different thing." He smiled.

"We want to go round the table and get them to say what their biggest issues are."

"I'll capture them on charts," *for no real prep this is quite a good double act*, "and I'm ready with my own points if I think they're missing important elements but I'm hoping that won't be necessary."

"Then we'll go around the table again and ask them what would solve their problems. If we're lucky and the discussion gets going, we might get them making suggestions about how they could help each other."

Arthur breathed in and raised his eyebrows.

"In all honesty, we're not expecting much from that, but, once again, I'll capture the points that are made and that's all we want to do with the first session, but here's where we need you, Arthur." He had his serious face on, but he was listening.

"We want to run a bigger session at eleven by bringing in all the people Claudia has spoken to this week. You'll have to sanction that."

"Including the truckers?"

"Arthur!" Claudia admonished him. "Not the truckers. I'm there to represent them" and she flashed him a little girl smile. *I think you're a dear man, but I'll use whatever tactics I need to in order to help you.*

Arthur looked a little sheepish, but nodded.

"What we want to try to establish is that the ideas we need are in the room, but that people will have to reach across divisions and levels to solve them together."

"We're not going to solve the problems today, but we'd like at least to see if there's a readiness to work together to solve them."

"So, what do you need from me?"

"Arthur, you have to open these sessions," said Marybeth. "You have to be clear that you're looking for new ways of working together. You have to give the initial push."

"We can guide and orchestrate the sessions, feed bits of data in to prompt more ideas."

"But if my colleagues don't see you giving a lead, I'm sorry, they're just going to go back to their plush offices and close their doors."

Arthur turned to Rod, who nodded slowly. "They're right Arthur, and if the guys won't come with you, I'm afraid you need new guys."

"I don't think it will come to that," said Claudia earnestly, "I do get a sense of loads of commitment in this place. Lots of goodwill and lots of pride."

"Even amongst the VPs?" asked Rod.

"Very much so," said Claudia, nodding her head, "but they need to work differently."

"Very differently," added Marybeth.

"Do you think they can do it?" asked Arthur.

"If you guide them, sure!"

"And if I can't, we change the chairman" and he laughed hollow and loud.

Henderson shrugged, waiting a long while with that thought hanging in the air. "You said it, old buddy, and I think you'd rather have a business than have a job, am I right?"

Arthur looked shocked and took a few moments. "Well, well... I guess you're right at that."

Claudia sat still, but she dearly wanted to hug him.

"Guys, we have seriously overrun and Claudia, I know, has a plane to catch. But first let me thank you for the ideas. I've never seen so many pieces of paper stuck on these walls. And I thank you for the engagement you've shown, and the enthusiasm, and most of all for the hope, I guess, at least that's what I'm feeling." Claudia could see Tania beaming at the back of the room. "But my biggest thank you, of course, has to go to Claudia for helping us through this process," and there was a spontaneous round of applause, even the VPs, she noted, were joining in, "and I'm sure we'll be seeing her again soon when she and Marybeth work out how we're going to take this forward" and there was applause again. Claudia could do no more than smile and nod. She was caught up in all the positive feeling but very conscious that much else needed to be sorted. "Anyway, I must close it there." He turned to Claudia. "I know your car will be here soon." He looked at his watch. "Oh, I guess it's here already. But thank you very, very much for coming to help us, my dear."

"I must just say," and she stood up, "many thanks for engaging so wholeheartedly. This hasn't been easy for you, or for me, and I was very unsure about whether we'd find a way forward, but everywhere I looked I found pride and goodwill, so I would have been very disappointed to be leaving today without this big feeling of hope for you all." And they were applauding again as they stood to leave.

She walked back to Arthur's office with him. Tania went with them. "I have to admit, my dear, to feeling quite emotional. And I really do feel very hopeful, especially if we can see you again. I won't keep you now but, from what Rod tells me of your plans, we might become your first client — well, maybe your second. It sounds like he's keeping you tied to a contract with Collins."

"Ooh, Arthur, it's a splendid thought. I'd love to make it happen, but I've got a couple of weeks of hard thinking to do. But anyway, with Marybeth and Tania here, you have the nucleus of your team." She turned to Tania. "Give me a hug, girl, I really have to get going," and it was a big long hug, "and as for you, my good sir, as long as nobody tells HR, you can give me a damned big hug too" and she embraced him. "I really do hope I'll see you soon. I'll call you next week anyway to follow up. Now, I'm sorry, but I am late already, I just didn't want to stop them in there."

And she hugged Arabella too before dashing off to the stairs with Arthur and Tania hurrying behind, keen to wave her off.

29

Not that she had doubted it would come, but, exciting as the morning had been, it thrilled her to feel the mounting fever that she would be seeing him soon. Nothing could now go fast enough for her but at least the car journey and check-in were trouble-free and, in spite of leaving late, she was at the gate in good time. The flight would give her an hour to organise her reflections and it wasn't until the plane had left the ground that the more momentous thoughts began to come to her. It seemed that nothing now would stop her starting out on her own. Something completely inconceivable two years ago now looked almost inevitable. She had three clients already! But all based in the US and that leaden thought seemed to settle in her stomach for a while. There would be answers, though, there always were when you thought things through — and the projects themselves? Well, Collins was up and running, that just needed someone to take over her role, someone who could take some guidance; Molloy, with Hank out of the way and Eddie to lead the programme, would work well, she had few doubts; Giddings, well, she'd meant what she'd said. With Marybeth and Tania in position, it should stand a good chance if the enthusiasm of the morning was genuine. So maybe, just maybe, nothing would take excessive amounts of her actual presence — *if it seems too good to be true, it probably is* — but she returned to her original thought. The programmes had to acquire their own momentum anyway or they wouldn't work. But she would have to stay close enough in the early phases to make sure they did. That would need some travel. When she'd danced around with those thoughts a few dozen times the plane began to descend, and she was only half an hour away from seeing him again.

Sod the inhibitions! She flung herself at him when she got to the end of the jetty and they held each other tight even with other travellers jostling by. She wanted his arms around her and his hands on her body. It was a while before they eased apart.

"Your bags?"

"In the car. I got here an hour ago; I had time. Let's go!"

Google got them more or less straight to the house, but his driving was not helped by the distraction of her hand on his cock for parts of the journey.

"It's still daylight," he'd said, though when she began unzipping him. "I don't know that I want to give the lorry drivers that much entertainment."

The woman was waiting when they got to the house. They pulled in beside her car on the drive.

"It's gorgeous!" Claudia couldn't help herself. *It's huge, too.*

"You got kinda lucky with this late cancellation or I'd have had to put you in the smaller place. I normally have this booked out all through the fall. Let me show you things quickly. You'll rattle around in here, I guess, we've usually got six in and some families bring eight."

Claudia let Jack take in the details of kitchen controls and TV and audio options while she wandered around the rooms. She was relieved to hear the woman say quite soon, "Well, you guys have my number. No point in me talking too much, you can probably work things out for yourselves. Just call if anything puzzles you."

Jack at least appeared polite as he waved her goodbye. Claudia knew she was showing her impatience.

"Jack, this is wonderful, I know it is, but I can't concentrate on anything until you've fucked me."

"Come on, let's at least have the first one in bed."

But, once she was naked and sat on his cock, she managed to slow down and take everything in, his hair, his eyes, she touched his face, kissed him lightly, all the while pushing herself firmly down onto him, leaning forward, sometimes, to place her breasts in his mouth; thrilling to his teeth clamping on her nipples, then pulling back to let him admire her. "You have such gorgeous tits." Then the kisses became more passionate. She felt his hands on her arse, pushing her more firmly down onto him even as his hips were grinding more — he was coming, she knew, and she would soon follow.

They probably dozed, she wasn't sure, she was draped on his body, her pussy on his thigh, still feeling damp, still feeling tingly when she moved, as she did gently. She felt his body shake slightly as he chuckled, "Are you feeling greedy again already?"

"I might be."

"Well, if I promise to fuck you again before dinner, will you come out for a walk along the sand and have a look at the water."

"Before dinner and after dinner, then you have a deal."

"Deal!"

She didn't unpack, just pulled shorts, tee shirt and flipflops from the suitcase, lifted the work clothes from the floor and draped them over the chair.

"Come on," he said, "shower later, let's make the most of the sunshine."

They left through the kitchen, over the sheltered veranda with its big sofa and dining table, across the small sandy garden which melted into the tall pine trees separating the houses from the shore, all in shadow as the sun was near setting. It was still high enough to light the houses on the opposite bank, maybe a quarter of a mile away across the calm water of the widening river. They turned left, his arm around her shoulder, and walked along the sand towards the open sea, less than a mile away up the estuary. The trees and the houses petered out after a couple of hundred yards and they found themselves walking between the grass-covered dunes and the river, or maybe it was the sea already as the estuary grew wider. They were alone and, it seemed for the first time in months, at peace, enjoying the sand in their toes and the feeling of nearness of each other. They slowed to a halt, turned and gently kissed.

"I love you, do you mind?"

"That's OK, I suppose. How about if I love you?"

"As long as you fuck me."

"I can do that."

"Well, I might just trade one of those for a dinner. It was all such a rush, I haven't eaten today."

"Me neither, same thing, and a bag of pretzels doesn't count. Let's go eat."

They'd passed the place not long before they'd reached the house, just not quite walking distance. It looked colourful and cheery and advertised lots of seafood. It was filling up when they got there but the waitress found them a small table against the back fence with a view out onto a dock and the brightly-lit jetty with the restaurant's name above it. One boat was disgorging some older, clumsy passengers, who would certainly struggle to re-embark later if they drank too much.

"Crab cakes? It says it's the specialty."

"You said specialty." She smiled, amused by his adopted Americanism. "Yeah, crab cakes, let's keep it simple."

They ordered without looking at the menu and he picked a chardonnay after a cursory glance at the wine list.

"It feels unreal to be here with you, finally." They held hands across the table. Water, wine and bread came quickly. "Fast service is good, I need to get back for more of what we had before."

"Don't think my need is less urgent but we do need a few provisions. I think there's a convenience store back a little way."

"We'll have to be quick, I want you again already."

He smiled and took her hands again. "I love you. But we should use the enforced pause for you to tell me more about today."

And she talked but, even in her animated retelling, she avoided mentioning Henderson, then realised she would trap herself if she said nothing.

"Henderson was there" got added clumsily to the story.

"You never said that."

"Well, he didn't say much. Arthur and Samantha held court at dinner. They were very funny, and that doesn't seem to be Henderson's style. But he is an old friend, I guess, they must get on. He didn't come into the meetings this morning, but he sat with Arthur,

Marybeth, she's the HR VP, I like her very much, and me, first thing, and he was encouraging Arthur to do something."

"Encouraging?"

"Well, yes, there was a little bit of 'an offer he couldn't refuse' about it."

"Some friend. It's Arthur's company."

"Well, he owns less than twenty percent. He's got to keep it performing and the stock price hasn't been going anywhere lately. Anyway, it got Arthur focused and he did a brilliant job with his people. He has a lovely personality, he's very sunny and engaging, but I think it must have been the first time most of them had seen him like that. By the end I was quite hopeful, maybe I'll start with three clients."

"Three?"

Thank God for electric lighting and the fading twilight, her blushes wouldn't show. "I don't see why I couldn't keep a relationship at Collins."

"I'm pretty sure Davis won't go for that. He'll see you as a traitor if you leave."

"Maybe you're right. Well, the other two would keep me busy at the start. What do you think Davis knows about us?" *Thank fuck we're off the business topic, girl, and what's happened to your commitment to openness?*

"I don't know. Maybe there's gossip, maybe it's made him check itineraries, I know he'll want to know, but I don't think Monday's got anything to do with that. It can't really be trouble, I don't think, I'm the only one of the big regions beating my numbers. And the Old Man didn't make a big thing of it — he just mentioned it in passing, except he never mentions anything in passing, if you know what I mean. Anyway, I'm tired of being furtive. I love just coming out like this, just us being us, not worrying about anything. I am thrilled for you about the consultancy, even if it does get you into some bad company," and he smiled, "I do hope it's right for you. I think it would be wonderful for us."

"I'd like to think so, but I would be very busy."

"I don't exactly get a lot of you now."

"No, nowhere near enough, but we don't know what they'll be saying to you on Monday. You really have no idea what that's about?"

"I honestly haven't a clue; these things always come as surprises. I'm surprised I've been given the weekend to stew on it, except I don't plan to get distracted, I have some naughty ideas for us." He smiled at her and squeezed her hand but then the food arrived.

"You see," she said, after they'd drunk more wine, "you're the only really bad company I keep. How's your other bad girl, by the way?" He looked taken aback. "I'm sorry, I know I got a bit silly about that. It was very stupid of me — you'd managed her for a year before without a problem, and I like it that you keep in practice for me." He relaxed a little. "I expect she's been again."

"She has, last week." He still looked a little cautious.

"Don't worry, I'm really OK with it now. I do want to hear, though, that she complained about the previous time. Did she admit it had been painful?" She looked around. The nearby tables were occupied but all seemed busy with themselves. "The new bit, I mean, did she struggle with that?"

"Are you enjoying this?"

"Honestly, I am, especially if it was painful for her. I was silly to react like I did, I'm sorry, I like us being open. So, I want to know if she wanted that again, did she?"

"You're outrageous."

"So, she did. On the bench?"

"Yes, but she wanted to start with that this time. She wanted to do it properly, she said."

"So, did you start with toys and lube, to make it easy for her?"

"Yes, but just the smaller one."

"The one I got for you?"

He shook his head with a resigned smile. "Yes, the one you bought for me, it was all she could manage."

"Really, heh, heh, so how did she get on with him?" and she nodded down to his groin. "I know he's not supersize but he's OK and I can always feel it the next day."

"I think that's a compliment. I'll take it as one. Anyway, he was patient and careful."

"Ha, I love his independence. It was him who was patient and careful, not you. Well, he and I have some business later, I don't know that we need you."

"I'm the life support system."

"Batteries can replace you. Let's face it, big boy is bigger anyway, as well as more reliable" and they both laughed. "So, did she take the full twenty-five?"

"She had to but…"

"Ah, wait, no, no, wait, I think I'm getting a picture here, was your enthusiasm waning? Ha! Is it not the same if he's not standing to attention?" He smiled slightly sheepishly and nodded. "So now we know," and she leaned forward to whisper, "that means you did come in her arse."

"Shhh!" but he laughed, obviously relaxed now, as was she. They were together, miles away from any cares — *in love, I think* — and free to do and say whatever they wanted.

"I still hope it was twenty-five big ones."

"It was, my lady, I am on this earth only to serve the ladies' pleasures."

"It's funny, I have a peculiar desire to see a picture of your handiwork. And to reassure myself that her bum's too big."

"Would you like a picture of yours?"

She considered. "Actually, I would, but suitably disembodied. I got caught last time, remember?"

"I do, but in a funny way..."

She grew pensive. "Yes, I wish that had happened differently. It meant I was in the wrong somehow and feeling guilty, but then it might not have made the break so decisive and I'm much happier now."

He took her hand. "Truly?"

"Very truly!"

"Me too."

I'm even content enough to encourage you to thrash Martha again as a favour to Henderson. Although letting you fuck her arse is a bit beyond the call of duty.

"What are you thinking now?"

"Just thinking about Martha. I'm not worrying, honestly. You'll tell me if I need to, won't you?"

"You don't need to. I've told her I love you."

"Wow," and she shook her head, startled, "wow, thank you, that's lovely. Wow, but I suppose that relates to what I was thinking. Where does she go for that — love, I mean?"

"I don't know. If I ever get near broaching the topic — I mean, I think I'd feel more relaxed if she had some sort of relationship — but she just says 'look, we have something good here, let's just enjoy it'. And I have fun, I admit it, so I'm OK with that as long as you are. I'm just not going to make a big thing about it. Anyway, even you've had to come clean about having your own pleasures on your little boat trip — *and you don't know the half of that, my darling.* And did you enjoy your Wednesday evening in the hotel room?"

"Yes," she smiled, "but I want a real one next time."

"I'll organise two for you."

"Promises, promises."

"Be careful what you wish for!"

And, as they raised their glasses, it seemed a strange thought passed between them.

The basket they'd picked up for cereal, milk and tea bags became so full they almost went back for another but then he said, "This is ridiculous, we'll eat two breakfasts, max."

"I know, I'll stop."

And the drive back was so short she barely had time to unzip him and get her mouth on his cock, but that at least made him park very slowly and carefully back at the house. She looked up. "To be continued. I want you on the sofa on the veranda. I'm not wasting a warm evening." They threw the bags into the kitchen and went straight outdoors.

The sofa was big and deep, and she made him lie back. "You did your bit for Martha, now I'm in the gentlemen's service business." The neighbourhood seemed very quiet, but she spoke in whispers. "Take these off!"

"But…"

"No buts, do you want your cock sucked or should I look elsewhere?"

"Hmm, you know I find that thought intriguing."

"So do I, but at the moment you'll have to do. Now get those shorts off" and he was sliding them down anyway.

"Ah, my dear Mr Cock. I've missed you, it's been almost three hours" and she slowly slipped her mouth over its head. *Mr, you are going to have a wonderful time for the next twenty minutes and I am going to find out what I can do, so I can't let you come for a while.* She lifted her head. "Take all the time you want but Miss Pussy will demand the reciprocal services later" and she went down further this time.

She spent most of the time sucking its head, that seemed to keep him breathing most steadily, occasionally pulling away if she felt he needed to relax a little but keeping gentle pressure on with one hand, stroking his balls with the other. Then, every minute or so, she would try taking him deeper. She started moving around the sofa to try different angles. "Stay still for me, baby, I'm trying to see how much I can take for you."

"I'm staying still, I'm staying still. It's heavenly, just don't make me come."

"I'm being careful, just let me control" and she kissed his lips but then went down again. When she tried very slowly, she was getting further and further but then she felt his excitement rising as her throat squeezed on the head of his cock. She came up again. "This is going to work, eventually, but it might take hours of practice, I'm happy to say."

He smiled at her. "I don't know how long I can hold on. Wouldn't you like to sit on my face so we can both come?"

"Know what? That's a good idea. I'd love to stay out here but I'm worried we'll get noisy." She stood up, looked at his stiffness, and quickly removed her shorts, "But I'm not missing the chance of a quick fuck outdoors" and she straddled him and sat down quickly on his cock. "I'm sorry, my darling, but he just looked irresistible," she moved slowly up and down, smiling and looking into his eyes, "and I was just feeling terribly slutty."

"Well, slut, am I going to be enough for you?"

"I'll have to make do tonight, I think, unless you have some friends around the corner."

"I think it's just me and big boy tonight. I'll get some guys organised tomorrow."

"OK but make sure they're big and rough. I'll want them to fuck me real hard. I want them just to do what they want. I want to be their sex toy."

"I want them to strip you naked and then pin you down and fuck you everywhere. I want them to put you over that big sofa inside and take turns sticking their cocks in you. I want one to make you suck him real deep while the other fucks you from behind and slaps your gorgeous arse."

She was moving faster and faster. "Yes, yes, I want them to come in my mouth, I want them to come everywhere. I want to see you holding your cock and watching while they do everything to me."

"I want to watch you sit on one while the other gets behind you and sticks his huge cock all the way up your arse. I want to hear you screaming fuck me, fuck me!"

My God, I did love that. I would love it again.

"Yes, yes. Let them fuck me, watch them fuck me, watch them fuck me!"

And neither of them could wait any longer.

As they lay in each other's arms and their breathing slowed, they began to hear only a gentle breeze through the pine needles above and the swish of small waves running up the sand.

"That was a lovely story. I hope we weren't too noisy."

"Ha, how terribly British of us: please don't frighten the horses! I'm glad you liked it but it's your turn to tell a story now."

"Why?"

"Because we're going upstairs and for the next twenty minutes my mouth is going to be fully occupied with your pussy."

"Heavenly, let's go." They picked up their shorts and went upstairs, pulling their tee shirts off and collapsing into each other's arms on the bed they'd left unmade.

He pulled her to him, her breasts squeezed against his chest. He slid his fingers to her clit and began massaging gently.

"That's lovely, and I do want you down there but I'm in absolutely no hurry."

"Me neither and he won't be ready again for a while yet."

"Who says he gets another go?"

He looked into her eyes. "I do. You'll do as your told!" Oddly, it thrilled her, it always did when he spoke like that. "I'm going to slide down soon and slowly lick your pussy. I will take my time. I want to pleasure you, but I love licking your cunt anyway, so I am not going to rush. I like keeping you on the edge. But when he wants you again, my tongue and my fingers will excite you to screaming and then, as you're slowly subsiding, you will do exactly as I tell you and take him as I want to give him to you. I may come down your throat, I may come up your arse, I may come in your pussy, I may make you suck me and then come all over your tits when I'm ready, but it will be whatever I decide."

She nodded. "I love it when you tell me what to do, love it when you talk dirty, but I'm supposed to tell you a story when you're eating me out. I'm not good at stories."

"You were doing very well just now when the guys were fucking you."

"I was just following your lead."

"Would you always do that?"

"I always have done, haven't I? And I have to admit, I've always had fun."

"So, if I want to watch two guys fucking you rough?"

"I can't honestly say that was a fantasy of mine."

"Two guys, rough sex, or me watching?"

"Any of them, really, but I enjoyed the story just now. I guess that was pretty obvious, wasn't it?" He nodded. "And I never know with these things what I've buried. Ooh, keep touching me, it's lovely, I am trying to think of what to say, really I am. Shall I talk about someone sucking your cock while you're licking me?"

"That doesn't really do it for me."

"You're more turned on by two men fucking me?"

"Yes, it's odd, but I am — and I've no idea where it comes from. It's like spanking you. I can tell you from the first pictures of naked ladies I ever looked at that I've been an arse man and later I always found spanking stories exciting, but I've had no direct experience of it at all, not until I slapped a girlfriend's bum when I was about eighteen and she liked it."

"I was amazed by how much it turned me on when you did it to me, but I had rather buried the girlhood memories of Mandy being belted by her dad and then showing me the red marks on her bum. I know it disturbed me, but I couldn't really process what I was feeling. I was too young to just think about it and play with myself, but I knew I found it exciting in a funny way. I admit when I was older and I'd started thinking about sex, I did sometimes imagine being handled roughly, being pushed against a wall and having my knickers ripped off. I used to come to the thought of a big guy just fucking me as he wanted."

"But not two?"

"Not two, no."

"But you found the idea exciting just now?"

"And with you watching, yes, that was the funny thing. I wanted you watching. I guess it made it feel a little bit safe, but I also wanted to show off to you."

"Just tell me more about that. I'm going to slide down now."

He slid his hands under her arse cheeks to lift her cunt higher, allowing him to lick everything voluptuously.

"Mmm, you do that rather well. Are you sure you don't want someone sucking your cock while you do that?"

He lifted his head for a moment. "I'm not sure, no. If it ever happens, I don't suppose I'm going to turn it down, I'll take it as a birthday present if you insist, but it doesn't excite me like the thought of two guys fucking you senseless."

"I've got to admit, I'm more turned on by that too."

"So just tell me about that some more" and he buried his face in her pussy again.

"I love it when you pin me down and fuck me. As soon as I saw the big sofa when we came in, I wanted you to push me down over the arm, pull my knickers down and just stick him in me. I know when it happens, I'm going to want you to kneel down after a while and lick me but that's not the fantasy. The fantasy is you just have me, you just do what you want, you make me take it. You're so sweet about always reaching for lube but when I fantasise about you, and I've masturbated more in the past two years than in the previous twenty, when I think about you like that, you're very rough. I put pillows under my tummy at home to keep my arse up while I play with myself and you're just sticking him in me. You pull my bum cheeks open, spit in my arse and just stick him in there. I'd never have thought of that before, it really was completely new to me, but I find it thrilling now.

"Keep licking, it's lovely!

"So, if I'm going to think about the guys tomorrow, they're going to start by stripping my shorts off and pinning me down on the arm of that sofa and they're going to take turns. I want them fucking me real rough, I really do. I want them to use me. And now you've told me, I do want to think of you sat in that big chair down there watching us. Then I want one of them to sit on the sofa in front of me so I can suck his cock while the other one fucks me. And I want them to be big boys who can keep going. I'm not going to come while they're fucking me. I'm going to make you make me come later. I'm going to make you eat me like this and after I've come with you, I'm going to suck your cock as well. You'll be the third, remember, but, just when you're ready, I'm going to pull back and watch you squirt loads and loads of your cum. You've been waiting so long, watching these two big guys fucking me senseless that your balls are full, so you've got big fat blobs raining down on my face and my tits, on my belly, in my hair and, just when you're nearly empty, I take you in my mouth again and suck those last drops out of you. But that will be later. I want more from the big guys. I want them to use me. I want to be on the sofa arm still, they're taking turns again. I want to hear one of them say 'bitch has a beautiful ass, don't she?' And he slaps me really hard with his bare hand and says 'don't that look fine' and he slaps me again. He's got his hand on my back so I don't move and the slaps are coming harder and you're just smiling and holding your cock. Then one of them spreads me and licks me and then just sticks his cock in me. That will hurt, I know, because he's big and he's rough, but I want his big cock up my bum. I'll probably scream but I want him to force me. I want his friend to say, 'don't come yet. Let me fuck her ass', and I want that other big cock pushing all the way up my bum and I'll still be screaming but I'll be looking at you smiling, knowing you're going to be sticking your cock in my face later. But before then, one of them lies back on that big sofa and says 'sit on me girl' and the other one pushes me onto him. I sit on him. I want that big cock in my cunt. Then I feel the other guy push my shoulders down. I know what's going to happen. Yes, he just forces his cock again, all the way up my arse. I love having two cocks in me, you know I do, that's something you've taught me. I know they're going to come now. I want them to come and come and they're starting to shout. I can feel it building up. I want this. I can see you holding your cock. I can see you're excited. This is going to be fabulous. It's painful, they're big and they've been rough but I want them coming and coming — and they do, I can feel them pulsing and it's wonderful. They come and come and come and keep pushing their cocks in and then, only after ages, only when they start to soften — and that takes a long while, they love their cocks being inside me — only then do they pull out very slowly. I climb off, I come over to you, I kiss you. You kiss me deeply — and I've just been sucking two strange cocks — you keep kissing me but you move me upstairs to this bed, you push me back like this, you lick me like this and finally, finally, I can start to come. This is coming now, it's huge, keep eating me Jack, keep eating me, keep eating me!" And she seemed to burst into one glorious orgasm, panting heavily as he continued to eat her, slowing down gently, letting her movement become less violent, letting her breathing slow. Then he slid up beside her and cuddled her while she subsided into him. She moved her hand towards him.

"I thought that might wake him."

"It got him very excited. I loved your story."

"I only repeated what you wanted to hear — but now I have to deal with him. What do you want?"

"We said it already. Sit up!" She sat up and he piled pillows behind her. "Lie back a bit. I'm going to fuck your face and then come all over you."

"Give me some blobs, I want to swallow some blobs."

"You'll swallow some blobs. The first ones will hit the back of your throat but then it's your face and your tits."

"Yes, I want to watch you coming. Give him to me."

He puts his cock in her mouth, just the head, in and out, in and out. She pulls him deeper, as far as she can, he pulls back. He's very stiff now and, from his movements, she knows he's going to come soon. She wants this more than anything. She hears him shout 'Ah' as the first blob comes and then he pulls back and she watches the big blobs come quickly as he wanks himself. He points at her face, he points down to her tits, then her face again and she opens her mouth to take some. Then her hand takes over from his — she points more at her tits. There are loads of beginning to form small pools. But now, as he's easing, she takes him in her mouth again to take the last ones, then lets him push the pillows around so they can fall into each other's arms and drift into sleep.

30

She woke in the middle of the night. Not usual for her, but neither was the sound of someone breathing beside her. His arm was still around her and she snuggled in a little closer, enjoying the warmth of his skin but trying not to disturb him. Is this what she wanted? His body next to hers every night? She was sure it was. Is it what he wanted? She thought so too… probably… maybe… She knew she was important to him, but was she essential? But, as all the other thoughts crowded in again, it seemed almost absurd to hope. Singapore and the US for him, and who knew what next. London and much more travel for her if she made this step, and two people who needed her attention still and would do for a few years yet.

Could it carry on like this? They had managed well for two years. She wanted much more of him but those brief times with him had brought her so much joy.

Some heartache too? No, maybe it felt like it sometimes, but she couldn't really say that. The stories he told, about Joanna, about Martha, about his little Asian lady, were painful but she was managing them, even finding them, when she could sit with him, hold his hand, look into his eyes, even finding them almost amusing. She wasn't sure she'd had all of the stories. What happened during his 'hermit' phases? Nothing? Really? But when they came together again there was always love and passion — and imagination! Much more than she ever expected — and now a little maggot wriggled in her heart. She hadn't been open with him, not completely. Was she naïve to think he was entirely open with her? She knew the boat was not a threat, just as Peter's dungeon hadn't been a threat. She had just opened herself up to being more adventurous, it had been exciting, she was in touch with herself like never before, it helped her open up even more to him. Her old self would never have spent so much time sucking his cock, trying to work out how best to please him, and how best to have fun herself.

And tonight's story. Would she do it? Could she? Would he really enjoy that? Would she? Obviously not, was the immediate response, but why not be open? She'd never had a stranger. But now she had tried one-night stands. But Alphonse was no longer one night. But he was a friend, not a danger. He was lovely, but really not a danger. Alan had been just one night, a lovely night, but now he was a friend who emailed occasionally. The idea that fucking was fun was so new to her — and she and Jack now seemed to be fitting it into their lives, well, maybe he had always done that — but doing things together, exploring new things together, just maybe. Before the boat, could she have imagined that happening? Andy and Alphonse together, and then Peter and the public spanking? Not remotely. But it had been weirdly exciting. And how would it have been to have had Jack there and to have fallen asleep in his arms later? She found herself almost smiling; he would, of course, have fucked Jen and Yvonne and, yes, she would have watched and then let him take her to bed. How is it to be in Jack's arms now? She felt very full of love. She pulled his hand to her breast; she wiggled her bum gently against his dozing cock. She felt this was how it should be, maybe could be, and maybe, even with all the complications and difficulties, how it eventually would be.

Making love in the morning was slow and easy. He was awake first. She'd woken to his arms wrapped around her and his cock nudging gently between her legs. She wiggled a little and adjusted her pose to make it easier for him. That made him stiffer, made it easier to slide between her clit and her hole and she could feel herself getting wetter.

"I want to sit on you again."

"I want you sitting on me."

And they had gone very slowly, smiling and kissing and touching. She loved his face and his shining eyes. She loved his hands on her hips holding her down on him, then sliding around to caress her bum, then moving to her breasts to squeeze and pull towards him, 'beautiful, beautiful'. Now she wanted to make him come. "Go nice and easy with me, baby, don't make me sore this morning. Remember those big, rough boys are coming to fuck me this evening." She felt him stiffen. She felt his hands move to her back to press her down. "You're going to watch, baby, while they stick those big cocks everywhere. You won't stop them, even when they pin me down, even when they stick those big cocks deep down my throat. I can't take it, but you won't stop them. You won't stop them because you know I want them to fuck me. You want to watch them taking turns in my cunt while they hold me down on the sofa." She could feel him thrusting harder. "You want to watch while they take turns sticking those big cocks up my arse. I'm screaming but you're just watching and smiling and playing with yourself. Then they make me sit on one of them, and I want to. Then the other one pushes me down and I can feel that big, fat cock being pushed all the way up my bum." She could feel him coming. "I can feel them coming, the one underneath me is coming in my cunt. Oh, I love it. And now the one behind is coming in my arse. Oh, that's fabulous, that big, fat cock, he's coming and coming!" And Jack was coming, and then she had to let go, she was coming herself. She was shocked, she was telling him the story, but it was making her come.

She came round again, as he was getting back into bed, putting mugs of tea by the bedside, then wrapping his arms around her. She snuggled into him.

"What's the time?"

"Around ten."

"Wow, that was a good second sleep."

"I didn't want to wake you. You've had an amazing week. I thought you needed some rest."

"I guess I did. Well, I know I did. Wotcha been doing?"

"Getting the day organised. I want to just walk around the old town hand in hand, just like a simple pair of lovebirds." She squeezed her arms around him. "The best restaurants don't open until the evening but there are still plenty that look good. Of course, you can guess what the specialties are."

"Crab cakes?"

"Crab cakes!"

"That's OK. When they're good I love them."

"It's OK, there's plenty else besides — mostly seafood."

"I think we know we're not steak people."

"Well, not here anyway."

"But you didn't want to do dinner?"

"No, we're busy this evening."

And she didn't know, but she just let the thought stay there and cuddled into him.

"Do I have to start moving?"

"Maybe. We know what will happen if you don't." He reached between her legs. She jumped away, laughing, and moved towards the bathroom.

"Not now then, I have to save her, don't I?"

It was a perfect autumn day. They kept their sweaters draped around their shoulders as they wandered the streets of the old town and the waterfront, both amused and entranced by its colonial tweeness, by so much being done to preserve the spirit of the antebellum South but preserving truly only the facades; all of them, of course, heavily renovated. The land of the face lift!

"Shall we live by the sea?"

"Where else?" Best to throw that off light-heartedly, not to read too much into it.

"Do you mind that being a serious question?" They were walking hand in hand, just looking ahead. She stopped and turned to him.

"I would love the idea, you know I would."

He smiled. "I don't actually. You've never said."

"I've never said anything at all about living together. Neither have you until just now."

"Reluctant?"

"Let's walk," and they moved off hand in hand again. "Reluctant to say anything, of course, reluctant to be thought of as trying to pin you down, and maybe reluctant to hope. It seems such a remote prospect. We have such complicated lives."

"Maybe about to get more complicated."

"Exactly, so I'm blundering on just hoping to hold on to what we've got."

"But what we've got, with everything else swirling around us, just seems like the most important thing. Well, not true." *What's coming now?* "I know the kids are more important."

"They are, Jack, but, as you've found, their own lives soon become the only thing that matters to them. I doubt whether even your ex sees that much of your boys."

"Ha, that's true. When we talk, which isn't often, it's usually about wanting me to ask them or tell them, which is a bit of a joke, to spend more time with her. And I've seen them myself only once each a year. Admittedly, when they come out, we've had a full week each time and those weeks have been wonderful. She tries to get them to go on holiday with her and they won't" and here he laughed gently. "I haven't really been applying a lot of pressure."

"So, I don't like the thought, but I know that's how mine will be soon."

"So, by the sea?"

"Anywhere, Jack. The sea would be lovely," she squeezed his hand hard, "but just anywhere."

"I like the thought of being together." *Let him speak*, "I think we're very good."

"I think we're very good too. And I'm very happy to think of the seaside cottage as our goal."

"I was thinking of something maybe a little grander."

"Why am I not remotely surprised?" They laughed, "I love you. I'll take what I can get."

"I love you."

There was an odd formality about Grill 225, all dark wood and leather chairs, and it was quiet. Too quiet for indiscreet conversations like the previous evening when the noise from the neighbouring tables had allowed them to speak so openly.

"Have you brought me here so I can't ask you about Martha?" she asked in a loud whisper.

He smiled. "And what more did you want to know about Martha?"

"Will she want more of the same, do you think, or has your little big boy put her off?"

"Honestly, I think she'll be back for more, however much she squealed."

"Did she squeal? I do hope she squealed." She was smiling broadly.

"Well, let's see if you squeal this evening." He was looking directly at her.

She stared straight back. "A moment ago, you were saying you loved me."

"And you know what a big and complex thing that is. I do love you, and I have a great deal of fun loving you. Are you going for the scallops? I'm guessing the crab cakes are not going to tempt you today."

"I suppose remembering the scallops could be considered romantic but since I nearly always have them wherever we are, I guess I make that easy for you. But yes, I'm going scallops. Today I don't mind making things easy for you. What time are they coming?"

"Six."

"OK. Yes, scallops, no starter," and the strangest feeling opened up in her stomach. The boat had been spontaneous. This would be weirdly premeditated, but the anticipation was already electric. "What are you going for?"

"The tuna tower, but I'm already dreading the size."

"Of the tower? Or the boys?" They both laughed very loud and the tension was gone. Now they could just chat and eat.

One course was ample, but the food was beautifully prepared, and he'd ordered Sauvignon today, that would be better with this. A few tables filled up, but they could talk normally about his job, about hers, about Pat and her new-found friend Penelope. "I'm looking forward to meeting her. I think I'm going to learn a lot and, much as I love Peter, I do need to get this set up properly for me and it sounds like she'll be a big help."

"Every day it feels more real, doesn't it?"

"Well, more real than a seaside cottage."

He raised his glass. "Let's just drink to somewhere together. Anywhere."

"Somewhere together, anywhere," she touched her glass to his and she felt strangely — *unreasonably? No, dammit, just believe*— warm and secure.

They heard the car pull up just before six. Jack had closed all the blinds — *sensible*. She went to the stairs. "Where are you going?"

"I need a pee!" *I need to make an entrance, I think. Let me approach this my way.*

She went to the bathroom but did nothing. She'd been half an hour before. She came part way down the stairs, staying out of sight, listening to the voices. Pleasant voices, Southern accents, one very deep. *Promising, I love bass voices, will he be black?*

"Oh, we'll keep going if she's as pretty as you say she is."

"And she likes evrythin', you're sayin'?" Jack had obviously nodded.

"Can we slap her a bit? Does she like that?"

"Stick to the arse." Jack's voice sounded strange in the mix. "She likes that a lot."

"Man, well I like that too and I slap real hard. You just tell me if I'm too hard. I ain't gonna listen to her." *Wow, not so sure about this but it's too late now.*

"And you wanna join in? Or you just watchin'?"

"Not planning to. I'm just thinking I'll take her away when you've finished."

"Sure, man, whatever you say. Some guys like to watch, some like to join in. You can join in if you want, we're easy. You say she never done this before?"

"No." *Not quite true, buddy, but not with strangers.*

"You neither?" She assumed Jack shook his head.

"Well, we just have our fun until you tell us we gotta stop. Like we said, we don't listen to her, that's the deal, right?" He must have nodded. "That's our usual deal. Little lady likes to pretend she didn't really want it, like we're forcing her or somethin'." This was the bass talking.

"Course," said the baritone, "that don't work so good when we get asked back" and they all chuckled.

She stepped down. "Good evening guys." They were leaning back, side by side, on the sofa. Jack had stayed in the big chair opposite.

"Wow, man." This was bass, and he was black — *a cool dude, I guess* — and big. "You weren't kidding, she is real pretty. You're real pretty, ma'am. What are we gonna call you?"

"Most of the time it's just bitch," said baritone, blonde, taller, still well built, late twenties maybe, like his partner, but it was hard to judge, quite handsome really, "but a name's nice sometimes."

"Jane is good. And bitch is OK." *Why not?*

"OK, Jane, now show us what you got." She hesitated.

"Get naked, bitch." She caught Jack's eye. He was smiling. *OK, calm the nerves, think of undressing for Jack.* So she slid her shorts down slowly, pushing her arse out towards them as they came down. She stepped out of them and turned round slowly.

"Man, that's beautiful. You sure she never done this before? She done that real well. You're doin' fine, bitch, but show us them titties!"

She pulled off the strappy top quickly, no bra, of course.

"Wow, man, I'm gonna love bitin' them."

"Just lookin' at you bitch, that's getting me goin', but you're goin' to have to do a little more work to help him." Blondie unzipped himself and slid his shorts down. He was half erect — *I must have put on a good show* — "Get down there and suck!"

This was a first: her first contact with a man would be with her mouth on his cock. She knelt between his knees, her forearms on his thighs, took his cock in both hands and felt it stiffening quickly — *smells nice, freshly showered* — then slowly slid her mouth over its head. She pulled it towards her slightly so she could look up at his face. His head was back with his eyes closed but, as she pulled him, he looked down to her and smiled. "That's real nice, but I know you can take more" and she could. The practice with Jack had helped, and she slid down deeper. He put his hand on her head and pushed — *uh, oh* — but not too firmly. He wasn't trying to push it all in — *yet*. He let her move up and down and move her hand in rhythm. He was very stiff and breathing heavily but it didn't feel like he was near coming. She was starting to relax — it was a nice cock, a little like Jack's — would he be playing with himself yet?

"OK, bitch, time for a change." Bass talking. She turned to look at him. *Oh my, this is different, it's not quite as thick as Andy but it may be even longer.* He was standing beside her. She left baritone and took the black thing in both hands.

"Nice, man, that is one nice cock!" *I can do this. Are you listening Jack?*

"Well, you're going to get to know him real well tonight, bitch. Now suck it!"

She did what she could but kept both hands on his shaft. When he put his hand on her head and pushed, her hands saved her, but, even like that, her mouth was full. He didn't force it — he seemed happy with her rocking to and fro on its head. "Nice rhythm, bitch, but now I'm gonna sit me down and you're going to bend over this arm here. You carry on sucking, but I think my buddy's got something for ya."

He sat back on the sofa, holding his cock vertical. She went to the arm, bent over and took him in her mouth again, surprising herself that she was wanting to take him again. She knew what would come next. She spread her legs. She also knew she was ready. Come on, Blondie, I want you to fuck me now! She felt his hand on her back — *yes please* — and then he pushed in easily. "Wow, bitch is real ready, she loves it, man, that is one real nice, wet pussy."

A moment's alarm. She freed one hand, slipped it between her legs to stroke his balls but mostly to feel the reassuring rib of the condom. The other danger was the black cock. With only one hand to save her, she was pushed down firmly. She pulled back sharply, choking. Bass laughed. "Guess you're gonna have to give this little girl a bit more practice, man." And he let her find her rhythm again. Her mouth was very full, but this was gorgeous. She had both hands on him again and was managing it perfectly, enjoying it now. "But don't you go thinking, bitch, that you can pull away like that when my little friend down there wants to go all the way up yo' ass!"

That was a bit frightening, but she felt her pussy getting wetter and softer around the white cock. He was holding her hips tightly now and pushing deep but she didn't feel he was coming anytime soon so she was surprised when he pulled away. "This is one beautiful ass, bro. Thing is, it just needs a little bit of colour. He stepped to one side, put his left hand firmly in the small of her back, then delivered a huge stinging slap to her right cheek. She jolted up but the black hand kept her head in place, then the next slap came on the other cheek, even harder if anything — *wow, that's warm* — and she jolted again but was held firm.

Blondie moved behind her and stuck his cock in deeply again. "Now that looks real pretty, bro, but I guess yo' gonna wanna slap this ass too."

"I got time, bro, bitch is doin' a good job on my cock." *I am, big boy, and this is nice but my jaw is starting to ache.* And they settled into a rhythm again.

Blondie was sliding his hands up and down her back but then began stroking her arse, pulling her cheeks apart. "Mmm, nice, that looks too sweet, bitch, yo' ass is gonna be busy." She wiggled. "Woah, sassy" then he slid out but she felt his face quickly on her pussy. She went up on tiptoes a little to let him lick her clit easily. The boy was good, finding the spot quickly, moving around, changing the pressure when he felt her moving too much, but she was getting excited. She was taking more of Mr Bass in her mouth.

"You doin' good, bitch, careful you don't make me come now!"

She lifted her head a moment. "Tell your buddy to be careful or he's going to make me come."

"Get yo' mouth back on me, bitch, and don't you worry, you come or you don't come, we just carry on fuckin'."

Blondie stood up and stuck his cock in her again. "Oh yeah, but we deal with bad girls who come early.

Hey buddy," he was talking to Jack, "You got that lube?"

She heard Jack move. He obviously handed a tube over. He must have had it with him.

"Thank you, brother. I think I'd like a play with this sweet little asshole." She felt the big, cold dollop land between her cheeks. He kept fucking but she could feel his thumb playing with her arse. It amazed her how much she had grown to be excited by this feeling. She felt him pull his cock out slowly. *Fucking my arse already? No, not yet* — and he stood to one side and squirted more lube. More fingers now, this was becoming a nice stretch. The nerve ends were jangling but now the pinkie went to her clit. *Oh, no, has he told them?* The sweet voluptuousness of lots of fingers in her, her clit mesmerised by a touch — she was sucking harder on the big one. Blondie must know I'm coming, he must feel it. "Mister, you have one greedy bitch here." He pushed his fingers deeper and pressed harder on her clit, speeding his movement as she did. *Oh, no, I'm coming already, I'm coming.* She started to scream but was held down on the black cock. She just made strangled moans as she came and came and then slumped almost lifeless on the arm.

"OK, little darlin', we take it just a little easy now." Bass was standing up, laying her head gently on the sofa. "But we gotta keep these boys going. You just stay like that. It's time I had me some pussy." *Oh, what's this going to be like, he's huge.* "Oh, my, my buddy sure is right, this is one beautiful ass, but that comes later. You just take this ol' boy in yo' pussy." *I want you brother, even now already, but go slow, please.* Bass obviously understood the problem. He put its head gently against her hole. "I'm gonna go easy now, bitch, you just enjoy this" and he pushed very slowly, easing in and out to move it forward in gentle stages. *My God, it is huge, it's gorgeous.* She felt full already but wasn't feeling his belly on her arse. Somewhere deep in her belly it was becoming uncomfortable. "Man, yo' bitch likes a big cock." She could see Jack nodding. "We takin' it easy fo' a while but this bad girl gotta take some slapping. Gotta learn not to come so fast. But, meantime, I'm loving this pussy.

Meantime Blondie had sat on the sofa again. "Suck, bitch!" Mmm this was easy, just move the mouth up and down and enjoy the huge cock in her pussy. She was already recovering, already wanting more.

Bass was moving gently but he'd picked up the lube as well and squirted more — *oh no, not yet* — but he just started playing with his thumb inside her — *oh, yes, just a little deeper, that's gorgeous* — and she was wiggling again. "This is one bad girl, bro, what do ya think?"

Blondie was moaning gently as she moved her mouth on his cock. "Mmm, bro, I think twenty."

"Each?"

"Oh, yeah, each."

"You want her over your knee?"

"Oh, yeah, over my knee like this."

"OK, I'm gonna keep her on this arm. Reckon I can slap harder. Bitch needs a lesson."

"OK, I'll just hold her down." And he slid along, taking his cock out of her mouth and held her shoulders firmly down on to the sofa. She felt very exposed with her arse even higher now. Bass put his hand firmly in the small of her back. "Know what, I just want a little more play with that pretty little asshole" and she felt him slide a finger deep inside her. "Mm, sweet," and he wriggled another in — why do I love that? It feels so good, but the third stretched her. Oh, that delightful discomfort — but when he started playing with her clit, she was embarrassed that she was ready again. "Yep, this is one bad girl, man, reckon she needs a lesson. You wanna come back here man and see an ass get real red?" *and Jack moved, the bastard*. Thoughts quickly left her as the first slap landed. Her scream was stifled by Blondie pushing her face into the sofa. Wow, it wasn't a cane, but it was harder than any paddle. The next one came, just as fierce. The two behind were enemies. Bass thrashing and Jack watching, enjoying. Only Blondie seemed almost a friend, two hands touching her, merely restraining her, sliding his hands over her back between swipes. The third came. This was just pain, and it was intense. She wasn't getting outside herself, the fourth came and now, slowly, she began to get to that other place; to somehow lift herself to see this big man thrashing her bare arse; to see Jack, behind, enjoying the view, and Blondie alternately holding her down and then caressing her to comfort her. But the fire was spreading out all the way from her arse into every part of her body, and the big man's hand kept pounding — *Jack, are you watching, are you enjoying my perfect arse going brilliant red?* — and the fire felt intense and total and carried on burning, even as she felt hands on her hips; even as she felt the huge cock slide slowly into her again, monstrous, but somehow now easier. Was she that aroused? That excited? That easy? Oh, no, not that easy. It was still huge, but this time she could take it. Then he pulled away. "What do you think, man? Ever see that colour before? Beautiful!"

She heard Jack move back to the chair. She turned her head. He looked concerned. She lay across the arm, her arse on fire, her pussy wetter than she could ever remember, juices running down the inside of her thighs, and she smiled at him. He smiled back, relaxing visibly.

"OK, bitch, come here," said Blondie, opening his arms wide above his lap, as Peter had. She stood up slowly and moved round, her eyes meeting Jack's all the way, even as she draped herself across Blondie's lap. How this would be, she did not know, but the spanking could hardly be more severe and the fire in her arse had reached almost a point of numbness. And Blondie's approach was different. It was bare hand, and hard, less intense, but after every two he would slide his fingers to her clit. He had a perfect touch, and brought her so close to the edge. She was looking directly at Jack and watching him smiling, and then Blondie would take his fingers away – *no, not yet, not yet* — and then slap twice more and then repeat the touch. *This time, please, let me come this time.* But no, another two, and she tried counting but was lost in the numbers. The fire through her body and her trembling clit screaming at her until finally it seemed to be over, his one hand was stroking her burning arse and his perfect fingers were stroking her clit slowly. He was feeling her moving with him; he was finding her rhythm as she pushed against him. Now she knew, now he would take her there, she could let it come. She looked to Jack. He was smiling and nodding. She could let herself go. Oh, oh, just hold those screams, loud, not too loud — and it was such a delicious coming — *is the second always better? Yes of course it is! Oh, this is wonderful, this is wonderful* — and she slumped on Blondie's lap.

"Wow, man, that is some wonderful bitch you have there, man. Beautiful body and so, so sexy — but now my buddy and me are gonna have our turn. Over the arm again, bitch!"

They lifted her and pushed her, like before, over the arm of the sofa.

"No offence, bro, but you go first," said Bass, and, turning to Jack, he added, "I guess she gonna love yo' little guy in that ass. Me, I'm thinking, she gonna find it a little uncomfortable. You good with that?"

She looked at Jack. He was nodding.

Bass held her shoulders. She felt Blondie squirt more lube. He pushed fingers in her arse. They went in easily. Then she felt his hands spread her cheeks. She had come to love this and, with the pain in her cheeks subsiding. It melted away much quicker than after a caning. She enveloped Blondie's sweet cock in her arse. *Oh, push it in, give me more, oh, that's gorgeous.* He grabbed her hips more tightly and pushed deeper. She felt him thrusting and thrusting, she was sure he was coming. Then, suddenly, he pulled away and slapped her once again. This time she hardly felt it; she'd wanted to feel him coming. "You can wait, bitch, I'm gonna have that ass again in a while, but my bro gonna give you something to think about first!"

For the first time, she felt worried. She looked to Jack. He was smiling smugly and nodding. Now Bass moved behind her and Blondie held her down. This could be more than painful. Bass at least squirted more lube on her. Then he caressed her flaming skin tenderly, sensually. The feeling was coming back. One hand was on her back again, now the fingers were entering her again: one, easy; two, pleasant, stay there a while, move and turn; three, uncomfortable now, how far are you going to push? Then two large hands on her cheeks, spreading her, admiring her. "Man, that is one beautiful ass!" and then she felt the cock head pushing at her. *Oh, this is getting seriously painful now.* Jack was still nodding. Bass was pushing, this was seriously stretching. Her ring was screaming. She felt like screaming but now this was a challenge, she now wanted this, she could show them. And Bass was good, he kept it slow. "You take this, bitch, you gonna love it" and he was in. She had this massive thing inside her and she felt wonderfully full, more than uncomfortable, but wonderfully full. She felt more than disappointed when he slowly pulled away. "Well, bitch, now we ready for you. You are one beautiful lady and my buddy and me, we gonna come together in yo' beautiful body."

As if choreographed, Blondie stood, held her hands and lifted her gracefully. Bass lay himself on the long sofa, holding his cock in the air, making a joyous feature of rolling a fresh condom down his cock. "OK, bitch, you come here and slide yourself down slowly on my little friend here."

She wanted this big cock coming inside her. She straddled him and, wrapping one hand around him, she lowered herself down. It was still huge. It was very uncomfortable, but it wasn't painful, it felt wonderful. He pulled her down onto his chest and whispered, "You are one very beautiful, very sexy lady." But that little moment of almost-magic was broken as she felt Blondie behind her. But this is what I want, she thought, as his cock pushed into the tight space between her cheeks. He went deep. Now she was more than full. She could feel them start to come. She sat up a little. Blondie let her move. "Come to me Jack." He looked transfixed. "Come to me, I want you in my mouth." He moved towards her, his cock erect. She wanted this. "Fuck my mouth, Jack, I want your come down my throat." The boys were starting to come, she could feel them beginning to pulse. Jack's cock was deep in her mouth now, one hand on her head. He was pushing. She was almost gagging but he just held himself deep enough and then, as the boys were coming, she could feel him pull back a little, ready for his own explosion. "I'm coming," he shouted, and she felt the blobs in her mouth. He pulled back a little — good boy, Jack, let me suck and suck — and the blobs came and came. Had she ever sucked so many, and still they came, even as she felt the other cocks slowly subside inside her — *oh, Jack, your cum tastes gorgeous, I want those last few reluctant drops* — and she was still sucking and licking as the bodies slumped around her.

They disentangled slowly. Jack fell back into the big chair, she fell on to his lap and wrapped her arms around his neck.

The two men collapsed, side by side, on the sofa, their softening dicks glistening with lube and juices. *At least they have the decency to look exhausted.*

"Guys," said Bass, smiling, "that was just the most beautiful fuck. You be sure and tell us if you ever come to Charleston again. Bro?"

"That was so beautiful ma'am. I sure hope you enjoyed it as much as we did."

"Guys, you were amazing. I especially loved that big black thing, but I thank you both for being so careful. With things like that you surely need to be."

"It's a pleasure to give pleasure, ma'am. And Jack, my man, you are one lucky guy. This lady is so beautiful and a free spirit. You hang onto her, d'you hear?"

"Yeah, but bring her back soon" and they all laughed.

The boys stood and dressed quickly. Still naked, she hugged them both and kissed them. "That was truly memorable, guys, thank you. My body will remember it for days. I will remember it forever."

"Turn round for us, one last time!" And she turned, and wondered if anybody had ever seen an arse so red.

"Goodnight guys, and thank you," said Jack, and they left.

"Cuddle?"

"Yes, just take me in your arms and hold me."

31

The place was quiet, but they were early. The waitress put them at the same table by the white fence and handed them menus. Claudia began looking.

"Not crab cakes today?"

"No, Jack, not crab cakes."

"They do scallops."

She laughed. "Fuck you! I'm having a look." She studied the menu briefly. "I'm going jumbo prawns, in batter, with loads of fries."

"Two of the jumbo prawns, please, and I apologise for my wife's language if you caught that on the way over. She's from Scotland, I'm afraid."

"Scotland, really? No, I didn't hear nothing, sir, 'cept two jumbo prawns with fries. Y'all want wine with that? Same as Friday?"

"Yes, lovely, thank you. I'm impressed you remembered."

"It's the job, sir," she smiled pleasantly, "and you two sure make a sweet couple with them lovely accents of yours. Chardonnay coming right up."

Jack looked at Claudia's screwed up face, "Are you in pain?"

"I'm all right, arsehole, but I kicked the table when I was aiming for your leg!" He laughed loudly. "That's not my only source of discomfort. I hope you didn't mind being careful this morning."

"No, I wanted to be gentle. Are you OK?"

She smiled. "I guess I'm going to have reminders for a couple of days but I'm fine. I love you, Jack."

"I love you, very much."

"Is this going to be it? Stolen dirty weekends and journeys to the airport? When do I see you again?"

"Next weekend."

"Next weekend?" She was stunned. "You never said."

"I only arranged it this morning. I have to stay here longer. I don't know for how long and it's a bit pointless to head back midweek so I'm going back to Singapore via London."

"That's wonderful. Will you stay at the flat?"

"Yes, I'll get in Friday morning, fly out Sunday."

"I think that's OK. Wait, I've got Peter Friday morning, but that's easy, that's only the morning but I did say I'd have lunch. Why am I worrying? I'll make it OK."

"You're wondering what the kids are doing?"

"Yes, I'm trying to think if they have plans."

"They do. I have four tickets for The Lion King on Saturday afternoon. I thought we could do Chinese after that."

"Jack, no," but she was thrilled, "really? How on earth did you manage that?"

"Did I say it was cheap?"

"No, of course not. I know you and your dodgy connections. I'm just stunned. Thank you."

"Well, this wasn't dodgy. Connections don't work so well on a Sunday, so it's just expensive, but so worth it, I think. You don't mind me meeting them?"

"Well, I mind a bit, but they'll be thrilled."

"You mind?"

The water, wine and bread came. "Quiet today?"

"You guys are early. We'll be full after one. That's why we can only give you an hour, sorry."

"No, that's fine, we've got planes to catch anyway."

"Where y'all goin'?"

"DC, to start with."

"But you've had a great weekend?"

"We've had a wonderful weekend, thank you," said Claudia, with such enthusiasm that even the waitress was taken aback. But maybe the waitress hadn't had too many days like yesterday. *And I certainly haven't had too many days like yesterday.* "I only mind a bit, Jack. I'm sure we'll have a wonderful day and they'll think you're dead cool, but then they won't see you again."

"I'm going to have to build in more London weekends. We will just work round it. I'm not looking for anything else. I want you."

"Somewhere, anywhere?"

He nodded. "Somewhere, anywhere" and raised his glass. "To us, somewhere, anywhere."

32

She just caught the kids on their way out. She stopped herself saying anything about London. She needed to tell Pat first. Tell, or ask? Let's just handle this carefully, she thought, it's a tell, but it's got to feel like an ask.

"You've got some time free, haven't you?"

"Of course I have, my love, we've got a lot to talk about. Well, you've got lots to tell me. Have we got a business?"

"I'm almost certain" and they laughed and hugged.

"I'm so thrilled for you, Claudie, I really am. And don't worry, we'll make this work. Brodie Associates, it keeps going round in my head. I am so chuffed! I'm even getting emails from Penelope."

"Really, what's she saying?"

"Ah, no Claudie, sorry, strictly private and confidential" and she kept a straight face for just long enough to see Claudia's brow furrow before bursting into a huge laugh.

"Pat!"

"Sorry, boss!" and she smiled again, looking rather proud. *Of herself? Of me? Of the business? No matter, just thank God she's here and so committed.* "It was their terms with that Peter. So, she did stress it was absolutely only for you and me. It threw me a bit. She used a different email address. Are we going to have to get into this cloak and dagger stuff?"

Henderson came straight into her head. *I'll call him Rod to his face, but he'll always stay Henderson otherwise.* "We are, I'm afraid. I'm hearing and reading more and more and becoming aware of how much leaks out from other businesses. We're going to have to get very disciplined. You and I will need separate accounts that we just use for each other. Well, no, it's probably even more complicated than that. Maybe we can ask Penelope who we should get in to advise us. I mean, our clients are going to insist we're completely secure and we'll have to prove it to them. I've got some people I could ask but I'm starting to wonder about who I can really trust, now."

"Do you want something to eat? You should." Pat was pouring tea. "Shall I just do some toast?"

"Yes, that'll do, thank you. I have been eating well, mind. Crab and jumbo prawns and scallops, all things I love."

"So you've had a lovely weekend, too?" Pat paused expectantly.

"Yes, I should start with that." Pat, the bread still in her hand, sat down. It made her hesitate.

Pat reached out and put a hand on Claudia's. "Don't worry, love, I know you've moved on. Even

David's starting to get serious with this girl, well, woman I should say — and she doesn't seem a bad sort. She's not you of course, but I'm getting the best of both worlds at the moment. And now we're starting a business, I've stopped worrying about you moving away. That was my only big concern, you taking the two of them somewhere else. So, what is it? Does he want to get married?"

"Ha, no," and she laughed, "actually, I don't know whether I'd want to. But he does seem to want to get closer. He wants to meet the kids." She was nervous.

"About bloody time! They keep asking me about him. I say 'ask your mother' and they don't. I was going to tell you actually, when I found the right moment."

"I love you, Pat, I really do, but you and I haven't got time now for this 'finding the right moment' crap, have we? I know I'm guilty."

Pat smiled. "I think so, my dear. I will if you will. So, what've you got to tell me?"

"He's flying though London next weekend. He's got four tickets for The Lion King on Saturday afternoon and he wants us to eat Chinese afterwards. Is that OK?"

Pat tried to look grumpy. Claudia knew this was not going to be serious. "Only four tickets, I've been wanting to see that for ages" and they laughed together again. Pat was plainly thinking. Finally she said, "This may be a silly suggestion…"

"What are you plotting now?"

"You're going to want to stay up there, aren't you?"

Claudia felt herself almost blushing. "Well, no, I have to bring the kids back."

"No, you don't. You can take me to the Chinese, I'll bring them home afterwards."

"But Dave, what will he say?"

"That doesn't matter. If he asks, I'll tell him. I need to know who you're keeping company with. He should have let me meet his girlfriend before he took the kids out with her, I told him that. And I want to meet this man of yours. So, Chinese, am I invited?"

"I'd be thrilled. He's got to ring later, I'll tell him then."

"He won't mind?"

"Pat, as they say in politer circles than ours, who gives a fuck? I'll just tell him" and they laughed again. "But I actually think he'll be delighted."

Pat nodded knowingly. "I'm sure he will when he realises he gets the extra night with you."

"You're awful," now she did blush, "but thank you. Are we going to get down to some serious business now?"

She covered Molloy and Giddings in a lot of detail, stressing how she thought there were people in the businesses who could manage the programmes. This wasn't just to reassure Pat. She knew it was the only way she could make it work for herself. Pat was suitably curious about all the issues and all of the people. Maybe a little more about the people than about the issues, but that was probably to be expected. She told her less about Collins, only that there was a good chance of getting a contract. She didn't want to talk about Henderson.

"Three would be a good start," she had a cautious look, "but they're all in America."

"I know. It's worrying me a bit too, but if I can't keep to my fifty max rule, then it's not going to work anyway. I'm seeing Peter on Friday. He's the one who says he has the businesses that need me. He'll have to direct me to European ones."

"Yes, he will," said Pat, nodding, but she didn't look unduly perturbed.

Pat left before lunchtime. They could have carried on talking, but they were managing to be more business-like now. Claudia also had her day job to attend to — and even Pat had to pay the long-suffering George some attention. She was glad she had calls to make. She tried to put Jack's Monday out of her mind. What could happen? When might he ring? She told herself six would be the earliest, his lunchtime. She'd be out with the kids. Chinese had become a very convenient habit. And there would be a sweet tickle of revenge in telling them over dinner about the Saturday plan.

She had one thought about Brodie Associates in her head that she wanted to follow up, but the discipline had to hold: two hours on calls and emails for Collins before a Brodie break.

Two hours later she rang Alan.

"Hey, stranger, wonderful to hear from you. What's going on?"

"I'll come straight to the point. I might be setting up on my own. I could be propositioning you as a client, but I'd like to describe it to you to see if you might be interested in coming in with me."

"Wow, bolt from the blue. I have to say, straight away, I'm intrigued."

"With which alternative?"

"My God, woman, you're being very direct, but, being frank, you've rather cut yourself out of the first one by giving me so much help at the start. It's going well here, although maybe it's worth talking about whether I could take it up a level. But no, I'm more interested in what you're doing. Should we meet for a drink one evening?"

"That's what I was hoping you'd say. Could you do it this week?"

"Just a sec. Wednesday any good? Your pub, like before?"

"Wednesday's great but I don't want gossip. It was bad enough last time — although I enjoyed my brief notoriety as a scarlet woman with a toy-boy. Where's good for you?"

He took a while. "Do you know The Weyside on the river on the way into Guildford? It's on your side of the town."

"Yes, that's good, I can drive straight up. Six o'clock?"

"Perfect. Let me book a table for something to eat. Can you do that?"

"Er, yes, I think I can. My mother-in-law will see to the kids."

"Excellent, but have you got time to tell me a little bit more about it now? Like I said, I'm intrigued."

She tried to be succinct. She realised, too late, that she was trying to impress him. He was good, and she might need him if there was as much work as Peter was suggesting. She wished she'd made more notes before the call to give herself a script to follow. But he was asking interested questions and it flowed like a normal conversation, so when he closed with, "I'm really glad you rang me. I'm looking forward to Wednesday very much, but I have got to get on with stuff here now, I'm afraid. I've made myself late for a meeting. Thank you ever so much for calling me." She relaxed. She hadn't fucked up!

"I'm thrilled you might be interested. See you Wednesday."

And that felt good. She couldn't do anything before the Peter meeting, but it would be useful to go into that conversation feeling that she already had a team, potentially.

The email came at five thirty, obviously at the start of his lunch break:

'Exciting things here, lots to talk about, hope you don't mind waiting until 10.30 your time but I'd rather make sure we have plenty time to talk. How are the kids about Saturday? XXXX'

'Haven't told them yet. Telling them about it in the Chinese shortly. We have a plus one for dinner on Saturday. Pat thinks you won't mind because it means I can stay the night while she brings the guys home. I admit I blushed, but I did like her point. XXXX'

You could have told me more, Jack. I've now got five hours to wonder what you're going to be doing, she thought, but at least he still had a job, that seemed clear.

The guys were thrilled about Saturday; about The Lion King, but mostly about meeting Jack. And when she told them about Gran coming to dinner as well, she got a very knowing look and a smile from Abbi. "So, you'll be staying up there with him, Mum, yes?" — *You're only fourteen, my dear, you shouldn't understand these things* — but it looked like it augured well.

There was plenty to catch up on still after the kids had gone to bed, but the time dragged. Most of her felt drowsy but a part of her brain felt it was plugged into the mains.

Ten thirty came. Nothing!

Ten thirty-one a text:

10 minutes, please, sorry XXXX

Well, that was something.

At ten forty-five her phone rang.

"What is it?"

"We understand you have been in an accident recently. Our team of insurers..."

"Jack, for fuck's sake, what is it?"

"It's America."

There was a very long pause.

"You know you're going to have to help me on that. It sounds exciting. You're obviously excited. You've been tied up with it all day. But what the fuck are you telling me?"

"They've pushed Mike Harris out."

He left a pause. It didn't help her much. This was a name she knew. She knew he was a senior guy. But she had no real idea what he did. "That doesn't really help me understand, Jack."

"He ran all the Americas region. It's the biggest regional job. In sales terms, it's sixty percent of the corporation. It's always been seen as the step before

COO. The Old Man's asked me to dinner tonight. He did the job ten years ago."

"Jack, that's amazing, I think. What am I not seeing? Does that mean you run the place when he retires? Fuck!"

"Well, that's a leap too far. The COO is the number two. They'll expect him to take over as CEO in a few years. Maybe the Old Man will tell me more tonight. I guess he's thinking he'll split his chairman and CEO jobs at some point. They had Harris lined up for it, but it looks like they decided that wasn't going to work. He'd only been doing it two years. They can be brutal on decisions like that. They have to be, I suppose. Well, I know they do. In my own little way, I've done the same."

She was utterly thrilled for him. But what did it mean for them? When was he going to come on to that? It was obviously on his mind. Why wait all day to call? But what a brilliant job for him! Not the time for her little worries.

"So, no more Singapore?" That was the easiest way of asking the question.

"No, no more Singapore, not in the new job anyway." *What will Martha do? Why the fuck would I worry about her?* "Lots of travel still, though, I'm afraid." That was the word she was waiting for: 'afraid'.

"What's worrying you? Is that why it's taken you so long to ring me?"

"No. Well, yes and no maybe. I wanted to have time to talk properly, although even that's getting squeezed now with the Old Man's dinner."

"When have you got to go?"

"Don't worry about that."

"But you're worrying about it Jack. What's really bugging you? This is a fantastic job. I think it's amazing." *I really do, but I'm feeling other things as well, and so are you.*

"It is, I'm staggered, I admit, and what's been nice is that all the guys in the region, the ones who'll report to me, well, all except one, have been great about it. The guy running the US thinks he should have got it, so he was a bit sour. But generally, I don't think Harris was well liked. Well, not that that matters. The point is he actually wasn't respected. Anyway, I've been on the phone all day to each of them since the first meeting."

"How did that go? What happened? Tell me about it."

"The Old Man wandered by first thing and just said casually 'ah, glad you're back, I suppose we'd better talk, come over' and he led me into that meeting room beside his desk. Davis was there with Saunders. Do you know him?"

"He must be the COO now, is that right? I'm just guessing. He's the one that sits nearest the Old Man."

"Exactly right. Well, he and Davis were in there already. And the Old Man just sat down and said, 'don't know if you heard, but Harris left on Friday'. I saw Davis raise his eyebrows. He knew where I was on Friday, of course, this is why he wanted me around but couldn't say anything. It would have given the game away, but then the Old Man just said 'we want you to take over from him'. I was a bit blown away."

"Well, I'm blown away now. But why do I feel there's something you're not saying?"

"It's all the travel, I guess, and being based here."

"Do you want to explain why that's worse than what we have now?"

"I don't suppose it is, really, well, I can't exactly pop into London easily — I won't be flying round the world. But I have just had one of the most amazing weekends of my life. I love you very much and I was hoping to move us forward a bit."

"Is that all?"

"Is that all?" he exploded, "Is that all?"

"Calm down, Jack," *I'm going to pretend I'm calm if I can,* "somewhere, anywhere, remember. What's changed?" *I'm going to give myself time to think.*

"Well, nothing really, if you put it like that."

"I could have three American contracts. I could be there more often."

"You haven't given up the Collins idea?"

"No, Jack, I figure I've got someone important on the inside helping to make those decisions; someone with influence." *And you think I mean you. I don't like tricking you but...* "I don't think this makes anything worse, does it?"

"No, I suppose you're right, but I was hoping we could find a way to make things much better."

"I refuse to get disappointed when you get a big step up and a rise. I assume there's more money?"

"Well, nobody's said, but there will be, yes."

"OK, so now I can plan a big house on the coast instead of a cottage."

He laughed. "I adore you. You are absolutely wonderful." *I know I fucking am!*

"Anyway, don't stop me being thrilled for you. Go and see the Old Man. Call me tomorrow."

"I love you."

"I love you too. Now, off you go."

And a welter of thoughts and feelings spun round in her head. She knew she had to make herself believe what she had just told him: it wouldn't be any different; it might even be better. But a little maggot of doubt was crawling around inside her. No matter, take three days, she'd learned how to do that. She'd be clearer by Friday. Much clearer about everything by Friday. And she would be seeing him then!

33

"You look bleary!" she said as she dropped her bags in the flat's small hallway and fell into his arms.

"I don't sleep as well on planes as you do, but I don't feel bleary," he said, as his hand moved over her arse.

"You can forget that for now, my darling, my meeting's at ten. You can get some sleep, you'll need energy this afternoon."

"Are you ready?"

"Honestly? No, but I don't see how I could be. There are so many open questions. But I had a good meeting on Wednesday with a guy who might want to work for us as a consultant. If Peter has any European clients, I'll need help quickly. And this guy's good, I've known him a couple of years."

"Is he in our business? That wouldn't be so good if you're trying to get us as a client."

"No, he's in pharma. It'd be good to have some very different experience. But I'm babbling. I've got half an hour. Can we sit down and have coffee?"

"Of course, I'll get some. Pop your bags in the bedroom and go sit down."

She sat on the sofa, looking up the Thames. "I love this view, I really do."

He put the coffee down and sat beside her. "You can use the place whenever you're in town, you know. That might be a lot more often now."

It was an obvious thought, but one that had never occurred to her. "Wow, that's very sweet of you. It's a marvellous idea, but I think I'm always going to want to get back for the kids."

He smiled. "They're fourteen and twelve. I'm taking a longer-term perspective on this."

"Ha, you're right, I suppose. I'm struggling to see past this morning's meeting."

"Where are you seeing him?"

"In Sandy Nicholls's office. I need to leave at half past. But how was the rest of your week?"

"Interesting, but I can't do it justice in twenty minutes. I think we'll both have a lot to talk about this afternoon."

"No doubt, but we're not going to start getting our priorities wrong, are we?" She leaned towards him and kissed him. "First things first this afternoon."

It was almost a shock to see Peter in suit and tie, but the formality didn't get in the way of the beaming smile and full embrace as he greeted her in Sandy's main office. Sandy had shown her in. "I'll see you guys later." Peter merely nodded.

"You look very imposing, sir." She smiled at him.

He smiled warmly as he positioned a chair for her at the round meeting table. "Thank you, my dear, and you, once again, look absolutely enchanting. This is, I think, the first time you've really met my full Dr Jekyll."

"Yes, but I have had quite a lot of your Mr Hyde, thank you — but you had your Dr Jekyll face on when we talked about this on the boat. Although one drop of your magic serum seems to let you switch very easily."

He was nodding, as if pleased with her observation. "I think it's very important to be able to compartmentalise. You seem to do that quite well."

She pondered. She didn't think she did, but this was an interview, of sorts, and she reminded herself not to fall into a trap of loose, self-critical observations. She was sat next to a master of interpretation — and espionage, she now knew. She didn't respond.

"Be that as it may, are you going to tell me what you want to do?" He smiled and seemed pleased she hadn't just filled the space with words.

"I'll put it simply: I want to do this. I can see the market out there in general and I can see some specific opportunities that could get me off the ground. I can also see how I would want to operate. We have to establish teams in each client business who, effectively, do all the work. We assess, we set up, we monitor, and we advise. We will never be a permanent presence."

"We?"

"I'm already thinking of, ultimately, a team, but I have identified my first recruit. A guy I've known for two years and been impressed by." Peter pursed his lips and nodded slowly, as if pleased. "I have to feel that there is a positive culture for acceptance in any client we take on. Andy will have that when he's made a couple of changes, changes he seems prepared to make. Giddings I was sceptical about, but I think we've had our breakthrough moment, so I would take them on. Collins," she paused and looked directly into his eyes, "will, I have on good authority, engage us to continue overseeing their programme. I will want you to tell me a little bit more about our Mr Henderson but I do accept, from the outset, that his role is supportive."

"And essential, I'm afraid, but we can come back to that later. Why don't you tell me more about how you see your assignments working at Molloy and at Giddings? You'll have to give me a little more background on the latter. You seemed impressed that I came up with Arthur Gunter's name when you mentioned them, but my knowledge is quite superficial."

She looked hard at him. "Shall we come back to that when we're talking about Henderson later?"

He looked coldly back. "We can, but I've told you my knowledge is superficial and that describes the situation accurately. You seem to be surmising, admittedly quite correctly, that I could know more if I wished to, but I shall make two points about that: first, until you mentioned your involvement with Giddings a few weeks ago, that business was of almost no interest to me whatsoever. I merely maintain a general business overview, prioritised in part, I admit, by the connections of people with whom I have connections — that may sound more mysterious than I wanted it to. Are you clear about that?"

"Let me see. If Henderson, or anyone in a similar relationship with you, has a connection with a particular business, you keep a closer eye on it."

He relaxed and smiled like a proud teacher. "Exactly! And secondly, this is very important, I have a relationship with Henderson — and one or two others, it's true, but he's an important one — that is both ethical and commercial. It is vital for you that you understand this: he tells me things that he is legally permitted to tell me; I pay him an annual fee for general advice. Our aim is always, however, in any given situation, to ensure and enhance the success of the businesses we're interested in. That business success is a proxy for maximum benefit for interested parties. Yes, that's stakeholders and employees but it's also, unless you feared for a moment there that altruism might be intruding, for the maximum benefit of, ultimately, myself."

He was, for Peter, quite animated and unusually serious. Nevertheless, it had to be risked. "Has the reverend finished the sermon?"

He leaned back and laughed uproariously. "Oh, dear, oh dear," still laughing, "was I really pontificating?"

It needed no more than a smile and a gentle nod.

"OK, I suppose I may have been. No more, I promise. Of course you get the point. You do seem to have a wonderfully intuitive understanding of some thorny issues. We will come back to Henderson, I promise you. There are some things, arising out of what he knows, that you and I need to discuss. But that's for later. Tell me how you're going to deal with your first three clients."

Molloy was simplest. The issues were clear cut and Andy was receptive to the important changes. Giddings took more time to explain because Peter really did appear to have only a limited knowledge of the business — but he did know about the former HR VP's affair with Samantha — *had Henderson really needed to tell him that?* — and about Henderson's relationship with Marybeth — *wow, you were cool about that, girl* — and Collins, the biggest and most global, but the easiest to deal with today since she'd covered it before when talking to him on the boat.

"But there are big changes afoot at Collins, if I understand the situation correctly. Changes that impact you considerably, personally?"

"You know about Jack and me, Peter, and his job's changing. It looks like a big promotion." *Maybe it's good that you know about that but am I going to become more vulnerable to what others know and do?*

"So I hear. We'll come back to that." And a small voice somewhere said 'this, too, is ominous'. "We're talking about establishing Brodie Associates and I think you're saying that's what you want to do."

"Yes, I completely want to. I said to Gunter and Henderson when they took me to dinner that I would be interested to see how these ideas worked in other places, but now, having looked at Molloy and Giddings, there is so much need for these ideas that I really want to try if I can."

"If you can?"

"That's why we're here, isn't it? I need connections. I could maybe manage assignments at Molloy and Giddings, but I wouldn't know how to go about getting new clients without the sort of connections you can offer and, for all I know, keeping a contract at Collins is dependent on Henderson's support which is probably also dependent on your say so."

He merely nodded.

"But I need set-up money too. There will be expenses, of course, but I even need a living wage until the money comes in."

"And what has Sandy told you?"

"He said he worked like stink but found out, only more than a year later, that he'd earned far more than he'd ever done before."

"Yes, well, I wouldn't expect you to be so ignorant of your ongoing financial status as he was, that wouldn't be your way. But I'd expect you to be at least as successful he was in the first two years and, longer term, you should be much bigger than he is if we set this up right. I will cover all the set-up expenses and the business will guarantee you, personally, one hundred thousand a year for the first three years. That's OK, isn't it? Sandy, of course, earned much more but that's the minimum I guaranteed him."

She nodded mutely. A *hundred grand, minimum!*

"Penelope will help you manage that. I think you've made contact, yes?"

"Indirectly, yes." *How on earth to describe Pat and her role?*

He smiled. "Don't worry. Penelope is a superb accountant and the most scrupulous person I know. I admit she was my plant when Sandy started up, his taking her on was a condition of my support. She will, nevertheless, it's important to understand, be working for you when you, or your PA, contact her" and he smiled. "I think they're getting on well, aren't they?".

"They seem to be." *Pat, what have you done? Bless you!*

"Good. I know that she's been impressed by the contact they've had. Penelope is a resource you will pay for via the fees you pay Sandy. My sole condition is that your operations are completely transparent to her.

Importantly for you, however, is that she will only contact me if you are going seriously astray or ignoring her. Actually, those two conditions may be effectively synonymous. OK so far?" She nodded. "Just to set your mind at rest, she called me twice in Sandy's first year and hasn't done so since.

"She has probably acquainted you with the," he paused and smiled, "strictly confidential financial terms and conditions of my relationship with the Nicholls business." He looked at her with raised eyebrows. She nodded. "Good. If you want to hire this guy you were talking about, she can also tell you about contract conditions for taking on extra consultants. You might, by the way, want Sandy to meet him so you have an alternative view. Would that help?"

"Very much, thank you."

"Good. Now, there are two European businesses I would like you to look at straightaway, one based in the UK, so you may need help quite soon."

"Peter, woah, can we stand back a moment?" He looked puzzled. "You're talking like this is happening. Am I seeing that wrong?"

"Are you telling me it's not?"

Stay cool, Claudia, try to ignore the stomach's gyrations. "I wasn't aware that we'd actually made that decision."

"We haven't. You have. I told you that if it was what you wanted, then it's what I want. You will do a superb job and some of my businesses badly need you. And I'm only talking about the ones that know they do already. Beyond my network, you know you will find Sandy a useful source of contacts and most of his work is Europe based, which will please you. But on the bigger stage, you will find Henderson, as you insist on calling him, quite useful."

"I know I need to be a big girl about this and I think I understand the importance of his role, but I can't help finding him a little sinister."

"That comes with the territory, I'm afraid. I hope my Group is big enough now to cope with the sort of shocks he exposes but there were one or two episodes he brought to light in the early years that might have taken me under. The high probability is that you'll hear nothing from him. If anything happens that concerns us, you'll be more likely to hear from me. I think he may have hinted at a potential issue?"

"Something to do with Jack?"

"I'm sure he talked about discretion and the need to alert people to potential issues and let them make their own decisions." She nodded. "That's all we ask, and people are given the space to sort out their own problems. If we, on a rare occasion, appear intrusive, it's always done with our person's, and our businesses' best interests at heart. We've not had a single case of an intervention being unjustified or resented. I think one case I can talk about, without details of course, is Andy and Jen. That looked like going astray, so we tried to help."

"She said a little about that."

He smiled. "Good, I'd rather hoped she would. As you know, I'm a great believer in relationships. When they go wrong for our people, the damage can spread very wide and be devastating, so we like to be comfortable about the relationships people are in. I know how very fond you are of Jack and you seem to manage that very well, so I'm comfortable about that. But if that basis were to change, I would like you to discuss it with me. Is that asking too much?"

"No." *It probably is asking too much, actually, but I don't think it's relevant.* "I can't see it changing."

"With his move and his new job, or his reaction to your new job, he might want to change something."

"All we've talked about is trying to see more of each other."

"Well, maybe US-based clients are a good thing for you."

"I really would like to think so. But why do I think there's something you're not telling me?"

"There's nothing to concern you. I would just like you to talk to me if anything changes. That's got to be the basis of our relationship. Do we have a deal?"

"Do I actually have a business? Is this real?"

"It is. You know the terms and conditions — the same as Sandy's. You'll get some independent legal advice to vet it but, unless you hire an idiot, nothing should change the proposed arrangement and we can get that signed off next week. I'm due here again next Friday. In the meantime, please take this card." It was similar to Henderson's: dark grey, with simply 'Peter Dickinson', a mobile number and an email address. "You're in my system already. If you call, I'll know it's you."

"Can I hug you? I am so thrilled!"

He stood up and opened his arms, smiling. "I am also completely delighted, my dear. I'm certain you'll have no regrets." They hugged for a long time — she felt very emotional. He eased his embrace. "I think you're approaching it in absolutely the right way: arm's length to clients is right, they must create their own teams under your guidance; and then you can give priority to your home life. Just remember, talk to me about any changes, OK?" She nodded. "Good. Let's get Sandy in and we can talk about how we work together in practice and if that spills over into lunch, so be it. We'll walk round to Square, do you know it?"

"Ha, how sweet, that was my first date with Jack."

34

"Do family weekends mean we're restricted to vanilla sex?" They were lying naked and lazy together on the Sunday morning.

"By no means! But he needs a little time before we can start again."

"Seriously, old man? Am I going to need a toy-boy?"

"I don't think that will be necessary, but if you do decide to take one, you know I'll look forward to hearing about your adventures."

"Touché. I suspect I'm going to be a little busy for toy-boys. But where are you going to look for a new Martha?"

"At the risk of appearing soppy, I think things are going to change."

"I think my kids think they already have: The Lion King and Hakkasan; it's not Vue cinema and the Shanghai Jade. They're spoiled for life now, and I've not seen Pat like that, ever. I really do think she fancies you. That looks like competition to me. After all, she's closer your age than I am." She moved away swiftly before his hand could catch her.

"I thought she was lovely. I don't know what I was expecting but she really gets what you're trying to do with the business. Well, I thought they were all lovely, and I'd forgotten how kids that age can eat."

"Well, Abbi's starting to get fussy, but you wouldn't know it from the way she tackled everything. And that wasn't Chinese as they know it. It must have been like my Singapore team nights for them."

"No birds' claws though."

"No, thank God, that would have stopped even Jonah in his tracks. But you got a big seal of approval, though. Abbi whispered 'he's lovely' as she hugged me when they left."

"You could have said!"

"Mr Stephens, as soon as we waved them goodbye you had only one thought in your head."

"And I met with reluctance?"

"No, of course not, and I want more before your car comes at four."

"It won't be vanilla."

"Of course it won't be vanilla."

"I keep saying it, don't I? I love this view." They were sat on the sofa looking up the river, just in tee shirts and underwear. "You can tell it's Sunday, somehow, it's boats, it's traffic, it's people walking. I wonder when we'll do it again."

"Well, it won't take me long to hand over to Robert. He's effectively been my number two for a year or more. You remember him?"

"Of course. He started the conference off when I thought you were avoiding me."

"Let's not restart that one."

"That's what you always say when you're in the wrong."

"Are you becoming immune to that paddle?"

"No, I'm still tingly — I did like it though."

He hugged her. "I am pleased they've given it to him, we finally get an Asian in the president's group. He's very good, he'll do well, I think, but it's good for the corporation as well. Anyway, I expect to wrap that up in a week or so but then I've got a lot of travelling to do over there. Some of it's tough; we get much more security. There are plenty of bad men down south of the border."

"How much time will you be travelling when it's settled down?"

"Hard to say, probably fifty percent is a good guess."

"And fifty percent in DC? Can you get an apartment like Henderson's? It was gorgeous."

"Wouldn't you rather have a house?"

"It'll be your home. What do you want?"

"I want it to not just be my home. It'll be my base for five years at least, maybe ten if things work out the way the Old Man expects them to and I told you, I want to take a longer-term perspective. So, what you want really matters."

"Am I missing something? I'm just starting up a business here."

"Most of which might be US based."

"Jack, I think I like what I'm hearing you say, but I'm based here until Jonah is eighteen."

"You wouldn't consider moving them?"

She felt like a floundering fish. "No, well, let me think for a minute. No, I just can't see that being realistic. But I'll think about it, not today, not tomorrow, but sometime soon."

"I do want to marry you. That's not today or tomorrow, I know, you're still married. But that's why I'm asking these questions. I want us to be together. I've told the Old Man we probably will be. I had to say you're probably leaving the corporation. He didn't seem surprised, which surprised me."

She was stunned. "It would surprise me if he even knew who I was. But wait, what did you say at the start back there? There was an 'm' word, or did I mishear something?"

"No, you didn't mishear. I said I want to marry you. Am I going to get a yes?"

"You take two years to ask a question and you want an answer in two seconds? Of course it's a yes" and she threw her arms around him and kissed him. "But somewhere, anywhere, remember? Yes, I'd love to think of your US place as our place, I'd love to spend more time there eventually. I want us to spend more time together than we are doing now and I'm sure we can make that work. So, yes, yes, yes but I will want to make the most enormous success of Brodie Associates."

"Of course you do, and of course you will, but I also want us to make a success of us."

"Oh, Jack, my love, please don't let me make you think that that's anything other than the most important thing for me now. Please come back to bed with me. Bits of me are tired and sore but I want your naked body in my arms for this last hour before you go."

35

Peter, I won't call you since you might be in the wrong time zone, but we should talk about some unexpected developments with Jack. Best, Claudia Brodie.

Writing to him was an easy decision. She wrote that evening, but she spent ages wondering whether to put Brodie or XX after Claudia. Once she'd pressed send, she realised that the alternative would have been completely wrong. This was Brodie Associates dealing with the Dickinson Group, this was not a party in Barnes or even the in-between world of the boat.

That new business relationship seemed to characterise the slightly strange phone call from Peter. He rang at six thirty the next morning. She was already up and dressed.

"I'm in China. Sorry for the hour but I thought it best to catch you before you got into your day. What's happening?"

"He says he wants to marry me. I thought you should know, given our Friday conversation. I can't do anything about it, of course, I'm still married, but it seemed like the sort of thing that you wanted to know about."

"It is, my dear, it's exactly the sort of thing I want to hear about. It's not going to make any difference to Friday for you is it? I'm planning to be back to sign papers."

"No, I'm completely committed to Brodie Associates."

"Good, me too, but before you also get completely committed to Jack Stephens, I would like a conversation. I'm here until Thursday though, so I'm going to ask Alphonse to seek you out. He'll explain everything. I should emphasise that he doesn't know about this, it falls into the deep discretion area, but I will have to brief him and, of course, I trust him completely. OK?"

"Yes, OK." But she was very taken aback.

"Good, well Alphonse will be in touch later today. Oh, and congratulations to you but I suppose it's a little early for that. See you Friday."

"See you Friday, 'bye." And she felt a little numb as she put the phone down. This felt mysterious and unsettling and she changed her plans about talking to Pat later that day. That would have been an awkward conversation anyway, since it would have to cover divorcing Dave and spending more time in the US. Best to try to understand what was behind Peter's concerns first.

Alphonse rang at lunchtime. "Hello, my dearest, I gather I have the chance to see you again soon." She immediately felt better. This was Alphonse at his smooth and smiley best, no hint of concern in his voice. "Which evenings work best for you?"

"As soon as possible. I'd like to understand what this is about."

"I thought you might say that. Can you get to Coworth this evening?"

"Oh, yes please."

"Now don't misunderstand my intent, but I have already booked a room. From what I understand we need to have a very private conversation, although I don't yet have the full picture myself. I'm expecting another call this afternoon. Can you get there around six?"

"Yes."

"I know you're feeling a little tense, but Peter just wants you fully informed before you commit to anything. I'm thrilled for you about Friday. Peter and Sandy are very excited about your business."

"I am too but I'll admit this is giving me a wobble, but I'm sure I'll cope."

"I'm sure you will too. Sensitivity and resilience. That's two more reasons why I love you."

She found herself smiling for the first time that day. "That and…?"

"Yes, and your perfect arse. And don't worry about this meeting, my love, there are merely things you need to know about in this big, bad world. I'll see you at six."

She was there early, not worrying about betraying any concerns. They were too obvious anyway. "I'm a guest of Alphonse Newman, he's saying here tonight."

"Yes, madam, but he has not checked in yet" *The sweet, careful elocution of a French woman speaking English.*

"Thank you, I'll wait here" and she took a seat in the lobby. Would he make it out in the rush hour? Had his phone call gone to schedule? What about his own business, doesn't he have other things to do? But at five to six he strode in. Dark green suit today — very unusual colour — and a green striped shirt.

"Elegant as ever." She had spotted him the instant he came through the door and stood up to greet him. He picked her out almost immediately. The place was quiet. He swept towards her and embraced her.

He then stood back. "I know you're very lovely but somehow my memory never quite does you justice." He leaned forward and kissed her lips lightly. "I'll just check in." The porter with his bag had spoken to the woman on reception and she was preparing his room card. "One card or two, Mr Newman?"

"Just one is fine."

"Will you be dining with us this evening?"

"I believe I've booked for eight o'clock. I know it's only the bar."

"I'll check and confirm, sir."

"Thank you" and Claudia, behind him and looking at his back, knew instantly that the woman had just received one of his smiles.

The room's tall windows looked out over the rolling fields with the lake below and the polo fields in the distance. Two small but comfortable chairs were either side of the small round table in the window. Shafts of the setting sun broke through the striated clouds. Was this a scene that would fix itself in the memory by its attachment to some dramatic event or news?

She sat down, he tipped the porter, hung up his jacket and joined her at the table.

"You booked a meal?"

"Only bar food tonight, I'm afraid, but we have your new business to celebrate and the champagne choice is excellent."

"Do we? Doesn't that depend on what you're about to tell me?"

"I don't think it should. I don't think it will. Peter just thinks you should know more about Jack than perhaps you do."

"Well, I'd guessed it must be something like that from the way he set this up. You'd better tell me quickly."

"I was talking to Henderson this afternoon. You know him, I think."

"Yes, not well, but I have met him a few times and I had one very revealing conversation with him recently."

"And he told you about an issue in the Far East where he'd had to intervene to prevent a situation becoming embarrassing."

"Yes, he gave no names but he let me know of a situation where a very senior executive had exposed themselves to the danger of being blackmailed."

"And this senior person was?"

"He didn't say. I just assumed it was Martha. She's the regional head of a major bank based in Singapore. I know a little about her and her tastes, and I could understand why it might..."

"It was Jack he was speaking of."

The punches she'd felt in the Henderson conversation were nothing compared to this. He let her stay silent and look out of the window while he fetched glasses and water and poured for them.

"Thank you," she said, distractedly. She huddled into a ball, feeling very small, feeling very silly, feeling humiliated, continuing to stare out of the window. When she allowed herself to glance at him, he was just sitting, relaxed, looking at her.

"I wish you wouldn't keep looking at me."

He stood up, leaned towards her, kissed her head and slowly unpacked his bag. It was a small bag. It took him little time to put toiletries in the bathroom and a few items of clothing in the wardrobe but when he sat down again, he looked out of the window.

It was a long while before she said, "I suppose I need to know more about this, don't I?"

"I'm not going to tell you any more unless you ask, but if you go home without talking to me, I think the questions will grow like weeds."

She turned to him. "I know you're right, really, so I guess I'd better listen. I feel so silly though. From the way Henderson described it, I felt sure it was Martha. It seemed to fit with her dropping out of Jack's life for a while and then re-emerging after, I'd assumed, Henderson had talked to her."

"Well, now you know, Henderson had talked to Jack."

And, feeling helpless, she asked, "What had he done?"

"Nothing really bad. Well, nothing that you or I would consider bad in itself, but he met bad people…"

"And he wasn't open about it. He didn't say anything to me."

"And you and I understand the serpent of silence."

"But I thought he was being open."

"And he thought you were being open. Does he know everything about you?"

She shrugged weakly. "No, I didn't tell him everything about the boat."

"Would you? Will you?"

"I don't know. I don't know what I'm going to be doing now. What has Peter really been worrying about?"

"Principally about you and then he will laugh and tell you, of course, he's only worrying about his business but really, in all of this, his biggest concern is you. Just as you are my biggest concern at the moment."

"Can you hold me?" She looked to him. He stood up and opened his arms. She melted into them, relieved to feel his embrace. "What am I going to do?"

He kissed her forehead. "What you're definitely not going to do is expect me to answer that question for you. Claudia doesn't do that."

"No, Claudia doesn't do that. Claudia's a big girl now."

"It will help, I think, if I tell you what Peter is concerned about. Shall we sit down again?"

"Yes, time to get my game face on."

"Yes, something else I love about you. You don't make my life easy, but you do make it more interesting." She felt herself smiling, she left his lingering embrace reluctantly and sat down again.

"We all ask for commitments to openness, we try to minimise uncertainty in our lives, and when we give commitments to openness we believe ourselves, but then things happen: little things that we think don't matter; little things that could upset but needn't; so we start to keep secrets, unimportant, trivial secrets —

we're showing tact, showing concern, showing care for someone's feelings. But really, we're hiding ourselves, trying to present a better self — to the world, or to the one we love. Now you have uncovered a new Claudia in the past two years, a Claudia that is confident, vibrant, adventurous, dazzling even. She's surprised you, yes?"

"Yes. More than a little."

"And you're quite proud of your new creation, or you should be — but it's not really a creation, you've simply discovered yourself — you don't know if Jack will really love this whole new person and you've not yet come to terms with what might need to change in the new Claudia to make the relationship work, if anything. I'll just ask you one little question, and it really does not need an answer. It's just to make you think, but, if you marry Jack, will you still sleep with me?"

It took her a long time to answer. "If I marry Jack, Alphonse, will you still sleep with me?"

His face softened even more. "I will still want to, and I hope you can make that work in your life but we're getting close to the central point here, and why Peter is so concerned. If your relationship with Jack is to become closer, it must be on the basis of openness and understanding. Too many big secrets once you are committed to each other and your relationship will fall apart very badly, with all the consequences that brings, for you, for your business and, further out in the fallout zone, for Peter. So, just as Jack must understand you, you must understand and accept and embrace Jack."

"So now you have to tell me what he's done that is so bad."

"So bad, it isn't, I don't think, but he exposed himself to dangerous company. Take away the dangerous company and he is not at risk, which is why Henderson let Collins go ahead and promote him. If I understand Henderson correctly, Collins doesn't actually know about this. He tells me that if his interventions are successful, he doesn't take the information further — but his arrangement with Peter is a little different. The point here is that what Jack does may undermine your relationship."

"I have to hear it. What was he doing?"

"You know about Martha, obviously, and his relationship with her — and you, to some extent, share some of his dark tastes." She nodded slowly, remembering Alphonse watching her over Peter's knee. "Well, he began pursuing them more widely and more avidly than merely with Martha. He got into larger parties that were attended by people on Henderson's lists, dangerous people. We're assuming that you knew nothing of all this."

She sighed, "Yes, I only knew of Martha, that was hard enough."

"So, you would not have reacted well if he'd told you?"

"Probably not. Almost certainly not. I don't know how I will react now, it's worse that you've had to tell me and he hasn't. I admit he and I have enormous fun pushing our boundaries. But maybe it's just him pushing my boundaries, who knows where his are? We've been having wonderful times these past two weeks, but picturing him at big parties, orgies, I think you're saying, and it sounds like frequently, and not a word being said to me, I just don't know. Maybe I will be able to wave him off happily to Brazil and such places but now I will always wonder. And I will always wonder about how really dark he is. Is what he and I do enough? Is this his pursuit of a little more fun, or is it a dangerous obsession? I need to think."

"Think about Friday?"

She paused. "No, I'm more committed than ever to signing with Peter. And I hate how I'm feeling but I'm glad I've been told — and I understand why. I have plenty of time to think about Jack Stephens. But Alphonse?"

"Yes?"

"Can I stay with you tonight?"